KU-694-385

THE PRICE YOU PAY

AIDAN TRUHEN

This paperback edition published in 2019

First published in Great Britain in 2018 by Serpent's Tail,
an imprint of Profile Books Ltd
3 Holford Yard
Bevin Way
London
WC1X 9HD
www.serpentstail.com

Copyright © 2018 by Aidan Truhen

1 3 5 7 9 10 8 6 4 2

Designed and typeset by sue@lambledesign.demon.co.uk

Printed and bound by CPI Group (UK) Ltd, Croydon CR0 4YY

The moral right of the author has been asserted.

All rights reserved. Without limiting the rights under copyright
reserved above, no part of this publication may be reproduced,
stored or introduced into a retrieval system, or transmitted, in any
form or by any means (electronic, mechanical, photocopying,
recording or otherwise), without the prior written permission
of both the copyright owner and the publisher of this book.

The characters and events in this book are fictitious.
Any similarity to real persons, dead or alive, is coincidental and
not intended by the author.

A CIP record for this book can be obtained from the British Library.

ISBN: 978 1 78816 009 4
eISBN: 978 1 78283 425 0

Mixed Sources
Product group from well-managed
forests and other controlled sources
www.fsc.org Cert no. TT-COC-002227
© 1996 Forest Stewardship Council
FSC

This book is dedicated to my brothers:
good men to have at your back.

And also to everyone who has ever belatedly realised
what an asshole I am.

What could possibly
have taken you so long?

part one

I'M ORDERING A LATTE MACCHIATO because Didi is dead and that is sad. It's not like horrible sad but it's sad. She was an old lady and actuarially she didn't have long but it looks like someone couldn't wait. It's the kind of thing makes you uncomfortable in your neighbourhood and it's the kind of thing that's bad for business and just fuck it who needs this crap? It leaves open questions is what I'm saying and open questions are upsetting to a certain kind of person and that kind of person is the kind that I am. So coffee while I reflect on this situation that I do not like.

I am all kinds of reflective. I am deeply contemplative of the universe. I am fucking restrospect is what.

Yeah look it up so anyway this is me before it begins. It is morning and I am chipper. I am positively giddy with the love of all mankind because that is how I roll. This is me coming out of my front door and this is me walking down the hall singing a little song to myself, I have no idea so do not ask. I have no idea the sad shit that has happened so I am singing a little song.

This is me in the elevator and now I am not singing my little song anymore because: elevator music. And this is me pushing the button and I have my executive sippy cup of hand-woven organic honey seasalt rooibos and la la la. I am getting on with my day just ordinary is what.

This is the elevator doing that thing that it does shall we close or shall we pretend there is a fat man in the doorway and we must not jog his ass. Today we are respectful of his personal ass space, and so: no we shall not close the door we shall instead screw around. Juddadada juddadada but that is fine. All is right with the world. Even the elevator music is not terrible. Now the doors are closing and down we go. Eighteen floors and no one else in this building leaves this time of day so mostly I am all alone each morning, and each morning the elevator and I go by ourselves San Diego instrumental noseflute calypso all the way to the bottom.

This is me sipping my hand-woven organic honey seasalt rooibos and savouring the nutty and textured depth of the brew and the tang of dolphin ejaculate and this is the elevator stopping on the floor right under mine and making the ping noise. This is me smiling at the unexpected and preparing for serendipity.

Ping.

This is every single fucking cop in the universe standing there on the seventeenth floor and that is two guys in space suits collecting evidence and that right there is Leo my cop buddy and that means someone is dead. Someone is dead in my building. Someone is dead in my building right under my apartment. Someone is dead in my building right under my apartment in such a way that there are all the cops in the universe plus also Leo and that means they got dead violently and with malice in my building right under my apartment and you just have to take notice of that kind of happening.

Cops look at me. I look at cops. I do not rubberneck. I wait to go ping bye bye.

Oh excuse me sir!

Yeah hi officer hi. Hey Leo.

Oh sir right you know this guy sir.

Hi Jack yes officer I do.

Leo what is this?

You got this old lady down here named Desdemona?

Fuck. Desdemona?

What it says.

Desdemona?

Seems like.

Didi is what.

Didi?

Goes by Didi.

She's dead.

Yes I get that. I will say that she was a terrible person but not so that you would kill her.

Jack you hear anything last night?

No.

Uhuh.

They definitely looking for Didi?

Who knows man but they definitely got her.

I look at Leo. Leo looks at me. I say: I'll see you later Leo you need my statement whatever. Leo says he'll make some shit up. Cub nearby looks a little shocked but we are joshing obviously just joshing like black humour. Leo would not do such a thing and his upstanding citizen friend would not ask him to.

Ping bye bye.

Didi is dead.

I look at my executive sippy cup all the way down and then I leave it in the corner of the elevator. Fucking dolphin ejaculate is not appropriate anymore.

The guy behind the bar is called Mike. He's not a barista, he's a guy who works behind a coffee bar, not because it's authentic or because he loves coffee but because he shot a man in the knee in 78 and employment thereafter was hard to come by. He's pouring my macchiato the way you should so that it comes out in layers: milk, espresso, foam. Pale, dark, white.

Coffee is the judge of a person. Everything you need to know you can know about someone from their coffee, like I am drinking macchiato and why is that? It is the coffee of simple joy like coffee running naked in a field. You know who statistically and dispropor-tionately prefers bitter coffee? Psychopaths. They like bitter food and that is science, whereas I will tell you there is nothing profound about bitterness at all.

No no chocolate powder thank you Mike there are limits.

Yes I did say he shot a man. In the knee. It was not in Reno and you'll gather from his target that it was not to watch him die. It was because he wanted to express his annoyance at this other fellow trying to steal his fishing rod. It was an expensive one because back then Mike was the king of local TV fly fishing and he had used his second pay cheque to buy at a hefty discount some really nice gear. The next step on his agenda was to go and get a sponsorship deal but up comes this walking pissboil and shoves a knife in his face – not like actually in his face but close enough that he felt the breeze – and la la la.

Mike Sunby – that's the barman's name – took the knife and threw it away and then unfortunately went ahead and amputated the pissboil's patella with a .38 that came serendipitously to hand. The judge said that was stretching the definition of self defence to include basically just being fucking annoyed.

The judge actually said fuck because it was the 70s.

So after that he was a barman and not so much a TV personality because it turns out fly fishing is a namby pamby enterprise with a prudish attitude to gun violence.

I taste my macchiato.

Sunby says: haven't had anyone order that since 00.

Yeah well Didi's dead and she was shot like execution style and that requires some sort of fucking in memoriam but also some deep thinking. I do not say that to Mike.

What I say to Mike is I haven't drunk coffee since 00 either and that is a lie. I haven't drunk coffee since 01. Between 94 and 01 I was a coffee junkie but also a professional coffee person. I bought and sold coffee internationally and I drank it and I slept exclusively with women who tasted of it. I wore vetiver and black coffee cologne and dressed in coffee shades. I ruled coffee. No one called me the King of Coffee because everyone back then in the trade was the King of Coffee. There were so many Kings of Coffee you could have made a football team. Two teams of pasty desk-assed fuckers with incipient heart problems and bad sex habits. I was the Cardinal. Not the Cardinal of Coffee because that went without saying. You just said you were going to see the Cardinal or the Cardinal thinks this stuff is The Shit – or it's just shit, or whatever – and people knew who that was. If they mattered in coffee they knew. All the so-called Kings of Coffee kissed my ring.

And then I was in London one autumn and a friend called from his office, mid afternoon, says: Did someone crash a plane into my building?

Fuck. Are you asking me?

Guy says: we don't know what's happening. They're saying don't use the elevator but we're really high.

Use the fucking elevator.

But they're saying don't?

Use it. (Don't know why I said use it, but I did. I knew or I was too fucking stupid to know you shouldn't. Whatever. I said Use It.)

What if there's—

Use. It.

… Okay. Okay, I will!

Asshole did not use the fucking elevator. Nuff said. So you know what happened next? Apart from I cried the whole week and had to go and see a therapist until 04 and the therapist wanted me to have fucking electroshock to get it done? My fucking asshole friend live-SMSed his journey down the stairs and his last one said just: I'm burning. And what the fuck do you do with that? Why would you text it to anyone, ever? What the fuck does he want me to text back?

He was not my best friend. He was just this guy I knew.

I was sitting in a place in Green Park which is near Buckingham Palace and I was drinking – you know what I was drinking – and I got his message and suddenly my macchiato is ash. I don't mean like ooooh I'm so poetic. I mean like in my mouth I can taste New York air and ash. I'm drinking that appalling ash that's falling from the sky all across Manhattan.

I looked in the cup and it was pale and grey. There was a piece of a woman's purse in it, a charred lone survivor from a gold-strap clutch. The saucer stuck to the bottom of the cup and it fell. It fell dozens and dozens of floors screaming all the way down and then it hit the ground and it didn't break because catering. Fucking unbreakable catering china.

So that was a kinduva life-altering day, is what I'm saying.

Didi is dead. She was a rude old lady and I didn't really like her that much but someone shot her twice in the chest and once in the head like she was a drug mule in some ratfuck town wherever idiots smuggle drugs into this country from these days. I am not okay with that.

My name is Jack Price and this story is about me.

What I do next is go and see Big Billy. Billy knows things and Billy is known as Big Billy because: fuck irony this guy is just so big. Billy has inroads is what I'm saying because he is in construction and also because Billy. Billy has inroads into the traditional criminal substrate like the local demi-monde which is a nice way of saying that Billy knows some lawbreaking motherfuckers and he cannot entirely keep from talking about the shit they cannot keep from talking about because lawbreaking is some kind of cool.

Specifically the construction Billy does is he puts up and takes down scaffolding tubes. Billy is very particular about that word: tubes. Scaffolding is not made of bars, rods, or any other shit. Above all there are no pipes in scaffolding because scaffolding is not a conduit of any kind. Billy hates it when people talk all construction-y at him and then say 'pipe'. Homeowners in particular do this. Billy hates it. He's not a bad guy but he tends to express himself with some emphasis because he like most other men in his line takes a great deal of cocaine while he is working. This makes him impassioned.

The key thing about working scaffolding tubes while riding the Pale Peruvian Stallion – this being the brand of cocaine Billy and his guys are into and the imprint on the little cellophane twists in which it arrives – is that it is a fine fucking line. No not like it is excellent cocaine although it is excellent premium top-drawer award-winning snort-off-Miley-Cyrus cocaine but more like there is a hard limit to what is okay. Yelling at some wannabe handyman is fine. By the time that happens you're all under contract. Less fine is trying to juggle a hundred pounds of rolled steel and letting it go so that it drops two floors and impales a Bichon Frise. Blow your deadline, crash your truck into the outhouse, set something on fire? That'll happen. But shish one puppy and you are going to have trouble like you've never imagined.

Dropping something on a human is a cop issue. You may go to jail. But a dog? You're going on the national news. Your life belongs to the Million Angry Grandmas and they will fuck your shit up. They literally have nothing else to do.

One of Billy's guys had an unfortunate moment of inattention two months ago which resulted in a near miss. That is to say that a canine citizen was partially affected in an adverse manner by a mid-length temporary stanchion in free fall. That in turn is to say that a twelve-foot spear rolled off the decking and took out an imported corgi's back left leg. And that is to say surgically. Like that.

As it happens everyone involved was very fucking lucky because I was there and I made Billy pressure bandage the dog – if you can believe it he was a corpsman in 03 – and we did a whole thing so now Billy's company has a three-legged mascot and a reputation for speedy good sense rather than pet murder and people actually come looking to hire them because of the good coverage: Veterinary Veteran Preserves Pierced Pooch.

But it's been purgatorio for the whole tube crew in the meantime because obviously they could not be seen to be fucked out of their minds on cocaine during this sensitive period of self-examination and the tender scrutiny of law enforcement. This last was particularly vexed because some of Billy's employees are not entirely or even remotely white, and it may come as a surprise to you in this enlightened age but we have not entirely fixed racism in this world and white cops do still in many cases love the opportunity to be shitty to brown folks.

So all of Billy's guys have been on the narrow. This is actually easier if you take cocaine than it is if you're a dope fiend – not that anyone would hire a stoner to work scaffolding, can you even imagine? – because coke clears nicely in a few days and as long as you have no hair there is really no way to prove you've been using.

Billy's crew are not chumps. They've all been shaving their heads since they signed up. Some of them also manscape quite thoroughly. Hey it's the new century. Fuck am I gonna judge?

The one person who's okay with this drought is Jonah Jones, aka the Whale. The Whale is the resident religious old fart. Jonah tells everyone that the scaffolding gig was better when cocaine was expensive. He's probably right. Back then a tube crew would get well paid and save up. It was fucking social mobility in action. Now they pay for a lot of coke and go to girly bars. High, horny and depilated, they end up in bed with strippers in the same condition and voilà! A new generation of poor hopeless fucks is born to replace the tube crews and strippers when they get old and die. Stagnation, lock-in, death of the dream.

Fucking free market is a prick. Nature of the world.

Obviously the proximate bastard in this situation is their dealer, the scumbag who figured out he could hook a whole industry, lower prices and shift volume. The Pale Peruvian Stallion isn't even Peruvian. It's grown and processed domestically. Locally, even. There's almost no supply chain, so fewer opportunities to leak to the cops. That guy is responsible for these shattered lives, at least unless you're prepared to point the finger at traders and banks and speculators and at the whole apparatus that parcels up life in tranches of collateral so you can fake a profit, squeeze the decimals to produce an illusion of growth. That guy is to blame for everything that happens to and around the tube crews up to and including the severing of a corgi thigh and Billy getting dog blood all up his face while he tied off the stump. Full credit to him: PTSD triggers all over the place and he was stone cold. Billy once saw a man's upper half just levitate off the ground, propelled on its own blood rocket. Billy should not have to deal with blood ever again. That is why he declined the army's offer to put him through med school. They would have done counseling for him and everything, made him rich and useful. Except as it turns out the program was cut so all that he actually missed out on was six months of bureaucratic dicking, but you know there was no way for him to know that at the time. The point is that Billy should not have gone through that and the dealer is the man who sent him back into battle. That guy is an asshole.

That guy... I hate that guy.

Yeah it's me.

Obviously – everyone knows this now, yes? – obviously I'm not going round to Billy's office with a hundred grand of cocaine in one of those spy-game metal suitcases because I do not propose to spend my life in jail. I don't make deliveries. I outsource that. Used to be you used juveniles and a lot of the traditional dealers still do, but even though you won't usually get a juvenile sent to real jail, if you use the same kids over and over they get a sense of who you are and how you work and then when they get popped that information tends to become public. Kids are loyal as hell but they're also not stupid. They know when to turn you in and they actually don't believe they can die so they're not scared of you. Juvenile labour is a ticking time bomb plus it's unethical. Those kids should be in school so that they don't turn into tube crews and strippers. Which are both irreproachable careers in the abstract by the way but which owing to the deforming forces of late Neo-Liberal Oligarchy are professions whose outcomes are less desirable than those achievable by education and application and a small but crucial measure of luck.

Plus this is the digital age. My deliveries are ride share. They are zero-hour gig-economy microjobs. You want to move a fifteen-kilo file box from the East Harbour to the Point? There is indeed an app for that. In fact there are a bunch of apps and websites and lists and peer-to-peer services, above-ground legitimate regular people ones like City Fetch, which runs collection errands for busy PAs, and 1brokeIT, which gets you a copy of something you accidentally destroyed so no one ever knows, and mesh-substrate private nets for executive couples seeking convivial third parties and white-collar fight clubs and addiction counseling. You do not care about the technical stuff, the point is this: why bother with maintaining a workforce when there's any number of people who will work on a very occasional freelance basis, without knowing shit about who you are or who the end user is, especially if you can guarantee three things:

a) They are not assisting in the commission of an act of terror. (Deal breaker. You have to make them really comfortable about that.)

b) If they get caught they have plausible deniability. (Not that they assume that you're doing anything wrong, man. But like, in case.)

c) They get paid well for doing something they'd basically do anyway (like commuting, going for coffee in a nearby deli and meeting new people).

You're not inducting newbies into the shadowy world of international smuggling, you're just allowing stand-up citizens to turn an existing downside of the personal economy into a revenue stream. Progress is golden and I am Amazon. I am Uber for illegal drugs. I have everyone from executives in Beemers to old codgers with Z frames running cocaine for me. They know really that this is what they are doing but as long as it is never confirmed they do not care because money and maybe frisson. I do not make them do things they don't feel comfortable with. I do not serve areas those people would not like to go to. I only supply Billy and his tube crew because they work nice areas which is why that falling tube hit a corgi and not a homeless person. Think of it like I am Norwegian Airlines: I do not fly to any destination that is notably shittier than the airport you take off from.

Today I am not even here to talk about cocaine. I'm inevitably going to talk about cocaine because Billy takes a lot of cocaine and people who do that like to talk about it, but I'm even less interested in talking about cocaine or Billy's erection or Billy's previous erection or the various fucking appalling places he chose to deploy that erection than I usually am. I am here to talk about Didi.

Didi was about a thousand years old and looked older and she was bad-tempered and cranky and she smelled awful. She wore that spooky doll make-up that very old ladies wear. I met her once coming home and I honestly thought I'd walked into a horror movie. I thought her head was going to come off and bite my eyes out or she was going to explode and turn into cockroaches and they would crawl all over me. I hated Didi. I hated that she existed and she made my building smell weird and she hissed – like a cockroach she hissed – at my girlfriends when I brought them up here to look at the view and screw on the balcony and drink whisky and she called them loose women and me all kinds of words that meant I was bad. I do not blame her for that. She was right on pretty much all of that stuff. I liked that she was down there listening to me screw on the engineered hardwood with Danish models and hating me. I liked hating her and I was pretty sure it was mutual.

Fuck but she was good value for money. If you were in the market for a real ancient monster like one of those clams in old movies that shuts on your hand just as the shark is coming she was one hundred per cent your girl. She was stubborn and mean and awful. And she didn't even get in a few licks on whoever did it. You'd think she would but they were seriously intense about it. Didn't touch her. Didn't steal from her. Killed her. Not a sound. I slept through the whole thing.

See and that gives me the fucking shits. Could they have done that to me? Is that the whole point? Is that the implication? If so it should come with a pointer in that direction because right now I'm at sea. Maybe it's random. Fucking crazed killer acting all international hitman. Fantasy about being The Jackal and she's the secret president of Atlantis, got to die or the sea people will eat Manhattan. I don't know.

Or maybe she was a target. Or maybe I was.

I do not like that Didi is dead.

So this is not my softer side or redemption calling, this is management.

So I am talking to Billy. He is not my core client base any more precisely because he retains this connection with the lawbreaking motherfuckers of this city and very soon now it's going to be time to cut Billy and his guys out of my loop. They were my first clients but our social circles and our interests may be diverging. Although on the other hand maybe Billy is coming with me, coming upscale. I've been working on that. If he were to redirect his energies the cocaine business with him would dry up naturally, without negative emotions on either side.

Billy figures it is okay to tell me criminal stuff because he figures I must do a lot of murders in order to pursue my commercial project. This is the effect of television and cinema. In my business so long as you don't do a lot of murders and you are careful and smart and you are not leading juveniles into despair and addiction and you are selling to senators and day traders, then no one cares. If the cops even notice you they have better things to do. And if they ever catch you, you cut a deal and they don't have a problem with that because all you've ever done – assuming they can prove beyond a grain or two of it – is meet demand.

I'm infrastructure. I'm substrate. I don't make waves and I am polite. There's no collateral from what I do. None at all. When they decriminalise – and they will – I will go from here to there without doing anything except sending Forbes a press release. Most likely half of them are on my list already but I don't check. Client data is held on their own devices and double hashed because privacy is not something you tack onto a service it is something you build in. I am all about the seamless experience. I am not about noise.

So I ask Billy about Didi.

I say: Is anything going on right now?

Like what? Like construction?

Like warfare or something. Someone moving.

Shakes his head: No. No way. Everyone's happy, it's copacetic. Stable. Everyone's building, everyone's making money. I mean not working people. Legitimate working people in this country are fucked. Am I right? But all the big guys are making money.

I hear ya.

Of course I do. Crime has one-percenters too. And a pretty ferocious middle management stratum, which is another reason to outsource. Who has time to be taking finger joints in the name of HR? I mean what even is that? Fuck should I do with a finger joint? Necklaces?

The way I do things is about money. Like Billy is doing things now because I told him to. Used to be that his office – the only place I ever meet him, because I do not deliver cocaine to his office it goes direct to the sites – was in one of the shittier parts of town. Now the area has moved up a little and it's edgy and artsy and his brick-and-whitewash interior is a little bit authentic. He was going to sell it, cash in, I said no for god's sake stay in, rent out space. Consult. So now he consults on design, which is to say people come to his office and get inspired and go away and duplicate it really expensively using suppliers he specifies and he gets a cut for doing nothing. Additional revenue streams again. He even owns the salon where his guys get their manscaping done which is double economy because he knows all that cocaine-addled hair gets properly disposed of and not scraped into a fucking evidence bag by a drug squad asshole looking to make his numbers.

I thought about buying that place myself but I don't want the connect. I don't want Billy's guys in my place singing last night's hot dance track and breathing stripper fluids and dropping wraps of the cocaine that I sell them through a variety of really clever cutouts on the floor of a business that does not need to be linked to that sort of thing. I don't want the hassle of disposing of evidence in the form of butt-hair scrapings. It's a bad idea. You don't close the circuit. So I told Billy to do it and if it worked out he should pay me in information and it did and he does. He is absolutely straight with me because there are no areas of conflict in our holdings or lines of business and that is to our mutual advantage and we both know it.

I assume that one day he will fuck me on something and then we may experience a little turbulence. But everyone knows I'm not a violent guy so there's really no need to worry about that. I'll take it out in trade. Whatever. Everything goes better without friction.

I said that to Billy once and now it's written on the inside of the salon's glass window: #withoutfriction.

Sometimes I feel old and tired.

Hashtag.

Billy says: So I mean no man, no problems. No one moving, just like nothing. It's all good Jack. Why do you ask?

Because there's a crazy old bitch in my building shot in the head and she's just a crazy old bitch.

Someone's inheritance maybe?

Yeah, maybe.

Thing is Jack people get crazy waiting for old folks to die. When you're young you think shit: grandpa can't hang on long past seventy and even if he does I have all the time in the world. Then grandpa hits seventy and you're already thirty and he don't die and then he hits ninety and you're fucking fifty. Are you kidding me? So suddenly it's all about hey, grandpa, let's go snorkelling! Let's experiment with drugs, grandpa, what've you got to lose?

Fuck, Billy.

I'm saying.

Fuck, people do that?

Do what, Jack?

They try to get their grandparents to take drugs so that they'll die?

Heart failure? Sure Jack all the – yeah maybe not like all of – but yeah they absolutely do yeah.

There is a fucking thing I did not think of. This is why my relationship with Billy is profitable. He's like the perfect shithead. He attracts the complex and simple thoughts of all shitheads and he explains them to me. So now I'm making a note: I need an age ceiling on my sales, or possibly some sort of health check. That would actually work. The way Billy has his salon, I could have some kind of spa or fitness thing, hire some trainers, some medics. Yet another layer keeping me away from the bad, making me look legit. Who knows? Might take off so hard I could just shed the coke thing, back burner it until it's legal. Although you want to stay ahead of the curve on something like that, the technology, the consumer. Probably best to hang in there. Plus also I like coke not like to take but I like the product because it is elegant. It does exactly what it says on the billboard. Coke fucks you up.

Back to Didi.

Someone does pay Didi's rent, for sure. Did pay it. Can't possibly just be that person economising, not with a hit. Hidden costs everywhere in that kind of decision and it is all totally downside risk so why? Is someone maybe sending a message to someone else and it just happens I'm near the phone?

Billy says he wants me to come and see his brother Rex, who is in demolition, blow up a building. Someplace called the Triangle – yes there are three buildings arranged in a triangle because downtown civic architecture is nothing if not disappointingly predictable – and they will destroy the tallest of them and it will go straight down into the ground. Rex recommends that everyone come and bring a date because apparently the sight of this happening is almost certain to lead to coitus. Do not ask me why I do not want to think about it.

Rex is almost exactly like Billy except he destroys and Billy creates so he is like yin to Billy's yang except obviously do not ever ask Billy about his yang. Rex and company are if anything even more fucked on the Pale Peruvian Stallion than Billy's crew and that should fucking terrify everyone in the free world.

I say: thank you Billy I will put that in my planner.

Billy says that's cool and then I say goodbye and get on the crosstown train and think about the things that I have learned.

Snorkelling. For fuck's sake.

Crosstown rail. Getting so it's the oldest thing in the city, and it's not even that old. They say you're a local when you miss how this place used to be. Basically everyone these days. Mind you they say that about New York too and look how that goes.

Time sickness. Future shock. Information overload. All the bullshit ways we tell ourselves the world's getting faster. It's not. We're just older. Seen too much, just want to sit down and have a cup of coffee.

The crosstown is like death without all the drama. Just peace and quiet and everyone is grey. Briefcases and umbrellas and long coats. All kinds of people because this is that kind of city. White, black and brown people, Germans and Angolans and Brazilians, Native Americans and Dutch and Manchurians and Okinawans. World in a basket, all of them grey in the sleet.

Back where I came from – where the city is a kind of curseword or a bedtime story to scare your kids with – we farmed. Probably what sent me into coffee and then into cocaine. I know crop. Always have. Still keep my mother's place, got some livestock. Pigs in wallows. My thing now, notionally: organic goods and artisanal produce. Biologically fermented soft drinks and herbal remedies. Smoked bacon. Anything I feel like.

See how that works? I can buy and own chemical gear. I can travel and sell. I can carry powder samples. You want to guess if I ever carry cocaine in a pot of mustard? OF COURSE I DON'T! Ten points. Now you're getting it. I do all the things you should do if you deal cocaine, but that's not how I deal cocaine. It's completely clean and separate. I have letters from border authorities, from ministers, explaining to local law that I'm a legitimate trader in high-end edibles, that it's my endless and slightly amusing chore to move things that look as if they could contain drugs across borders. Everyone knows that I look like a coke importer because I'm not one, and all the time I am. If I ever get caught they'll be like: of course! Fuck, I should have seen that. Like a good crime movie. Should have seen it. And then they'll realise their careers are at an end because: judgement. They've got none, and they put themselves on the line for me, recommended me, explained me. They're done.

Or of course they could make my little problem go away. I could be very financially remunerative in the right circumstances. Or not.

I'm on the crosstown. I like the crosstown.

Grey crosstown people and rain outside and sitting all placid on the bockadabonk bockadabonk railway that being the noise railways make and reading this woman's paper that's sitting opposite and I am content like relaxed and in my happy place and then seriously it is just that day:

WWWWWUUUUUURAGH

Whut—

GONNA FUCKIN KILL YOU

Oh for fuck's sake—

GONNA KILL YOU MAAAN

My god it never rains et cetera.

This guy, with a – what is that? Is that even a real gun? Fuck. This is going to go so wrong. What's happening here? Not like, in this compartment. I know what's happening in this compartment. I'm asking: what's happening to my life now? You know how statistically unlikely this is? Didi gets executed under me and a dog gets shished and now this guy this asshole with his enormagun and his GONNA KIIIIILLLL YYYEEEWWW.

Who says that? Who has a gun the size of a – I mean if he fires that thing at someone – well fuck if that scaffolding pole had hit a baby horse then maybe that would make the same kind of—

Yeah fuck off it's a tube I know. You really going to do this with me now?

KILL YOU ALL NOW. SHOOT YOU INNA FUCKING HEAD RIGHT NOW.

Who talks like that? Is he even listening to himself?

Gold-plated Libyan dictator gun. Miami club owner gun. Fucking James Bond badguy gun. All the stereotypes. Big. Fucking. Gun. Is what I'm saying.

In my crosstown. In my fucking crosstown. There are many others like it but this one is mine. What even is that about? Is he asking for money?

I say: Hey! Is this about money? You want money?

My fellow passengers are not happy. Assholes. Do they think he's just gonna go away? Ignore him darling it's just an unwashed fuckhead with a hand cannon. Pay no mind.

Seriously what? Who thinks that? You want to live your way

through this? There are protocols. There are fucking procedures, man. There are ways and means.

First you got to make contact. Gotta get so he thinks of you as a person not a face in the crowd.

My name's Jack. What's yours?

Nothing. Just gooooogly eyes like gooooogly. Man's not on a crosstown he's on a ghost train. Seeing ghosts. What's he seeing? Evil alien lizards maybe. Could go wrong.

I say: Now you say Hey Jack I want all your money. All right? And I go in here and I get all my money and give it to you. And this guy here does the same and so on. Is that what you want?

KILL YOU?

Probably not me. You and I we're just on the same train, right?

I GUESS.

Is there someone here you were gonna kill? Like really?

FUCKING LUCILLE.

Fifty-fifty: there is a Lucille and she is maybe going to die, or he's not just heavily armed and psychotic he's also big into Kenny Rogers. Fuck me but the first one would be so preferable.

By the way where the fuck is everyone? He's got the gun pointed at the floor now. Is no one going to step up and just take it away? Mother fuck I can't do it! I'm a professional criminal. There are limits to how much media exposure a person in my position really wants.

FUCKING LUCILLE!

Pointing the gun again. Seriously my fellow travelers are a disappointment. Guy's pointing the giant gun at me for crying out loud. What did I ever do? At me. Away from me. At me. Away. At me. Away. Like that fucking tick tocker on the top of my piano teacher's piano fucking tick tock tick tock. I hated piano but she was hot and I was old enough to know that boobs were really interesting. Jesus Jack not right the fuck now you know? Tick fucking tock.

LUCCCCIIIILLLLLLE.

Shit on a shitstick.

I sing the song. Hungry children, crops in the fields. I always think that line is four hundred. Four hundred children. Like he's farming them on little allotments and they come out of the ground and he picks them and sells them off the back of a wagon.

Well, maybe I don't think that because it's Kenny Rogers not Pink Floyd's unreleased rural gothic album, but I did have a nightmare about it every week for a year when I was fifteen. Gun guy stares at me like we're communing with god.

Then I forget what the next line is.

LUCILLE!

OhfuckitSMACK.

LUCILLE!

Smack.

Bang.

Smack smacksmack fuck you smacksmacksmack fucking miserable smack bastard. What are the odds? They're astronomical. Like literally it's more likely I get hit by a meteorite than I have to deal with this level of crap this often in one week unless the city is really sliding into anarchy and it's not despite what you read in the news. Crime is down which is how a serious criminal likes it. Down, stable, controlled, profitable. Nothing to get excited about. Fact of life.

LUCILLLLLLE!

How are you even conscious, man? For fuck's sake.

Black leather gloves. I always wear gloves in winter. Hit him as hard as I want to, don't have to worry about hepatitis or whatever because gloves. Fucking loser with a gun. Shot a hole in my crosstown and now I'm going to be late because cops and whatever that I do not want. Sure my life is an open book and I'm this completely upstanding citizen pillar of the la la la but you don't want to be standing in the precinct house passing the fucking time because that is just an opportunity to fuck yourself in the face.

SmacksmackSMACKforgoodmeasureyouasshole.

Crunching sound is boots and they pull me off, my fellow travelers on my crosstown. Man down! Stop. Oh sure you're all heroes now that it's over. Fucking fat boy there will be on the news tonight like how he charged the perpetrator and made an opening for me. Fucking ridiculous.

This whole thing is fucking ridiculous. Statistically improbable. Absurd.

Is that a problem like my kind of problem? Is this part of the same shit as Didi? Is someone dicking with me? This is not how I would dick if I was dicking but maybe that's the point.

Ash taste again but this time it's mine. Belongs to me, not like me on fire. This is me as fire, salamander style. Who the hell understands how the head works?

That's what I tell the first responder. She says yes sir that's fine and puts me in the back of her car to settle down. Little while later the sergeant takes a statement and says I can go. Tells me I did a pretty good job: coulda been lighter but I'm a civilian and I haven't been trained and to be honest in that situation sir it's better to be like totally excessive because you do not want to leave the thing half done and get shot.

That's right. Just a civilian.

Back when I was the Cardinal (of coffee but we do not say of coffee because everyone knows) there were a lot of guys who would bet on anything. It was a pathology with them like they could not get enough of their buzz from trading a commodity that is already almost psychopathically weird anyway. They had to bet fifty euros or fifty dollars or fifty-nine-point-seven Swiss francs on which fucking fruit fly would fly out of the bowl before all the others. These assholes would put money down and then someone would start trading derivates and spread and before long one of them would owe like ten thousand and the others would make him stick to that or pay it in strippers. Even the women were like this. Like if someone ever tells you that women do not behave like assholes in that environment like no. The straight ones will just make all those asshole male colleagues go to a club with male strippers so that there are pictures of macho Don the King of Coffee (Delaware) sitting in a blue velvet lounger with nine inches of improbable dong right in front of his nose and of course then there has to be a bet on which stripper will have the most improbable dong. Your own dong size is what's really going on here but no one ever bets on that because once you know, where do you go from there?

You know what else they would bet on? Who had to pee first. Who could pee straightest for longest. Who could memorise more digits of the daily ticker. Who could guess the phone number from the beeps on a cellphone. Whatever. They would bet on anything, because sooner or later you're in a helicopter that's landing on a pad somewhere in the jungle and the pad has a fucking swastika painted on it because that's who you're talking to today. Fucking jungle coffee Nazis. Because coffee. Because humans. Fucking humans.

Because they did these things I did them too and because I was the Cardinal I always won and that meant I didn't have to bet. I can tell you the first ten items on the ticker for every day the whole of 1998. Still. Cannot get that shit out of my head if I want to. Whatever.

Fucking humans do fucking awful shit.

Such as killing my horrible neighbour for no good reason. Should I just let that go? Chalk it up to humans and forget it?

It just bugs me. I need to know why. Not like need to need to. Just like need to because if I don't it's just gonna keep bugging me and actually that is not good. Focus is important. Didi is a fucking productivity suck. She is like Candy Crush but with murder.

Inevitably there's a kind of temptation here. I am a criminal so I could go all hard-boiled about it. I could just go loco. Go rogue. Show this fucking city what it's like when I cut loose. I've been cautious and well-behaved this whole time. I've been polite. What would it be like if I just let go? Over the top. Totally out to lunch. Crazy Jack Price. Fuuuuuck yeah. Blaze of glory man like old school. And there is an argument for that if I am being dicked with because it is clearly not what would be expected of me and it is not something anyone will have planned for.

But it's not good business is what it's not. I'm all about the business.

Crazy Jack Price.

There's a line I've always joked about in my head. Standing on top of a bar with a broken bottle like fucking old school is what:

MY NAME'S JACK. YOU DO WHAT I SAY, OR I'M THE PRICE YOU PAY!

Could get myself one of Lucille's golden guns while I'm at it. I'm calling the fuckhead Lucille. Why not. Turns out he doesn't have much of any other name.

Now I'm at the precinct house and this face is a cop face: all jaw and Officer Krupke. Leo's not around. This is another guy who thinks I am a lucky fucking amateur. He's talking Didi but not like talking talking, like making a statement to someone on the outside. Which is good. I am on the outside. I am totally unfamiliar with the criminal milieu because I am a standup civilian is what I am.

Cop says: Well sir I can tell you what this was not. It was not a random thing. There is no one out there just doing this that we know of and we would know because this is not a first-timer. There is no hesitation here and there are no mistakes. So you should not bother yourself on that score sir. This person will not be back and is not interested in you unless you and Miss Fraser are connected which I understand you are not.

(Didi Fraser. Desdemona Fraser. I suppose I did know her full name. It's on her box down by the main door. Was. They've already taken it off. Now it's just a brass blank.)

Homeowner Jack: thing is I guess officer, thing is I guess, we're not connected except by physical proximity. You don't think someone was looking to use our building as what would you call it a vantage? I mean am I in danger from – I don't know – if somehow this is an ongoing thing?

Cop gives me a little pro-class smile like what am I six years old? Says: Like a sniper's nest or some such? Yes sir we also watch TV sir. So we thought of that Mr Price but there's really nothing in that line that we'd expect. There are no government buildings or what have you, nothing that anyone would particularly hate. There are no banks so it isn't a heist situation. There's no political angle, not like a motorcade coming down your street. And if you just reckon that this is someone looking to shoot randomly into a crowd then the angles are bad and anyway having done this the building is now off limits because we're aware. The whole point of that would be to leave us unaware until the Event.

(I can hear him say the E in Event.)

So it really is a puzzler sir but what it is not is a problem for you.

Cop face is hard-working and cooperative. He's giving me the best information he can within bounds. I am maybe a recent hero of some deal on the crosstown that he privately thinks was bare-ass and hare-brained and I am lucky to be alive but that does not make me a cop so I cannot have everything he knows. All the same he's telling me the truth. I can check with Leo later but I know already this is the straight shit.

Thanks officer thank you. I do feel better.

I remember to ask about Lucille. Concerned citizen is what. Like: oh that poor man is he being cared for? I was so distressed that I had to beat the shit out of him with my personal hands.

Lucille is in a secure hospital. Guy seems to be living on the far side of crazy canyon and could have gone off like a bomb so I'm this big exemplar of civic action and shit. That really was a role I had in mind for someone else. There was that huge college jock sitting two seats over. I was sure he'd have a go but he just fucking sat there.

Cop shows me to the door. Basically kisses me goodbye and waves me away. Tells me not to worry about it. Read that as: respect man but don't come back asking for more, this is what it is, we're on it.

Okay then.

My penthouse. My home which is directly above where Didi Fraser got shot twice in the chest and once in the face. You need a key to get to the top floor. I have one. No one else does.

They get me coming out of the elevator. Heavy hands and a billy club or a real old-fashioned sap. They stretch me out. Not white light but yellow and a noise like BOCK that is the back of my head and warm stuff down the collar of my expensive shirt. Falling down I see masks: those fuck ugly flesh tone ones that aren't of anyone or anything. And what the fuck are those masks actually supposed to be for if not for anonymity during the commission of a crime?

Inevitably: someone kicks me in the balls. I go away for a moment, puke some. Nearest boots dance away swearing. Seriously man you're gonna beat a guy down but you're scared of puke. Weak as shit. Come down here I got coffee breath.

Next one's my mouth. Teeth crack. Yellow light goes green-brown like a tunnel made of bugs all around my head. Crawling green-brown and some asshole is making a noise like a donkey or a violin like hee-yurr-hee-yurrr. Godfuckinghell they are breaking me and I can feel it happening and FUCK YOU for that feeling because now I will always know what it is like. I will remember this moment for ever. This is a body being damaged. This is fragility is the limits of life is the boundary condition and fuck you so much.

Who does all that in a fucking blank mask? Show some respect. Wear a fucking clown face or Gojira whatever I don't care. Be a monster not a parenthesis.

Fuck. It's going on and on. Cracked ribs cracked everyfuck-ingthing and pain and beneath the pain the knowing. You wanted to tell me something I get that and I'm a reasonable guy so what the FUCK is wrong with the phone?

Fuck.

One actual message right into my ear. One message in words: Forget about Didi. Fucking leave it alone.

They watch me, all just standing there around me while I crawl across the floor. Cold. Surgical cold. They watch me knock the phone down off the table. They watch me fuck up the numbers as I try to dial and I have to start again. They watch me call the cops.

That same guy answers, the enthusiast. Send the fucking car, send it, I'm bleeding on my own floor. Three men. Masks.

It comes out different. Mafkf. Vree meh' i' mafukuh. Bleeheh ow o' muh vluh.

One of the masks gets his phone out too like real demonstrative. Dials a number. Tells someone it's done. Just like that, like pro stylee like in a movie. Wow what a jackass. Almost had me believing you there believing you were actually someone competent. Fuck. Fucking bullshit masks and now this. Just rude. Just fucking unnecessary.

Fnukng uknegegahy.

Phone guy shrugs and they go.

Hak. Hak. Fnukg rug gnuknegegahy. A hak hak.

Listening to my own voice: strangest feeling in my chest. Is that a rib in my lung? In my heart? Is that my death in there waiting?

Nope. Still here. What is that?

Man what is it? Perfect in the moment zen state like a religious thing is what. The opposite of death like birth but like being born complete as me. Like ash in reverse ash falling up and becoming stone and metal. Like getting beans from an espresso. I'm a little bit hazy—

They start in on me again like they were just having a break for a chat and a beer and then I know it, it's—

Clarity.

Clarity like the mute button like cold water in the dry heat. I'm back baby. No more hippy revelation shit. Yeah fucking kick me that's right get it done. I got places to be man ain't got time for this.

These boys have no idea how badly they have just screwed the pooch. And the pooch is being screwed so hard the fucking cat next door is screaming. There are wolves in Canada looking at one another's assholes right now like FUCK that's uncomfortable what the actual FUCK?

Masked men. Do you know who I am?

No. You have no clue.

But you just fucked up, my friends. And when you fuck up you know what I am? I am—

Yeah that line was cooler when I wasn't angry. Now it doesn't even begin. Lying on my own floor. Expensive fucking carpet covered in my own blood. Pissed myself, as you do. Don't tell anyone that part. Tell them about the broken fingers not the fucking swollen agonising balls. Hope that's not blood in there.

Does.

Not.

Begin.

Get better. Then we'll see. See if that line is funny.

Oh, shit. I hope that's not me dying. I can feel it coming up: huge shadows red and black but not really black. More brown. I'm not blacking out. Brownout. When I had to have my appendix done they gave me anaesthetic and it wasn't like this. It was like cold in me like a wave, and then I was back again and all hilariously doo-lally flirting with the nurses.

Not like this. Warm brown creeping in at the edges, seducing and cosy and what if it's the end? This 70s geometric print carpet. Wall carpet like in one of those Frank Lloyd Wright holdovers. I loved this carpet but now I'm not so sure. I'm worried it's like a little too post-ironic like maybe it's just tacky but hell it's gone now right? No way I can get this much me out of it. Pain in the ass.

Stay away from Didi? Forget about her? Fuck Didi. Are you fucking joking? In my own house? You're fucking joking. You do this and you expect me to go away? Boy did you ever misread your fucking audience.

You made me see mortality you pricks. I'm scared. Scared of dying on my own floor, dying of vintage funkadelic wallcarpet.

But I won't die. This is personal but it's also more than that. Because there's a business issue here too, and business never dies. There's an issue of criminal territory and reputation.

Money never sleeps, and I'm the Price you pay.

Been staring at this ceiling for a while, and I know my mood's all gussied up with high-spec medical opiates. It's like the local speciality: go to hospital, get whacked up with some appalling fucking painkiller you'll never quite see the back of, like a bad relationship you can't leave because the sex is so good. Doesn't matter you wake up and she's looking down at you with a carving knife in one hand, stone drunk and calling you all kinds of things you've never heard of, and fucking thank you yes I have and I never want to do that again.

Still staring at the ceiling. Can practically see the outline of her face, perfectly still and calm. Face and chin and breast and knife, this stunning outline like a goddess, like something from a temple where the hand and the eye and nipple and blade say something meaningful and eternal. I had sleep paralysis for a while and this was one of those times. She thought I was asleep with my eyes open. Lucia. That was her name. Gorgeous Lucia, the Milanese blonde by way of Connecticut. I got out that same day, it's not you it's me thanks for the memories changed the locks. Back in my pre-Cardinal days back when I was just a kid really. Two years later she opened a man's throat with a straight razor and then cut herself to ribbons. Both of them died and two EMTs quit on the spot.

But the drugs are so good I can remember the times before that and feel her arms around me and that is nice.

I'm going to hate tomorrow. That's when they'll turn this off. They'll tell me it's for my own good, don't want to make an addict, they'll start giving me fucking ibuprofen. Fuck's sake. They'll be right. I'll still hate it. But then I'm going to hate everything tomorrow.

Woman comes in, French African, face like a mother. Bedside manner says she doesn't like me: good. I know that look. She saves her compassion for when you're going to die. I smile at her.

Put that away, she says. Won't do you any good with me. I know your kind.

What kind? Except I can't say that because my mouth's got no spit. Clahhhkt gigh?

Kind comes in with a beating like that, she says. Did something to deserve that, didn't you.

No. But I'm going to. (Moch pfuh kgunn.)

Drink some water, tough guy.

I drink.

At least you're not humming any more.

Was I humming?

All the damn time.

Oh yes. I remember.

That's just great tough guy.

Mm mm mm hmm hmm hmm hmm.

That's just great.

I hum my little hum.

Days later. Can speak again. Make a call. Ringeddy ring and la la la.

Charlie you up?

Yeah boss I'm in the office.

Charlene works flexible time. She hates mornings. Statistically: more intelligent people are messy and like to stay up late. I don't care when she works which is why she works for me. That and the cocaine. Charlene is a designer and a semi-pro digital criminal and she is fond of cocaine. She and cocaine are not in a committed relationship, they are friends with benefits. She is literally the only person I have ever met who could quite happily just stop taking cocaine tomorrow. She does not take cocaine when she is working; she takes cocaine when there's not enough work. Then she gets bored of taking cocaine and she goes out and finds more work.

When she is not building card skimmers and running untraceable low-end bank fraud via the glorious new motherland of crime that is called the internet, Charlene designs wraps and other branding for the Pale Peruvian Stallion. The name is hers too. She said it evoked a classic 80s Escobar shamelessness coupled with ironic self-knowledge and a hint of porno, and that sophisticated people would totally put that up their noses. She was entirely right.

Charlie I need a makeover. I need a whole new look.

A thang?

Sure why not?

Cool beans can do.

Charlie my nose is broken, I've got some cracked teeth, what are we doing about that?

Shit boss really?

Really really for realz.

Don't do that you sound like my kid sister.

Well anyway.

Okay then something a little piratical maybe – wait are you going to get the nose dealt with, like surgery?

Not any time soon. Ten days until it's what it's gonna be for now.

Okay then definitely pirate, how do you feel about maybe some gold teeth?

Negatory Charlie I will need to move around unseen in the night no man shall know my name or recognise me by my exciting shiny teeth.

Cool just ordinary teeth gotcha. Take a couple days to tone in okay?

And then Charlie take the week off. Get out of town. Actually stay out until I call you. There is some heavy shit going down.

Things gonna get rough?

I'm about to take steps Charlie, I got no idea what's gonna shake loose but I figure no reason you should be around for it.

Received and understooded boss. I'm gone.

Bye Charlie.

I was the Cardinal. Now I'm Jack Price. Humming my little motherfucking hum.

Hospital administrator checking me out. Like prison but expensive. I'm shitting you I have no idea what it's like leaving a prison because I've never been in one and I never will.

Sorry you're leaving us Mr Price – just my little joke of course hahaha. We're always glad when people walk out on us please sign here and here to indemnify the hospital against any consequences of your early departure contrary to medical advice please do not seek further prescriptions of the drugs you have been taking as there is a note on your file.

Pops the absolute last thing I want is more of this fairy juice in my blood. I hate narcotics. Clue is in the name: a drug that makes you sleep. Enough people sleep their lives away. Sleep through school because it's boring, sleep through college and first jobs because the other kids are mean, sleep through a marriage, a divorce. Sleep through their own death. Fuck narcotics. And fuck meth and cocaine while we're at it, which make you too hyper to know that you're awake. Fuck LSD unless you are using it for all the medical applications we're not allowed to know about because that is a goddam hippy counterculture drug and we all know that drugs are for the one per cent not the fucking Occupy Movement. That's just the law of nature. Fuck all of those things. Give me booze and coffee and adrenalin and sex and I will give you a real person and I will give you a fucking Dalai Lama Gandhi Einstein of living from one instant to another and amen.

Pops signs me out and gives me the fishy eye because I'm limping off like a guy with a bat in his hands looking to Al Capone somebody's shit and that is exactly what I am. I am a guy who got the message and I have words. I have words and I have responses and emotions I need to express, like give voice to, like poetry.

Told me not to ask questions. Told me to mind my own business. Told me with their fists and their feet. Should have fucking asked nicely. No need for this at all. No need of any kind whatsofuckingever.

Should just have left me alone or killed me is all I'm saying. Seriously misunderstood who you're dealing with. Probably would have gotten bored asking about Didi and fucked off on my own account maybe. Maybe not if I'm honest. But I got a lot on my plate what with this whole commercial enterprise involving the distribution of branded cocaine to the digital city. There was just no need. That's the key. These cracked ribs and my fucking imperfect sideways nose which I have guarded my whole entire life so that I would not look like my sponging dad or my sour damp median middle-management-impotent-sweat-stained-front-row-of-the-strip-club-jerking-off grandpapa, both of whom got their looks rearranged at one time or another in discussions over late payment.

Just.

No.

Need.

And the thing is that now there's this perceptual issue this business issue that I have mentioned. There's a question of directionality, of who puts whose dick in the wringer. Sure I am like totally atomised. I am the criminal enterprise of the next century I got no structure no hierarchy no conventional apparatus as such, but all the same it needs to be understood that I am all the same the guy who does the dick-putting. I turn the handle. But right now there is this perceptual issue I mentioned in which during what you might call my personal time someone has – mistakenly and no doubt for reasons that seem good and sufficient to them – someone has reversed the natural course of human events. It's a mythical problem by which I mean that it's a classic not that it's not real. It is a Joseph Campbell issue is what. The whole order of things in the universe has been uprooted and unless that order can be restored there will be a vortex of destruction: rains of fish, snitches in the hedgerows and a plague of cops.

So this is a holy quest is what: a divine restoration of the flowing river of the wounded land.

But before that obviously: teeth.

This place is too damn white. White walls in high-vis like super reflective. Everything is white. It makes your teeth look very yellow in the mirrors which is what they want. Makes your skin look pale and sick which is what they want. Welcome to cosmetic hell and of course they can admit you to beautiful heaven – for a price.

A Price. Heh.

Hi Mr Mowbray how can we help you?

I need five minutes with your Doctor Greene if I may call it an urgent financial matter. I know it's real irregular Miss... oh okay I know it's real irregular Sonja but it's important and I will put this here – that's ten thousand dollars in cash – and if you in any way feel that you have been disrespected by me when I have spoken to Doctor Greene or if you feel your professional position has been diminished with him then it's yours okay? In your sole estimation right so it's entirely up to you.

I really – wow gosh that's—

It's what we call a surety Sonja it's like my bet against myself but don't worry this will be okay. He's between patients I gather so I'll just let myself through okay?

I gosh I wait well I—

Thanks Sonja.

Hi Doctor Greene how would you like to make five hundred thousand in ten minutes?

I beg your—

That's what five hundred thousand looks like. It's legal and entirely clean there's no downside here for you. It is quite heavy though so you will probably want to call a cab or something. What I want is I want these teeth fitted in my mouth with a – what is that stuff called I have it written down – anyway like a permanent bond fixture what you do with some kind of light-activated adhesive laser arrangement?

Yes we have that facility.

Well okay these teeth here they're caps made specifically for my recent injury and they are prepared for that kind of adhesion but I obviously cannot do it myself so what I would propose to you is I sit down here in this chair and you go right ahead and fix them and then I will walk out and leave the money and what happens to it thereafter is entirely up to you. Oh and by the way Sonja can keep her ten grand as well she's sweet.

Sonja would you ask Ms Miles to step in here we're going to oblige this gentleman and I'm afraid Mr Crofts will have to wait.

If he turns up it will be about ten minutes do apologise for me. Now sir let's get you all comfy. Oh. These are rather well done. They won't be as elegant as some of our top lines but they're certainly – yes they'll do very well and of course they're very durable oh I see yes there's a sort of force distribution frame that's very well done. Tell me do you happen to know who designed this approach it's novel but I rather—

I'll put her in touch she's extremely smart you'll like her but if you don't mind I'm on the clock—

Why of course. Ah here we go… Sir?

Yes?

Can you stop humming for a moment?

Oh sure sorry.

Here we go.

New mouth new clothes, haircut. Barber cuts my hair like I'm made of rice paper I got so many bruises. Fucking Frankenstein. Do not do not tell me that was the professor, I know. The monster never had a name.

I have a name. I have a name and a thin hard face with purple bootprints on it. I have thin lips split in three places and when I smile the teeth are like a quilt or maybe like geology. I have brown bedroom eyes that are swollen half shut, and my nose, my goddam nose, now is like a little bit of history repeating, like I should let my hair grow in Saigon and lose my job on the twenty-second floor and make a bad investment on a horse called Crossroad Guitar. Screw heredity and screw history and most of all screw you I have opinions. I have views. I am going to sit in the share chair and tell you a story.

I give the barber extra because the stitches on my scalp make her want to puke. I am a dramatic-looking motherfucker right now.

Mm mm mm hmm hmm hmm hmm…

See that right there? That is my little hum that I have been humming. It is my little happy hum. You know what else it is? It is the sound of a cellphone number. Because I was the Cardinal. I am Jack Price. I remember the first ten items on the ticker for every day in 1998. And now I remember this too.

I am Jack Price.

Dial the number. Nice lady in an office, got that midtown sound like expensive like corporate. Office has real walls not those fake ones. You can tell by the quality of the sound. These people own their real estate.

Good then. Good.

I get my briefcase and I go see a man.

Hi, sweetheart.

Guy on the reception desk does not like that at all. Fucking baseline homphobia still inherent in our society is what and I figure if he really sat down and thought about it and examined his soul he'd be ashamed and that would make him a better person but who has time for that in the modern world so in a way I'm helping him here.

Guy is big like a Texas farmer, round head round face round arms. Gym muscle with plenty of ring time. No hair to speak of, making sure to wear his elastine suit jacket just a little small so that we can all see that it stretches when he moves, like yeah okay (sweetheart) you're a really strong guy. Figure he goes by some name like Ted or Butch or Chuck.

Hi, Ted or Butch or Chuck says. Sir. Just enough of a gap in between to mean that guys who come in here with broken noses looking like hell generally leave again without taking a meeting or getting offered coffee.

I'm Jack Price I have a meeting with Mr Linden.

Actually I just called Mr Linden's temporary assistant and told her I was dropping by and she said no but I told her I needed five minutes with Linden and it was about Didi Fraser and she should tell him I was coming and then at that point her responsibility would be at an end and she said okay. Temps understand the nature of the world better than permanent employees.

I give Ted or Butch or Chuck a bored face. He gives it back.

I say: Men's room?

Through that door, sir. Dorothy? Yes, I'll hold.

I go to the men's room and pee. Then I go back to the waiting room.

I didn't catch your name, I tell Ted or Butch or Chuck.

I'm Oliver. Sir.

Well, fuck me in the ear. Okay, your name is Oliver, are you also a fan of Fellini and Truffaut and do you like postmodern architecture?

No, sir.

No?

No. Truffaut is overrated, the result of an admittedly successful promotional campaign conducted by himself in which he deified Alfred Hitchcock who was a sociopath. Fellini's persistent reputation rests on one shot in *8½* which film schools require their students to watch, and the postmoderns are negatively shackled to a modernist form that never entirely expressed itself because materials science was insufficient to yield actual instances of its highest form. They pre-dismiss what is yet to flower. Sir.

Are you fucking kidding me with this, Oliver?

In no way sir.

Are you security here or are you in law school?

I am both, Mr Price. Hold on. (Touching his earpiece.) Yes Dorothy. Yes. I understand. Mr Price I'm sorry Mr Linden will not see you. I regret sir. You should now depart.

Open the briefcase: got a hip flask in it. Show it to him. Stage magic.

Oliver, you'll be wanting to get your huge ass off that chair and come out from behind your desk.

Why is that sir?

Because I am going to count to three Oliver and then I am going to kick up a ruckus. When they find you, you'll want to be out in front of the desk so that it's clear that you made the effort or they'll fire you. Don't worry—

I was going to say it won't hurt, but, unfortunately, it will.

Oliver gets up. Takes awhile. Figure he's not actually as tall as Big Billy but he makes up for that by being filled with perilous intent. He's way wide, like a minivan. Guy no doubt takes up two maybe three seats at his local arthouse cinema when he's watching Frank Capra movies and eating my bodyweight in popcorn. I take a big step back and he follows, and I take another. Now I go, got my back almost to the door.

Oliver do you carry any sort of weapon or are you just meat?

Oliver has one of those telescoping batons which he should not have but that's fine. I thumb the door release and joggle the door as if I'm thinking I should get out. Door doesn't open. Wouldn't open because I didn't press the release all the way. Wave the hip flask. Sluice, spit it back in the bottle. Nothing special: high-alcohol mouthwash and low-toxicity disinfectant. Do not swallow.

Oliver isn't fooled:

Sir. I do not recommend this course.

Yeah, well.

It does not seem to me that your last physical entanglement went well for you sir.

Three guys jumped me, Oliver, on an off night, in my own place to which only I have a key.

Very well sir. Lay on.

The fuck? Lay on. What even is that? I take a pull from the flask, hold it behind my lips.

You got to understand that Oliver here and I have just built up something of a rapport. We are friendly now, and most people honestly find it a bit tricky to go from that position to the one where you're eating another guy's ear. And indeed Oliver is most people. He expects me to take a swing at him, or maybe he thinks I'm going to try to kick out his legs. That would be a great strategy if we were in some kind of sports event. No question, you take a man's base and he is going down. A few good shots by nimble Jack while huge slow Oliver swings haymakers would look great on TV. Of course, there's no reason for Oliver to be slow. I mean, he's big, but that doesn't mean he's a claymation puppet. He's taken time out to show me how damn slow he is, which means he thinks he's pretty much not. Yeah, well. I did not come here to demonstrate my prowess in some obscure Silesian fighting style. I came because I want to talk to Linden and the quickest way to do that is to run up the north face of mount Oliver and rip parts of his skin off with my teeth.

Plus also there's this perceptual issue and I need to address that. Did you see what Jack Price did to the security guard? And he fucking liked that guy!

Yeah well business is business and I am business.

I jump into his arms. I'm solving a problem like Maria: group hug! Oliver doesn't know what the fuck is going on. Big guy like him no one wants to grapple. They got compunction. Doesn't occur to them how bad it can get for Oliver before he can turn a hug into a submission hold. Climb him like a curtain. Did you see what Jack Price did? Fucking perceptual issue? Perceive this.

Get a good grip and bite down. One. Two. Three. Chomp and twist, spit. Repeat. Broken teeth hurt. They're fixed not healed. Call it an even trade. Between me and my teeth that is. Oliver is having a shit day. A day of shit. He's just all kinds of unhappy about this, visually he's gone from a wide Tom Cruise vibe to maybe if he's lucky one day cool scars like Tony Amendola in a second and a half. Plus you know: mouthwash in his open wounds. Stings like a motherfucker.

Yeah he's doing lots of screaming and yelling. Bellowing like a water buffalo: MOOO MAAAAH MOOO! UNNGH MOOO! Yeah guy whatever. Get your Discovery Channel on man everyone will understand. And now I really am hugging him because hey this is a professional situation. Not like there's any need to be a monster about it. There you go man let it out.

MOOO MAAAAAH AHHHH MNOOOMOO.

Yeah that's easy for you to say.

(Although pretty clearly he's actually having a lot of trouble. Life man it's a pisser.)

Blood all over my shirt. Quick swill of mouthwash from my flask, spit on the carpet. Very important when fighting with the teeth to maintain good hygiene standards, you wouldn't want to pick up anything nasty. All serious bar fighters brush their teeth regularly to be sure to avoid gum disease and so on. I like to go that mile and be sure about stuff like hepatitis although you know you wouldn't expect that from a guy like Oliver but I mean hep C man it's the silent killer.

Toss the flask back in the case and snap the clips shut because that's what businessmen do. Check the mirror. White shirt red. Excellent. Straighten my tie. See what I did there? No, course not. Because the hand deceives the eye is what. You're too busy looking at the blood to appreciate the fine details. Business is all about the details.

Temp assistant comes in. Hi, Dorothy. Mr Price to see Mr Linden he is right now expecting me.

Yes sir I believe he is.

Give Linden some credit, he's pretty cool about it. He knows Dorothy is outside on the phone to the cops, figures he needs to buy time: So Mr Price what can I do for you?

Well, okay, here's the thing. There was a misunderstanding recently involving violence.

I hardly call what happened just now—

No not that. That was all me. Forward me a bill for Oliver's medical okay? He seems nice.

Big smile: my clean teeth, all like rock strata.

No Mr Linden, I'm referring to a few nights ago when some gentlemen in the employ of someone to whom you are professionally connected mistakenly broke into my apartment and beat me down to my carpet and generally got in my face quite literally in my face. You will get that I disapprove. You will apprehend my general aura of disapproval.

Linden nods.

I cannot be doing with this Mr Linden.

Nod.

But here's the thing, this was a crossed wire and I get that. Okay? I am a reasonable sort of person and I get that. Your connection – no please Mr Linden unfortunately one of the gentlemen who disarranged my nose made the questionable decision to call your office direct to indicate that his obligations had been discharged and I chanced to overhear sir yes I have made something of a hobby of recognising numbers from tones Mr Linden and sir that all is information I have not confided to the police. Let us not say it was your client who arranged this because I understand you would immediately have to say it was not your client but your connection who tragically and mishappily used your innocent office as a relay for criminal business on the night in question through no fault of yours. That person – your connection – took me for the sort of guy you warn off. I am not that sort of guy Mr Linden. I was asking questions about Didi Fraser, because she lived in my building and I did not like her but she was kind of a part of the landscape do you understand? Like a touchstone for my private life, so I wanted to know what had happened to her. Now, this upset your connection who is not necessarily your client let's proceed on that basis. And they took an action they will now no doubt regard as precipitate, not to say rude, and you know I think it's pretty clear now that I am not someone to whom you address yourself in that way. I trust that is indeed clear. Excellent. And yet Mr Linden that is not my jam sir it is not my Tao it is not my way of being in the world my Urgeist whatever. It is not that. I express a preference for the deal Mr Linden over the closed fist I think that's clear enough and yet here we all are. And the whole thing has that air of going to shit. But I am a reasonable man and I am content that we should have a little what you might call restorative justice. Okay? I will even start the ball rolling I will take care of Oliver's medical bill. So I recognise that these things happen and that anyone can make a mistake. Would I be right in thinking that your firm specialises in managing discrete facets of the estates of the wealthy? I don't mean like comfortable I mean like oh I'm bored let's buy a country wealthy?

That would be an accurate assessment.

What I thought. In fact I happen to maintain a sort of a list of the kinds of people who do business with firms like yours is it possible you have a client named Driskol who basically inherited a lot of Apartheid diamond mines back in the day? Real elderly fucker? Or another named Barnes who has only one leg who made his money one of those times in the last century when the very rich fucked the very poor in the eyeholes?

I couldn't say Mr Price.

Great poker face man.

I couldn't say Mr Price.

So okay Mr Linden let's talk about my situation which is that I was struck. I was struck repeatedly and indeed my nose was broken and this has ruined the line of my face in a particular way which for personal reasons I am very unhappy about. In fact there are approximately fifty locations upon my body where damage was done. I believe it would be appropriate if we were to set a price on them as a collection.

That seems reasonable enough.

Understand: I do still wish to know about Didi Fraser, but I will waive that as a courtesy. This is all about courtesy now Mr Linden. It is about two predatory animals stepping courteously around one another in the forest because neither of them entirely knows what the other one is capable of. It may be that one of us is a bear and the other is an elk, or it may be that we are both wolves or that one of us is a crocodile. Perhaps one of us is an animal for which science presently has no name. There is simply no way for either of us to be sure of that at this time. As our interests have never intersected before it is safe enough to assume that we operate on discrete strata or in different sectors and therefore our present conflict is an anomaly. There is no reason for it to persist so long as we are courteous.

I agree.

So what I would propose is that you pay me one million for each of my bruises, making a round total of fifty, and we will go our separate ways in the forest without further conflict, and of course I will forget entirely that Didi Fraser ever existed. And I will pay for Oliver's ear. We should conclude our discussions relatively quickly because the police will be here shortly and I don't think we should want to pursue our matter through the filter of their excitation.

I cannot do very much about the police, Mr Price.

I will happily take care of that on my own behalf, Mr Linden, so long as you undertake to be muted in your description of events. Perhaps you might even arrange to lose the security camera footage.

That would leave us with the amount, Mr Price, which I think is high.

Do you Mr Linden?

I do, Mr Price.

Would you care – in the interest of a continuing courteous negotiation – to make a counter-offer?

I would say that twenty would be quite sufficient.

Four hundred thousand per bruise seems paltry to me Mr Linden. Perhaps we might say twenty as a blood gilt with a further thirty million in specific reference to my nose and the emotional trauma that entails.

You misunderstood me, I am afraid, Mr Price. Twenty. Not twenty million.

Ah Mr Linden. I did indeed misunderstand you. Very well. I will leave my offer on the table until midnight.

Our response will not change.

Let's see what happens at midnight Mr Linden. The world is composed of change after all. Goodbye Mr Linden.

I'm curious, Mr Price, as to how you will leave the building without encountering the police.

Oh Mr Linden. Why should I wish to avoid the police?

You're under arrest.

Yes thank you.

You have the right – and la la la.

Get ready to meet and greet.

In the precinct house and Leo is watching me on a crappy TV demonstrate Jack's theory of perceptual issues that I am right now addressing the shit out of to the viewing public.

Jesus fucking shitstick Price. Oh Jesus is that an ear?

Mostly lobe man it's nothing.

That is fucking cartilage motherfucker.

No wait no that's just – oh yeah no Leo you're totally right it is my bad. Yep. That's yeah but there's definitely no drum in that I have seen one—

Shut up shut—

Thing about lawyers' offices is that they record the video but not the sound for pretty obvious reasons. So the video shows me talking to Oliver and then him getting up and walking towards me, and I step back but I cannot leave the room, and then he gets out an illegal weapon and I swill some mouthwash and rip his ear off. So while I come out of it looking a little insane, I do not necessarily look like a criminal and they will be saying that to themselves in the office back at Linden Carver right now and they will be firing Oliver (sorry man but there you are and I really will pay for that reconstructive work) and the cops will be looking at it and they will be saying—

Price! What the fuck, man?

Sorry Leo.

So yeah Leo is this cop. Leo is this corrupt cop that I know. Actually that I pay. Leo is my cop and therefore in fact Leo is not a cop he is a criminal pretending to be a cop as the core of his illegitimate revenue stream but that is not how he sees it and there's no percentage in telling him otherwise so I don't. Leo is presently trying to work out how the fuck he will explain not arresting the shit out of me in his report. Leo obviously wants to punch me repeatedly in the face. Except that Leo thinks he is a cop so he cannot punch me in the face while I am being really polite.

That is Leo's life. Don't be sad for Leo. His life makes him very rich. Also he is a hero because he has the best sources on legacy drug industry players – that is to say my competitors – anyone has ever seen. Leo is an ace investigator except in so far as I just tell him what's going on and Leo goes and shoots it in the line of duty or puts it on trial and I pay him.

I am telling Leo that I am very sorry I bit a guy in the face but there were circumstances. Leo is trying not to find this funny. I like Leo. Also he can't stop himself finding this funny because it slightly is.

For fuck's sake Price.

Sorry Leo.

You're not covered for this, you know that right?

I know that Leo. I'll make it up.

You're damn right you will. Fucking bite a guy's ear off in a lawyer's office what even is that?

Personal matter. I'm taking care of the ear thing.

The fuck happened to your nose man?

Personal matter.

Same personal matter we're talking about here?

I think so.

Fuck's sake.

I know, man, what can I tell you? I got beat down for no good reason, went to discuss the matter in a civilised fashion but no takers. Restorative justice, Leo, is what I was offering. I went to make nice even though this whole thing with my nose is really – you know how I feel about the nose Leo we have discussed it.

Yes, Price, I do know and yes I recall that we have talked about it but even so have you seen what you did to this Oliver guy. This is a goatfuck.

One hundred thousand.

Two.

One fifty.

Plus expenses.

One sixty all in, I'll buy the drinks.

Okay.

Okay?

Okay.

So how?

Fuck if I know how yet?

Easiest thing is you violate my rights.

Get fired for that, man.

You got plenty cops you don't need.

Bunch of rookies, sure, no shortage, but the union—

Oh fine you're breaking my heart. One seven five all in, and I'll find gainful for the patsy. Construction, manscaping, whatever.

Manscaping? What the fuck are you talking about Price? Go from a cop to shaving guys' balls what even is that?

It pays.

How much?

When I tell him, Leo says fuck again and again like a metronome until my lawyer comes in.

Hey Sarah.

Hey Jack.

Sarah is a lawyer. She is not like Leo. She is a real person who believes in things like honesty and right action and legal representation for bad people. She believes in things like ethics which is why Sarah has a penny-ante practice in a terrible office. Sarah does not like me but I need her and so she feels an obligation. I do like Sarah and she knows this and it makes her unhappy. I pay Sarah more than all her other clients put together and this pays for the ones who cannot afford her and she kind of hates me for that and kind of does not.

It's complicated. I say:

Nice to see you Sarah.

You ate a guy.

I bit off one tiny bit of a guy it's not like – anyway it was mostly lobe.

Leo told me.

Thanks for getting me out.

You got yourself out. I just said Miranda like eighty-two times. Was it expensive?

Thanks for coming along and saying Miranda like eighty-two times.

You're welcome.

You want to go for a drink and celebrate how elegantly you said Miranda like eighty-two times?

No Jack.

Want to just go for a drink?

No.

I'm a little bit in love with you Sarah.

I'm a little bit not Jack but it's nice of you to say.

Is it?

No actually it isn't but I know you're trying.

Thank you Sarah.

Good night Jack.

Sarah has these cheekbones that should be illegal, some Swedish Haitian Lebanese mojo whateverthefuck that does things inside me that I don't control. I read where it's about your immune system that wants to meet another system that has complementary skills. I don't know. What I am wants Sarah. What Sarah is does not want me. Thus: pain.

Back at my place, no Sarah. No Sarah now or ever because she knows exactly what I am. I should let her go but when I try she gives me the smile and I honestly do not know if she does that because I pay for her other clients or because somewhere in between us there is something that could be something.

No Sarah. Never mind. I have work. Work is always there.

It's ten thirty-one. Linden has an hour and twenty-nine minutes to come back to me. I went high he went low it's the normal course of business. In fact Linden's probably out of the decision loop by now. Now I'm dealing with the client and we'll see. If it was me I'd pause and take stock and I'd want to see if there was business to be done. I'll take my fifty million in trade. Most-favoured nation, access. I don't need fifty million. I'm not an expensive person and I live alone. I don't even know how much I already have. Lots. Enough. The issue is perceptual like I said. Point is that I'm seen to come out richer. That's the key. Whatever happens, Jack comes out ahead which is why you want to work with him not against.

Make a call. Encrypted VoIP call, delocaliser service, clean handset. Basic comms hygiene these days.

Kto tam?

Hey, sister.

Jack Price?

Karenina is security. She's ex one of those Russian satellite states, used to do whatever demented and insane shit those tiny outfits had to do to keep from getting KGB'd or FSB'd or Spetsnaz'd back into the Moscow egg basket. Mother Russia does not fledge. She likes to keep her chickies.

Karenina: fifty-five and looks forty but silver, fists like pale hams. Got skills in all kinds of areas, computers and some Estonian street judo thing.

I say low and gravelly like in a spy movie: Da.

Snorting at my Russian voice: You sound constipated, don't ever say that again it hurts my ears. What is shaking Jack?

Karenina I'm looking to employ you for a short period. Rough and tumble. Weapons-free starting at midnight.

Nyeh. Cannot do it Jack, I am from two days back exploring a new collaboration that is delicate.

You went into business with someone else? Karenina I'm hurt.

Is not local Jack is long-term work mostly overseas. Very prestigious so I figure what the hell and also is still try-out. Maybe we are good fit maybe not.

Can you say who or is that uncool?

No is perfectly cool, we advertise. Actually you want maybe we are available.

I don't need a whole outfit.

Never can be sure of that in business Jack.

So who?

Is Seven Demons. Pretty fucking cool.

Get the fuck out of here.

Completely on the level-and-up.

Seven Demons for real? The bank job in Budapest?

Was never proved.

Okay but the hit in Krong Angkor?

Yes, was us. Them. Now also me. You know also the London Underground thing last year?

Bullshit, that was Basque separatists.

On contract. We got fifty per cent.

I did not know that.

Nor I. But they show me GoPro. Fucking smooth operation even after the cave-in. Great improvisation.

That is very fucking cool.

A week ago I get call, confidential interview, consultancy they say. They make like they're the Basque like you say. How could they improve? I tell them if they done right preparation then no cave-in. Get a big laugh. Then they game the whole thing, I do live commentary on first viewing of media. I say was brilliant live performance but fucking shitshow in terms of logistics. Best would be to arrange white noise in emergency systems, fog of war. Also is necessary a basic understanding of – well all that shit that I know. They say exactly which is why they want me.

That is very very cool.

Is cool if it works. We got option period. I worry they are too much Vegas too many Hong Kong movies not enough spreadsheet. They think I am too old until I run ten K faster than their ranger. Now is all about can I do lounges.

Lounges, what the fuck lounges?

Is for schmooze. They say can I also make rain, use cake fork, recognise good wine.

Wine tasting? Seriously?

No. I kid. But like that.

You're fucking European of course you can do all that shit.

Nyeh. Apparently I must learn to swim.

The fuck why?

Is requirement. I can see logic. So now I go every day to classes with Marco from Surf Sharks. Is me and four children under eight. I am worst. You want I see about the hire?

Yeah, go ahead it's massive overkill but maybe they've got a gap in the schedule and we can cut a deal.

I ask. Call back.

Disconnected.

Seven Demons. That's hilarious. That would be ideal, utterly gratuitous. It's like you see a mouse in your kitchen so you napalm your entire house and then you release a thousand hungry pythons into the ash. Probably it's too expensive to be worthwhile but then again it addresses the perceptual issue quite nicely and it's always good to make new relationships. Here's a softball and some easy money and we all walk away smiling so next time if it's more serious well hell we all know each other. We've got a track record of mutual satisfaction.

Binglebingle bonglebongle. I don't change ringtones. Factory default is fine. No one can draw conclusions about ownership from factory default.

Karenina?

Hi Jack. You're our next contract.

Well we'll need to discuss terms.

Nyeh. I don't say possible employer. You are subject. Subject of contract for Seven Demons. Full rate, unlimited term, Jack.

I see.

Da.

You're saying I'm the target.

Sorry Jack. I was not aware.

You should go Karenina. Thanks for telling me. I don't want you to get in trouble with your new crew.

Is legitimate response to service availability inquiry. Contract starts at midnight. Until then we are friends. After, more professional standard applies.

Sure.

Maybe best to resolve matter before then or leave town.

Yeah, well. I've got an offer on the table.

Jack, if we are hired is safe to assume your offer is declined.

The first rule is you go and I mean go like you're gone. Get your coat and walk out the door. It's a particular coat: the one you keep for this moment, not too long so you can run, nondescript so there's no place you can't be seen. Not a bag because bags slow you down. You pick it up and everything you need is in it. Passports and cards. Phone still in the plastic you bought from somewhere you never bought any other phone. You put it on and then you go.

And you are gone.

Leave by the back way, over the wall into the alley behind what used to be a warehouse, now it's expensive accommodation for artists who already have galleries. Easy mode: you drill this every month. Hop the crosstown, get seen at the bus station. Duck down and away, get on camera at the airport. Buy a ticket to Martinhal on credit, another from Martinhal to Frankfurt with cash, high-speed rail tickets to Paris and suck it because from Paris I could go anywhere. Go airside with the crowd then come back through arrivals. Junk one passport, open another and disappear in the crowd. They won't look for that because they'll assume I want as far away as possible because that much is obvious, and they won't want me to get away because that's the contract.

Uptown hotel, the Glasnost Park: Welcome Mr Cazarel, it's been some time but we're delighted to have you back.

Paolo Cazarel has only ever done two things. He has opened a couple bank accounts in Belize and he has stayed for a fortnight at the Glasnost Park. He is a private person and the hotel is pleased to comply with his request that they not store his photograph. Many guests feel this way. Paolo likes hot stone massages, Sam Adams and artisanal cheese steaks. Today he's only interested in items two and three but towards the end of the week he's booked into the spa and Sonja from Oslo has evidently been told to warm up the pumice and get in extra vetiver.

Beer and cheese steak on the balcony because why not? Jack Price is on his way to Martinhal. Contract starts at midnight. He'll still be in the air.

Fucking Seven Demons. Who even does that? I considered it because it was handed to me on a plate and I thought I might get a deal, but these guys went looking for it and paid the market rate. That is one massive motherfucking escalation right there. Like: hi, you want to play ping-pong? NO MOTHERFUCKER AND NOW YOUR WHOLE WORLD MUST DIE!

Yeah okay dude whatever it's just ping-pong.

Just no fucking reason for this behaviour. At. All.

They want me dead and gone and they want it now and in the worst way. It's totally unnecessary is what it is and you have to respect that. Gotta say it's also a big step up for me in terms of criminal social cachet getting the Seven Demons sent after me. You really only do that with an end-of-level boss. Downside… well that is obvious. I'm being personally nuked from orbit. The nation of Jack Price is being rendered unto glass and lava.

Beer and cheese steak. Use the rooftop pool. Look out at the city in a white robe.

Midnight oh five. My apartment block has just caught fire.

Midnight thirty and Linden's probably dead now. Hope Oliver doesn't work nights.

Charlie, tell me you really got out of town. Get the fuck gone girl.

Midnight fifty one my top-layer online presence has burned down, my disposable email accounts for dealing and the websites for my food business: Karenina's gone through it for signs of life. Some of my outsource kids are no doubt having a fucking terrible night and by dawn I figure at least a few of them will have tragically overdosed or been killed in a drive-by. Some others will have rolled over on me and made some shit up because they don't have anything to give up. Figure the Demons to know that, figure them to chase down the leads anyway and use that as an excuse to leave the kids alive. Point made already and no one wants to overcook it plus if you kill everyone in a city who's taking those jobs then who's going to do those jobs for you when you want them done? You going in-house with everything? Fuck no you're not. Not with Karenina running logistics because who do you think showed me how to set up? She's fucking allergic to long-term hire at the street level.

It's dawn and I have ceased to exist. Three deaths at a motel in Martinhal. Figure someone on the flight looked enough like me. Figure they'll know he wasn't and now they're stuck because they didn't find out about Frankfurt until after the connecting flight had left. In a while they'll find out about Paris but they'll know that could mean anything. No one checks you in on a train. Lots of places there's no CCTV. Maybe the guard remembers you were there, maybe not. Maybe that memory is accurate, maybe not. Maybe you sat in the bar. Maybe you got out at the border, maybe you caught a connecting train to Dijon, London, Trieste. Analogue, baby. Fucking analogue. They have to accept I'm in the wind, get ready for a longer game of seek and find. If I was running, that's how I'd do it and it would have worked.

Their trouble is that Karenina showed me her A game. I paid for it and she gave it to me and then I had my guy Tucker go over it and then I fucked it all around myself because when you have traded coffee for a decade you learn things about how to fuck with systems to your benefit. You know how to disappear a warehouse, how to hollow out a container, how to hide a single lot on a street so that it all but vanishes from the city and the world even when you're staring right at it. You learn those things if you're sharp and I am. Here's how sharp I am: there are almost no pictures of me on the internet. Why should there be? There are actor headshots for my mom-and-pop food operation, maybe a grainy team photo from the 90s but most likely that fucker was on actual film. But since then I've been all about invisible. Recently the border guys maybe have some shots of me with my old nose and old teeth, but now my biometrics are all fucked up. So likely if you've never met me you got no idea what I look like. Karenina's met me of course – but try right now picturing someone you know and love. Try and hold their face still in your mind and watch how it slips away. You know them. But unless you're a particular sort of person, you don't really know what they look like.

You don't know what I look like.

Two more dead at Frankfurt station. Emotional intensity, you got to give them that. Serious people these Seven Demons. I mean dedicated and completely without limits.

The Seven Demons are coming for me and they will never stop. They've taken the contract and that's it. They will never, ever stop. I'm a hunted man now, the walking dead. Can't have friends can't have a business and eventually they'll find something and then they'll find me. One day in a fucking bar in Lima or whatever: splat. Night night Jack.

I'm a dead man.

You know what this is? I got to sit down. You know what this is? This is.

The best.

Day.

Of my life.

Oh fuck yes it is.

I have sat and waited for the time when I would know exactly who I was and what I had to do and now it has arrived and it's almost too much. In this moment I am completely perfect. This moment is completely perfect around me.

You know what I cannot stand? Shades of grey and fine distinctions and issues of legitimate confusion. I hate the restraint we put on ourselves because we have to be polite and sensible and above all proportionate. I am good at those things but they turn the heart to coal. I read in a medical study where every time we say something we don't mean we actually damage the coronary muscle. Note that it does not say lie. You can lie and still mean it. You can say that you're a good person and all you want is to be happy and you can mean that and it's a lie because you're a professional leg-breaker. You're not a good person, but you mean it when you say you are. When that same person stands in court and says they're sorry for what they did they're killing themselves on the stand in front of the judge, taking years off their own lives with that lie. They can feel the bitter twist of cortisol and they don't even realise how much that is hurting them.

I'm under the eye of the Seven Demons. If I call Sarah right now she'll hang up and then I won't get through next time. She'll feel bad about that but she will do it because she's not insane. If I call Billy he will offer me a drink and if I go and meet him he will cold cock me and claim a finder's fee. I'm alone in the world. It's open season on Jack.

Best day of my life.

Because now I can try all the things I've always wanted to try and it's not disproportionate it's just fucking inspired. First thing I need is a little online time at the Glasnost Park's business suite.

Seven-thirty a.m. I call Leo. Leo's job is to arrest fuckers like the Seven Demons though in practice that is never going to happen. That does not mean it's not worth throwing some chaff their way. And then there's another thing. A lot depends on Leo's disposition here.

Leo I need to SWAT some fuckers.

Jack—

No Leo I'm not kidding I need to—

Jack—

I need to SWAT them but hard. I need those boys hopped up on some serious patriotic fervour and believing they are dealing with a live threat. Massive casualties. And afterwards there will need to be evidence that it was so, and I will provide that, okay, but—

Jack I am calling clause four.

The fuck?

Clause four Jack, the hammer is coming down. It's federal okay it's the fucking end of the world so meet me and bring my exit and I'll give you all the details and then I'm gone. I'm burned Jack. They don't know it yet but they're going to find me and then I am burned.

You sure?

Yeah Jack I'm sure.

Leo—

It's over Jack I am done.

Okay Leo I understand.

Yeah?

Yeah. As promised. I'm good for it.

Okay Jack. Thank you. Means a lot.

My word is my bond Leo. A man stands by his word. Otherwise the whole world just burns.

Okay.

You got to appreciate the craftsmanship here. They know I've left the country but they set everything in motion all at the same time so that my exits would be burning before I smelled the fire. If I hadn't gotten out when I did – if I'd had some idea of mustering the troops, fighting an organised retreat or whatever – this would fuck me up. Nice. But Leo is sad again.

I'm sorry I can't do more Jack but—

It's okay Leo, I get it, clause four. I'm good for it and I'll take care of Leena and the kids like college whatever until you can work out your shit. That's a courtesy because we're friends not just business associates. Escrow man totally permanent and isolated so don't think about it just go. You got your coat?

Yeah.

Okay good.

Where do you want to meet? I'm free now.

Go for a walk.

Where?

Doesn't matter I'll find you.

How the fuck you gonna do that?

I hacked your phone.

The fuck?

I don't listen in Leo I just like to know where you are.

Oh fuck you Jack you are the most—

I'm an asshole Leo that is my jam.

(Bullshit. I'm watching him from an empty office. No one thinks of that any more, it's always about the NSA but actually it's just easier in a big city to find an empty space and get someone to let you in. Realtor cost me five hundred dollars down, fifteen hundred to follow at end of day. Told her I was a management type taking a confidential client meeting over a celebrity sex tape case. But now I'm looking at Leo and Leo's looking at his phone like it just tried to put its tongue in his ear.)

Leo please just tell me out loud that you're not dumb enough—

No Jack—

Tell me you did not try to sell this both ways—

No Jack you're my out and these fuckers are crazy there is no way.

Okay.

Okay.

Okay man I have pushed the button it's done. Your money is on the move now you got to follow it because it is not coming home. There is no going back Leo none at all. Now get out of there man don't be a hero it's not the time.

See you soon Jack.

And he does man, he just puts on his coat. Good boy Leo. Good boy.

Clause four is goodnight. It's to say that Leo is burned and it's agreed that in that case I will take care of him, my preemptive counter to the moment someone offers him a plea. Run to me and I'll take care of it, get you to Ecuador, set you up in a house. We've joked about it but it's a solemn covenant between us. Leo is my keystone. If he goes the arch goes like the delicate balance of my criminal ecosystem whatever. Clause four keeps him strong. And here he is and the sky is falling. He walks like a guy waiting to get arrested like someone's gonna put their hand on him right now here by this fountain.

Hey man.

I'm sorry Jack they're on me. They're in my taxes for Christ's sake.

Jesus Leo don't tell me you pay taxes?

I—

Kidding, Leo. I gave you Tucker, remember?

Tucker does money. In and out of the world, and all around the mulberry bush. Tucker can make money dress up and dance or lie quiet like a dead thing. Tucker is Houdini is Svengali is Dom Pérignon.

Yeah, that's right, you gave me Tucker.

And Tucker's on this already, okay? Your problems are in the past you are leaving on a jet plane. Sing it man put a bounce in your step and a smile on your face you're financially independent as a fucking Rockerfeller and in a few hours this will all be a great cocktail story that you obviously will never fucking tell a living soul. So maybe just get your daiquiri and smirk at the waitress. I don't know man whatever opens your little paper umbrella.

Jack did you take on the Seven Demons?

Well yeah but no but yeah but there's actually only six of them right now plus the Russian, she's a try-out.

Jack it's the Seven Demons.

I am aware of that Leo.

It's the fucking Seven Demons, Jack.

Yes Leo. The Seven Demons are on me and that is their problem not yours. You're out now it's okay you are clear. But you know what's happening right now in their house? One of the demons, I'm gonna say Dong Ha Li, is calling home and his mama is saying like what's this I hear Dong Ha Li, that I hear you are doing? And Dong Ha Li is all like awww Maaa! But she's pissed, Leo! She's righteously pissed. And do you know what Ma Dong is saying to her son?

Well Jack I got to object to something there, I think you're going to find that in Korea he's Li Dong-ha, right. So she's not Mrs Dong, she'd be Mrs Li but Korean women don't take their husbands' names and you don't marry someone with the same name that's like incest there so in fact Li Dong-ha's mama would have to be like Mrs Park or whatever. That's a really common name in Korea.

Thanks for that Leo that's real constructive.

I'm pretty sure is what I'm saying.

Okay well I'll be sure and look that up later but let's just assume for a second that even if on this issue you're right it's maybe not the most important aspect of the narrative I'm giving you right now. Is that hard for you Leo?

No Jack.

Thank you Leo so to resume. Ma Park – thank you Leo – Ma Park is saying Child! What the actual fuck? Is it possible your dickless friends and you got all up in someone's shit without first asking if that person was a person of consequence? Is it – my beloved son who did after some considerable delay in youth eventually learn to tie his own damn shoelaces – is it possible that you and your five demon friends and the Russian try-out are right now getting into it with Mr Ballistic, the Bad Hand Clapping, the Butcher of the West Austin Marriott, the vast and borderline psychotic wrecking balls of the swinging scrotum of Jacob motherfunkin' Morgenstern Price himself?

And Li Dong-ha is all no Ma it ain't like that Mā, it's just a passing misunderstanding is all. And Ma Park says you better hope Mr Price knows that, sonny, because I'm fond of you and no doubt you're a terrifying force of nature at your natural level and everything but that fucker is craycray like Richard Milhous Nixon smoking toad, and he will fuck your shit up. You want I should call him and fix this right up? No Ma it's okay I swear! Well just you be polite to Mr Price.

That's how it's going Leo, is what I'm saying, and the fact that they've gone cop on you – that they would bring actual law and order down on you in your own place of business the fucking tax people I mean what the shit? The fact that they would do that just to get to me, that is just exactly the kind of unnecessary I have been seeing a lot of in the course of this sorry affair Leo. And I mean to discuss it and I mean to have words. I have views and opinions Leo. I have views and opinions. But I got to apologise to you Leo because you're a casualty of fucking inappropriate behaviour here and that is on me. I did not choose to make that happen but it is on me. These guys are really pissing in the jacuzzi I guess. They are just unreasonable. I am running a business here in a completely natural way and I am a man following his natural inclination and they have to get all unreasonable. Clause four man I hear you. So do you got a preference of where you go?

Where you got?

I got Canada if you want it, Vancouver, but you'd gotta get a different face and that is forever. Plus with North America I have to say there's an element of risk even with the best will in the world. I got island paradise coming out of my ears like Bermuda or maybe Turks and Caicos yes Leo that is a real place. I got Iceland you want a change of pace, real social democracy. Leo I tell you, that is a fucking amazing place and the women are hot like the geothermal power, hot all the way down.

How about Sicily I hear Sicily is nice?

Yeah I can do that but there's a language barrier plus obviously you going to set up a business there are local negotiations. You consider maybe China? I know I know it sounds crazy but hear me out...

And so on. Leo and I we're talking, and he is enjoying planning his future but obviously you have to be thinking what I'm thinking that if we just for a moment remove my longstanding promise to my friend from this calculation and if we once recognise that from this point out his life is nothing but downside for me, you got to ask if it's worth it. Leo does know things. Leo knows I am still in the city. Leo knows my mood and what you call it he knows my disposition. My personal way of being in the world and in a small way he knows me. Plus I mean there was that look when I kidded him about his phone I mean you got to ask is Leo getting paid on both sides? Well in a way that does not matter. None of it matters because like I said: a man stands by his promises or the world burns that's just how it is. The whole of life on this planet now is digital text which is to say rewritable and if you don't hold the given promise then where are you you're just in free fall and then who are you?

I am a fucking asymmetric criminal startup. I got limited expertise in criminal strategic warfare. I hotdesk and I outsource and I franchise but what I mostly have is a core concept, forward momentum and the unassailable fact that I'm crazier than a fibreglass hairball. I don't give a shit for territory. I don't care if the world burns. I'm a rapidly escalating nuclear temporary autonomous zone.

Hey Leo what about Brazil man? What about motherfucking Rio man?

Big shit-eating grin from Leo: Is it true that's where the wax comes from or is that just marketing?

No Leo that's true, that perfect landing strip for the pudendum that is absolutely Denominazione di Origine Controllata.

That's Italian man.

Pussy is international Leo.

Ain't that the truth brother?

Yes it is Leo.

So that's how we are together in this critical moment, this crisis moment. We make jokes and we know that we're crossing the Rubicon and what lies before will be different from what is past. We are brothers.

We hug. And then I shoot him in the face. Small caliber goes phht and one of his eyes goes red and that's it. Sorry not sorry.

Secure call—

Charlie it's me.

Hi boss I thought—

Yeah I completely am but – wait are you gone yet?

Totally.

You are?

Totally gone. I am the night.

You're still here.

No?

Get gone Charlie.

Yes boss.

Charlie get gone. Wait don't go I got a question about Korean nomenclature.

Boss this is awkward but I gotta ask you know I'm not Korean right?

Jesus that was insensitive of me. Sorry Charlie yes I do know that, it's just actually, it's just I got no one else to ask right now. Actually no one in the world.

… Shit boss.

Yeah that is fucking existentially challenging.

Yuhuh.

Shit.

Well okay can I ask you this question totally not because you are of Asian descent but because you're the only person in the world I am able to talk to right now?

Yeah that's totally legit.

(It turns out Leo was absolutely right about Korean names. I swear you learn something every day.)

Delivery, with instructions. Porter brings it up. Tip the guy and say thank you. This is the world now: people perform to specification and not beyond. Beyond is curiosity is initiative and these things can lead to ethics and corporations do not pay people for ethics. Employees do not get paid for beyond and they do not get thanked. The porter doesn't ask what's in the heavy box because rich people are weird and the tip says fuck off and don't talk about it and he speaks that language. We're all hotel people now. What's in the box? Sundries man. Client stuff. Could be a robot, could be a girl in a cake. Don't give an actual fuck. If it scratches the paint the hotel will bill the client and the client's credit is good. That being the case: who cares what's in the box? Satisfaction guaranteed is what, and no one needs to know.

What's in the box? Compressed air and metal pipe you don't want plastic because it can burst. Safety valve set high. Good welding. You got yourself a world-class grapefruit cannon. These days you can just fucking Acme one up if you're prepared to pay. Call the concierge service: hey man, frat reunion and I need a fruit cannon by tomorrow morning can you oblige? For money of course they can. Not an issue because I'm delocalised. My slush fund right now comes from the Belize accounts, good for a few days. When I leave here I'll empty them. I haven't even bothered to liquidate the ones I was using until yesterday, just left them there. Cops will watch them for months because they cannot imagine you would just leave that much money behind. Seven Demons will do the same. Huge waste of everyone's time, which is fine. I'm spending that money: paying for them to watch it rather than look for me.

Even Tucker doesn't understand about this. Tucker lives for money but he doesn't get this because money is how he measures worth. Money is capability is access but it's not the only form in which those things exist and as long as you have them money comes to you.

I have ghost money for operational expenses. The whole entire point of being illegal is to be disconnected from the mundane requirements of taxation and liability and so forth. The difficult part is at the interface between the two worlds of white and black economics but these days it's easier than you might think because everything is ghosted now. Everything is cloud. That's the modern condition. Plus frankly after the sub-prime thing so much bad money sluiced into the apple pie economy that half the world's oh-so-chaste banks are pregnant with dirty, dirty cash babies.

If you go online you can actually find out about the Seven Demons because they have a website. Grant you it's technically Dark Web which only means that it's hard to take down but it's entirely fucking revealing about what they do and for how much and they have this whole cult of personality going on that's really pretty major. They have like a million followers on Twitter and they post to Instagram a half dozen times a week, party shots mostly but very occasionally something like an infrared goggle shot of some compound in Bogotá going up in smoke, whatever. Celebrity assassins. I can see why Karenina isn't sure about the gig, they're real loud, not her thing at all.

This grapefruit cannon is actually more pomelo grande, done to my spec. Pomelo gun. Bolts to the floor of this flatbed truck. Hydraulic WYSIWYG aiming system. Conveyor-belt feed with a chopper and a hopper, so you can basically put a ton of fruit in one end and just let rip.

Park and wait.

The Instagram feed had only a few face pictures on it but these days you've got all sorts of massively powerful ID recognition programs kicking around just waiting to match for you. What once was a major intelligence undertaking is now a half day for a bored kid who would otherwise be serving at the local diner or working a sex cam because did I say gig economy yes yes I did. Even an outfit like the Seven Demons cannot buy or intimidate them all because there's just too damn many and they are too damn dumb. So I gave ShermansMarch6969 the picture of Johnny Cubano, who is the Rat Pack-imitating muscle for the Seven Demons whose name is not Cubano but Wexler and who is from fucking Michigan so he's a fucking white guy pretending to be a Hispanic guy because he thinks that's more fucking gangster and that is just straight out racist, and a few hours later ShermansMarch6969 gave me in exchange for ten thousand in cryptocurrency the name of the hotel and here I am.

The hotel is one of the new ones: called the Yohji, cool Asian modern, uncomfortable chairs in the bar. And look there – there's Johnny Wexler-Cubano coming out the door with a gaggle of party people young and pretty. Johnny's celebrating, a little bit careless but he knows I've gone to ground in Paris. Blue silk shirt like ooh la la say ooooh Johnny ooooh la la.

Low angle, near flat trajectory. Pluck him out of the pack like the pip out of a five of hearts. Fucking surgical strike, seriously, not what I was expecting at all. Pomelo gun makes a noise like THWUCH.

Johnny's last words are: Wha—

Not much for posterity.

Leo's head smashes through his chest halfway like if you imagine a golf ball driven into wet plaster at ten paces by Tiger Woods if Tiger Woods was on a fucking appalling combination of steroids and crystal. I keep my finger on the red button and other bits of Leo paint Johnny to the wall of the Yohji. Party kids are definitely not stupid, they're lying on the ground which makes it easy to miss them. Johnny slides a bit and then a couple leg bones right up nail him to the façade. Evidently the Yohji's frontage is covered in some kind of eco-felt that encourages plants to grow. It works like a pinboard.

I know it's a little much but we've definitely been suffering from a lack of communication. It's like they don't see that I've got a legitimate point of view here and that point of view needs to be factored into our discussions before we can get past this blip and move forward together in a new harmony.

VoIP encrypted call: dialling. Call accepted.

Hi Karenina.

Hello Jack.

How's it going over there?

I cannot discuss, would be in violation of terms of partnership.

Is it an embarrassment to you that I'm calling?

Is weird Jack but you want to talk that's okay. You have something in particular you want to say to us?

It's us now is it?

I am Seven Demons now Jack. That's like passport. Not undertaken lightly and not easily put aside.

Your English is improving.

Is quote. They got PR guy.

Yeah that would be Fred, he's like the number one of the whole thing right? I read where Fred was like some kind of sniper back in the day.

Is what I read also.

So who would you say was the toughest of them like hand-to-hand?

Jack you tell me. You been reading obviously website.

I'm gonna say Johnny Cubano. I read where he was the king of some kind of unregulated fight scene in Cape Town for a little while. On the website there's a really gnarly montage of a few of his wins. One time you know he actually gutted some guy from Lvov with his fingers?

Is what they say.

Would that be the same Johnny Cubano that's staying at the Yohji or is that some assfuckingly unlucky bystander?

Jack you're not in the league with Johnny Cubano. You want to surrender, work something out, that's cool let's do that. Be better for everyone. Maybe I can broker. You maybe get to live even live pretty well.

I read where the Seven don't make deals.

Client can always make deals, Jack. Is full service not some cowboy outfit from Kentucky.

Yeah, well.

Stay away from Johnny Cubano, Jack. Stay in Paris or wherever.

Karenina I'm gonna level with you. I'm not in Paris. I just needed a little breathing room. I'm in a bar like a block over from the Yohji and I'm thinking about walking on over there. Rumour is the sushi is to die for.

Yeah well is possible you do die for it.

Oh, what's that? I'm just watching the news in this bar, Karenina, seems like someone was – wow, that is outré is what that is – some guy was well there's no gentle way to express this... he was apparently killed in the chest by a flying decapitated head. Man, somehow they got footage of the attack and I have to tell you fuck me Karenina, it is ugly. It is the worst thing I have ever seen happen to a body in all my life and I am from a town where they do cow-tipping and I worked in a slaughterhouse when I was sixteen. And fuck me again if the dead guy who is like flypapered to the wall there, fuck me sideways if that is not Johnny Cubano, I'm pretty sure I recognise his perfect model brownface motherfucker hair. I guess this was probably a gang initiation, Karenina. Drive-by grapefruit mortaring with a human head. That is some outré fucking gang thing, right? Johnny Cubano, that guy must be the unluckiest man on the face of this Earth. Unless he had enemies. You think he had enemies? Because I fucking think he had at least one that I can think of.

Hold please.

You there, Mama Bear?

They are really pissed at you right now Jack.

Oh fuck are they? Damn that is disappointing. I figured they might be fucking enraptured at my welcoming manner and effusive people skills. Do tell them I'm as sorry as they can imagine I am.

Seven Demons not something you fuck with Jack.

Oh, man, I know. Except... well, that's embarrassing, but I guess it's Six Demons now?

Fucking fuck Jack.

Or should I maybe say Five Demons and One Reserve?

Fucking fuck Jack I—

Gotta go Karenina that sushi ain't gonna eat itself.

Time to say goodbye to Paolo Cazarel. Bye bye Paolo bye bye. These are shirt-front identities like those white paper dickeys you see in westerns: you put them on over whatever you're already wearing and lickety split you're somebody new – tuxedo guy. Yes I said lickety split, what? It's western like authentic. And yes it may also be the title of an adult movie, in fact no doubt it is and shame on you for noticing that.

Dickey IDs. When you take them off, they just stop existing. You're gone.

Bye bye Paolo, hello Gottfried. Losing track of where I'm from, doesn't matter no one asks. No one cares in the city. Take a bus, take a cab, fucking cycle: Airbnb is a fucking oubliette, you can just push a button and be gone. No receptionist to sell you out no hotel porters no lobby cams. Not gonna get me like I got Cubano. Going dark in the biomass like a whale in the plankton like a submarine in a movie. Thermocline is what. Going dark now. I'm always dark but this is the darkest. Look here's what it is: you're imagining me with stash houses right and container storage with those rolling doors that go up and they cut the padlock off in cop shows? I don't have those because that's how everyone thinks it works including cops and judges and what all because TV is a virus that gets in your head and people get assumptions from it about things they know don't work like that. Like people think fights are all swoosh chah zap and they're not they're like thump gouge roll on the floor someone loses an eye. No fucking Jean-Claude Van Ballet. Just pain.

So fuck photogenic container storage and fuck safety deposits. Fuck systems managed by people who know what happens in their system. That is not security that is stewardry and stewards can be paid off or tortured. That is the middle fucking ages and you might as well have a moat with alligators.

I do not have alligators because my money is ghost money. It exists in the First Bank of Nowhere, in the interstices of cryptocurrency and post-Geneva private financial jurisdictions. Places that make Panama and the Vatican look transparent like Sweden which maybe you don't know has the most transparent central bank in the world. Scores 14.5 out of a possible 15 and frankly they dropped that half point just so New Zealand wouldn't feel bad. Wall Street money is pirate money, loud and stupid and drunk, gets mugged in an alleyway and wakes up in the navy. My money is ninja money, strikes from the darkness, appears and disappears. Where do you keep your money Jack? Stuxnet baby. I keep my money in a digitally mobile distributed illegal wallet construct part-created by the NSA and stolen by @LuciferousYestergirl who is either a German anarchist or a Japanese–Nordic postdoc. When I want cash I push buttons and there is cash in a briefcase because I pay for it to happen. No one in the chain knows what they're handling or where it is going, just like my coke. The whole thing happens because water flows downhill. It happens the way an egg comes out of a chicken's vajayjay.

Well that image is gonna stay with me.

The service is called Poltergeist because it doesn't exist but it moves the world. Based out of Iceland where they really care about discretion in the digital context. Got data centres there under the snow, powered by fucking lava how cool is that? Ice cold and powered by the actual fucking burning core of the world. So Poltergeist is like the oasis, the place in the desert where all the animals come together and don't no one fight because everyone needs the water. Criminal Switzerland man. In fact it's absolutely Switzerland because that shit is federal. There's no one Poltergeist there's a whole crowd of them all hidden separately and different under the ice. I read where some of them aren't even on the island they're up up up in the frozen north like for real the North fucking Pole. Some of them are in other countries in places that don't even know they are hosting Poltergeist. Some of them are in your house like distributed computing. On your fucking phone. On the screensaver of every box in Dzerzhinsky Square. Poltergeist is everywhere and it is amazing. But Iceland is where it begins and ends. Cryptography is geopolitics is ideology is what you can get away with. Under the ice in a country of laws that say stay the fuck out of here: that's where you leave your key. And it ties right back to services in the real world. Concierge services. Cab firms. City courier bikes. Takeaway food. All good digital commerce, networked and legit and twenty-first-century cool.

Happenstance: means you can do what I do. Run crime without criminals.

Karenina helped me set it up but that doesn't matter because the service is asymmetrical. You can know how someone does it but you still can't fuck it up without access and she doesn't have it. Plus she doesn't know where she just knows how. She can look for me in the right places but I'm still invisible and there's no cure for that.

My money is protected, so I am.

All the same they're looking for me now and looking hard. I can hide but not forever because everyone makes mistakes, me and them. Fog of war, fog of crime. Time to go to Sunday school. Time to talk Demonology.

They're not called the Seven Demons just because it sounds killer. That's not a focus group name. It's one they earned way back in the day, when their whole thing was new. Back when most likely none of these Demons today were in the crew because you know even Demons get old eventually and step aside. The guys who got that name and began all this – before I was born okay? I mean in prehistoric times when Jane Fonda was the hottest woman in the world – those Demons are likely all gone on now to the giant hellish frying pan in the sky. What you have here is basically indestructible: an idea of a gang of seven that restores its losses and never stops. It is defined by a complete lack of compunction, by being more fucking terrifying than the gold standard of contemporary fucking terrifyingness. The Demons are the way they are because that's the way they are and when you sign up you take that on. The present roster supposedly includes – apart from Karenina and the recently headcannoned Johnny Cubano – two brothers previously from a Finnish freelance crew specialising in torture and logistical operations; a former private military contractor turned warlord; a doctor with a fondness for unlicensed human experiments; and a public relations executive. No one knows what it is that the PR guy does that makes him evil beyond ordinary PR but it evidently impressed the others so much they recruited him and now he's in charge.

These things have a rhythm and you have to accept that. Here I am riding high but I know I won't be forever. There's no way I get through this without losing some skin. Some stuff I care about. There's no way. I got a little Lao Tzu back there, like speed is the essence of warfare, or Sun Tzu, appear where the enemy does not expect you. I made a point. Now they'll make theirs. Some stuff I care about.

Someone I care about.

But this isn't a personal matter it's professional and you gotta have some integrity in your business. Plus right now I am Al Qaeda.

You know what Al Qaeda is? Al Qaeda is a business model. It's not an organisation and that is why it is a motherfucker to eradicate. Ooo but Jack no we bombed those fuckers in their caves and they are all gooooone! Are they dumbass? Are they really? Are they gone when a bunch of pressure cookers blow up in a crowd? Are they gone when there's a fucking nation in the middle of Syria and Iraq that belongs to armed fuckheadry? Al Qaeda is a concept, a way of working. Instead of saying that you are going to mount an offensive from a specific point under the command of specific generals you just tell people there's a war on and they should use whatever tools they can if they believe in the cause. You tell them that a section of downpipe stuffed with nails is as good as a tank if you put it in the right place and you tell them that anything is a target and you tell them to go hurt the enemy and the enemy is anyone they want to hurt. That is Al Qaeda. It is permission to be a fucking asshole in the name of god.

I am a fucking asshole already. I don't need permission. And I will never be gone.

Anyway look here's what it is: the Seven Demons are not really into jobs like this but their rep is so total that they don't really need to be most of the time and anyway, hey, how much trouble can a dick like me possibly be? Well, grapefruit gun much, fuck you to the maximum but still. This is what the playbook says they have to do: they must control the theatre. Full-spectrum dominance. They must have control of communications infrastructure and they must own the local authorities and the street cops and they must control the press and the landscape. They don't have to do this personally they just need to hold the city and that is what they have done.

This is the second thing they will do: they will isolate me. They will use their control to cut me off in so far as possible from my resources, my organisation, my soldiers. I cannot walk into any place I am known without dying. I cannot talk to anyone I know without dying. They will take the oases, the high ground, the castles. They will kill my friends and turn my allies. They will make the world my enemy. And finally they will reduce the area in which I can move until I am forced from cover and then they will kill me and that will be that.

Except that I don't have friends or castles. I just have me.

You've got to understand the business you are in, today's business not yesterday's. Know what the land looks like under your feet. Know the fucking substrate. I know the substrate, and they do not. Karenina gets some of it, maybe, but Karenina is a monofocus person. She does not do big picture, concept. She's perfect at seeing the shape of the stones. She'll never step back far enough to see the mosaic. Pardon me for the poetry.

So they are coming for me. But they're not really set up to operate in this kind of war. They think they are but they're not. They're great with killing presidents and blackmailing megacorporations and coups in countries and criminal organisations but I'm not one of those. I don't have to protect anything except myself. I'm a business plan walking, and this is my century not theirs.

In the bar on 3rd that used to be a Scottish punk dive I tell them I'm a skip tracer from the west and order a beer. Lots of those types in here: bondsmen, security guards and wannabes, PIs, fraud and even fire investigators, insurance folks. This is where you go if you got a cop job but you're not a cop so the real ones won't talk to you. Every fucker has a bar that's too good for someone or equally a bar someone else is too good for. That's what this is: low ceiling and low light and enough watered booze that no-crease polyester and bad skin look okay after a couple house specials.

This bar is for these people so that is what I say I am. I say I'm looking for Jack Price and I flash my geological teeth. Got a hat. Hat makes me look painfully fucking white like white from somewhere that's something people are unreasonably shitkicking proud of. The clientele here decides I am a lowlife, one fractional gradation closer to criminality than they are and they won't talk to me. That's fine. That's okay. I'm Bob Simons I'm looking for Jack Price he's got outstanding warrants in Filamore Bay. I show them a picture of Jack Price from five years ago, hipster-phase Jack with facial hair arrangements we will not discuss.

Anyone run across this guy?

Any reason we would?

Guy makes like he's upstanding like straight, sells cocaine is what I hear, got no organisation to speak of so maybe is what I'm saying. Maybe he uses people in our line to find other people in his line for reasons other than warrants.

(I have done that in the past. Then I realised these guys were fucking d-bags and I stopped but okay surely surely someone has to remember that?)

No one does. Fucking d-bags got no sense of professional opportunity.

I leave a card in case anyone heard anything about Jack Price: Call me there's a finder's fee okay?

Three more bars to cover. D-bag bars. Drink about a mouthful of beer in each one, bad beer you can feel in your pores.

A few hours later: phone call. Cell number to VoIP. Hard to track is the point.

Man who sounds like a sommelier says: Is that Bob Simons?

Phone's got what they call a confounder, fucks up your voice some. I switch it on.

Yeah, probably. Probably I'm Simons cos this is his phone and his dick is in my pants so I guess either I'm Simons or I know the guy reasonably fucking well. Who's this?

Call me Frederick.

Okay, Fred.

I understand you're looking for Jack Price.

You found him?

Not at all. I am also looking for him.

Well that's nice Fred I hope I find him first. No offence.

Mr Simons I will pay you eight million one hundred and four thousand nine hundred twenty eight and change for Jack Price if you bring him to me instead of to your present employer.

That's pretty fucking specific that amount you want to call it an even ten mill?

Acceptable.

You're gonna give me ten million dollars. An extra one and one half million dollars just because I asked?

I believe that is what I said.

Then why the crazy numbers?

If I had offered you ten million would you have said twelve?

Yeah.

If I had offered you twelve would you have said fifteen?

Yeah sure.

I find an ugly number concentrates the mind. There is ten million for you Mr Simons, not twelve, and you understand that now on an instinctive level. Do not ask me why that is a deeper mystery than I can answer.

Okay. I got conditions.

Name them.

I don't work with dogs.

Acceptable.

I don't work with dogs, Irish, or fucking crazy Sicilians. You work with any a those kinds of people then I ain't in it.

Noted.

Payment in bearer bonds. No crypto no cash no wire transfers and no fucking krugerrands.

You have very specific tastes.

This is not my first ride on the fuck you bus mister and the reason I am riding it again speaks to how I was insufficiently fucking particular last time around. If I'da been then I would be doing belly shots with Miss Nude Caracas right now insteada talking to you.

An evocative image, Mr Simons.

And no fucking women neither. This kinda thing is between men, women ain't cut out for it.

Indeed.

Yeah indeed is right. Okay if I find him I'll call you. This number okay?

Ten million. Bearer bonds. No women, no dogs, Irish, crazy Sicilians. You will call on this number. That is fine.

Fine.

Fine.

Bye.

In the general run of things I don't like to perpetuate negative attitudes towards women in the criminal professions because those attitudes are batshit ridiculous but as a practical matter there is one woman I really don't want to bump into. Coming face to face with Karenina would fatally cramp my style.

You have to ask why. Why are the Seven Demons here at all and what kind of asshole puts out that kind of money for just me? There's two dozen regular footpads between here and the waffle stand outside Baptist ministry who would have killed me for less than fifty thousand and a hundred more basic urban fuckheads woulda been grateful for the chance to make a name and pick up the keys to an inexpensive saloon. The crazy thing is that I would probably be dead now because I would've waited out that midnight moment and maybe gone for eggs in the morning and splat. Bye Jack.

So why?

There's a woman named Martine who works in the Probate Office. That's probate like wills and testaments not probation like crooks or prostate like the erection golfball in a guy's ass. The public waiting room is mint green like the inside of a sport sock and full of people who are not only grieving for somebody but now also pissed off because they are waiting for the government to admit that that person is dead.

Hi Martine how you doing? Beanie Paul says you're a lady does business o' the informational variety.

Go fuck yourself.

Martine that is no way to greet a member of the public in a government office plus also I am a friend to all mankind.

I ain't doing it whatever it is.

For the commonality and love of all mankind.

No.

For friendship Martine.

If I got friendship and peanut butter—

Yes you could have peanut butter sandwiches – if you also had some bread.

I was gonna say I could rub it all over myself and get off and you could keep the other part. Plus also I don't even know your name.

Simons. Bob Simons. I'm a skip tracer I guess.

Well guess this I ain't gonna.

I will give you cash money Martine.

Nope. Nuh uh.

Jewellery.

Nopety nope nope.

I can arrange complimentary manscaping for a partner or friend.

Fuck you say? Manscaping? What even is that?

The trimming or removal by waxing looping laser or other methods known and unknown of intimate hair from the male body in such manner as to produce visually attractive contours and more amenable tactile surfaces during intercourse and also as a hygienic measure to reduce unwanted odour.

You can make that happen? Even involuntarily maybe if I was to supply a name?

Martine I believe we can come to an arrangement.

Never underestimate the variety of human motivations: we do come to an arrangement and Martine copies all papers pertaining to Didi Fraser and puts them in a bag for me. It is white and made of biodegradable plastic and it has large black letters like moveable type printed on the outside. On the crosstown I skim through it. In an earlier life Didi worked in a school two hundred miles from here. Before that she failed to be either a singer or a garden designer. She was legally blind but too proud to have a support animal which also makes it very unlikely that she saw something she shouldn't have.

She was not the beneficiary of a trust fund or an unknown uncle with a diamond mine. She had some money – like middle class money not like exciting money – which was enough to cover her costs because she basically lived on air and water and she never went out or bought anything. No one particularly wanted her apartment – no real estate scheme relied on her death like in a bad TV show. The Probate Office does not have an official view on whether she killed Kennedy or Oswald or Ruby but I'm going out on a limb and say not.

In other words there's just no reason anyone would kill Didi Fraser and hire the Seven Demons to cover it up.

Didi Fraser was a boring, nice, nasty old dame. It makes no sense.

Sitting in my crosstown seat I realise I've made a mistake somewhere. Yes. Yes, I used Simons' name at the Probate Office as well as at the skip trace bars. Mistake.

The train car is almost empty but I'm pretty sure that's the doctor sitting on my left. Pretty sure because there's that weird cold like a breaking wave, like touching a live wire, like falling into space. Pretty sure that's nightfall.

She has lovely eyes, the doctor. Deep and full of fire like polished calcite. Mouth like roses covered in honey.

Count backwards from I'm dead.

part two

WAKING UP IS NICE IN THAT I didn't think I would. It's not nice because I doubt it's permanent. Open one eye expecting to be in a bathtub full of ice. Not a bathroom. Big expensive modernist living room, corner views. If not a penthouse then near enough. I could jump.

Memory: my asshole friend should have taken the elevator. Don't think about it now. Can't afford a fugue now. Think about the pale wood floor with the imported silk rugs, I'm saying Chinese not Persian but still. Tribal masks from South America. And then there's one other thing. I smell zagara flowers and Swedish–Haitian–Lebanese hair.

Oh hi Sarah. (Not out loud.)

Sarah the lawyer that I'm a little bit in love with. Sarah that is not a little bit in love with me. Crazy-cheekboned, long-limbed Sarah, all mystery and yoga and wheatgrass. Sarah Sarah. That Sarah in the chair opposite. Handcuffs like me. Sorry Sarah. And there's the doctor wearing a lab face. Clinical interest. They're the same height same build but so different. Sarah is all possibility. The doctor is all buttoned down like she's wearing a moonsuit all the time looking at you through a Lexan visor. Like you're a germ.

You going to experiment on us now?

It's good that you know who we are Mr Simons.

Well fuck me. (Not out loud but only just.) Fuck. She is calling me Mr Simons. She does not know who I am. That's great.

Sarah does know who I am. That is less great.

Will Sarah tell her who I am on purpose? Unknown but it's definitely not impossible. More important right now is that she might do so by accident. If she calls me Jack we're both dead. Certainly I'm dead. Probably her. I'd kill her if I was the doctor. It's just neater.

I wonder what her name is this doctor. What her life is and what it was before. She wears a charm bracelet with just a dog on it. Who does that?

Hey doc you like dogs? I'm definitely a dog man. Used to have Vizslas. You know what a Vizsla is? Great companion dog, proper animal.

She raises one eyebrow like: I'm not talking dogs with you maggot now fuck off you got five seconds then I'm going to knock you out again just for the quiet. All that from just one eyebrow.

Okay, doc, I'm gonna run with this a little you see where I go wrong and you let me know okay?

The doctor doesn't say anything so okay. Now, Sarah. How long have I got before the penny drops? Before Karenina comes by? Are the Demons in close touch? No choice. Talk to Sarah.

Hi, little lady, you must be Sarah Kessler am I right? You would be the legal representative of one Jack Price and the word is that he's a little bit in love with you. That's just what I hear. Is that who you are sweetheart? That's fine. I'm Bob Simons I'm a missing persons investigator that's to say I find people who want to be missing for people who want them found. I'd call myself a bounty hunter but there's that TV show now and people get all funny about it plus in my mind MPI has a ring to it. I'm thinking franchise in the fullness of time. Might could use a little legal representation if that individual had a discreet and appropriate response to ticklish situations. You ever think about the future darling? Probably behoves you to think about it now. Say yes Bob.

Yes Bob.

Eyes somewhere between shit scared and angrier than you've ever seen, cheekbones got tears on them but her voice is clear as a bell. My Sarah. Wonderful Sarah. Not my Sarah.

That's great. Now here's the situation in which you find yourself. That scary lady over there, I'm guessing she seemed kind to animals and good with children is that about right? You can say yes again.

Yes Bob.

That's great. So then she put a Mickey Finn in your cold milk or your Chardonnay. That's a polite and gentlemanly term for a roofie which is what frat boys and other ne'er-do-wells call Flunitrazepam. You might be a little bit young for Mickey Finn so I'm supplying those other names for your convenience okay? Anyway this lady works for a certain enterprise that has business with your client Mr Price. I'm also looking for Mr Price on an unrelated matter and I took it in my head we might combine forces. The good doctor (kind to animals good with children remember) she represents that enterprise in this room and she evidently has emphatic opinions about dispatch. That's to say she wants to meet with your client in a discursive setting sooner rather than later, isn't that right doc?

Tolerably.

Sarah you can say yes Bob again just so I know you're following.

Yes Bob.

Okay now I won't disguise from you that you and I – I think both of us I'm not entirely sure my being somewhat disinvolved but I'm here in the room and I arrived in much the same way as you did somewhat to my surprise but I'm inclined to overlook that owing to the size of my fee as agreed, but most definitely you Sarah on account of your close connection with Mr Price – we're in a somewhat ticklish position right now owing to that sense of urgency to which I alluded earlier. There's not a great deal of goodwill towards us here okay? It would be most unwise to do anything that upset the applecart. Let's keep all our apples exactly where they are right now. Yes Bob.

Yes Bob.

That being the case let me ask you and do please consider your answer real carefully, take your time and get it right first time out of the box because I'm quite sure our friend the doctor has alternative options regarding this conversation ready to hand: do you know where Jack Price is right now?

No Bob.

Then let me ask a different kind of question and you should feel free to improvise a little on your answer okay this isn't a courtroom you can spread your wings. Do you think you might be able to guess where your friend Mr Price might be? Where he might go and to whom he might speak in a time of great personal stress? If not to you?

He's not my friend.

He's just your client, I understand.

It's an important distinction for a lawyer.

Okay.

I don't know where he is. I don't really know him at all. He's this... he's an asshole. I have my own firm. He's my client. He doesn't launder money through me or anything like that. I do his legitimate legal. He's got someone else for that stuff. I'm straight Mr Simons I'm a good lawyer.

But you got this itsy bitsy practice.

I can't work for the bigs I got kicked out.

Boss get handsy and you broke his arm?

I found a key piece of evidence which sank my client. I was required to disclose it and I did. But as a practical matter I didn't have to. No one would have known.

You did everything right and you got fired?

I'm toxic waste now reputationally speaking.

Life sucks Sarah.

Yes Bob it does and now here I am.

Who's the guy?

What guy?

You said Price has a money guy do you know who? You can tell your uncle Bob.

Tucker.

First name or last?

Just Tucker and I only heard of him once. We don't talk about that stuff because I don't want to know. It makes me ashamed that I get near it. Price makes me ashamed and I'm ashamed now because I'm afraid and I shouldn't want to give him to you but I do. If I could I would. If he contacts me ever again I will.

I understand you sugar I really do. Don't worry, I think I can safely say you won't ever have to deal with Mr Price no more. You know how he reaches this Tucker? Is Tucker maybe local?

No Bob. I mean it when I say I don't know.

You think Mr Price really likes you Sarah?

I think he thinks he does. I don't think he likes anyone except Price. So if you're looking for a hostage I think I'm going to die and he's going to laugh at you.

Tucker.

Tucker.

That's it?

That's all I have for you Mr Simons. Is it enough?

She asks a good question, my lawyer. It better be enough because I'm definitely out of time here. When it occurs to the good doctor to run my name in any way shape or form it's going to turn out that there's no such man as Bob Simons. I can bullshit that, of course. I can say it's an alias and I've had some troubles of my own. If she sits still for that I can give her one of my dormant identities and hope like hell she doesn't have it already. But if she so much as thinks for five seconds about how I'm about the same age as Jack Price and the same height and weight and—

Well then I am dead.

Hey doc.

Mr Simons.

Hey doc I was wondering. I got questions.

Mr Simons I'm not really in the mood.

Naw, come on doc I got just two.

Go ahead.

Okay you want the easy one or the hard one.

I don't – Oh, for god's sake give me the hard one.

Is that enough or are you going to turn us both into lab rats for some freaky ass experiment you got going on?

Mr Simons I have already told you I'm not going to experiment on you. What could I possibly learn from a sample of two unscreened adults with no controls? It's like tossing a coin. I brought you here unconscious because I did not wish to argue but I am a scientist not a carnival villain. If I need to kill you I will kill you but there is simply no prospect of—

I like that if doc, I call that word if entirely heartening because it seems to me you're saying that at this time you don't need to and that means we're still partners.

Partners?

I told Fred I would find your guy in exchange for ten million and I will. I'm prepared to waive the issue of working with a female on the basis you're clearly a professional. I would consider it an honour on this occasion and I might even learn something.

How graceful of you.

Hell I ain't never been called that in my life.

Imagine my surprise.

So here's what I propose to do doc if it's all the same to you. I'm gonna take this lady Sarah home and maybe she'll show me round her place just in case there's any correspondence or other filings she might've forgot to mention in the course of our amiable discussion just now. Because you notice she is a woman of high principles and while she really don't like her client she feels some kind of priestly obligation to his worthless ass that maybe needs a little nudging to overcome. And then I'm going to find this fella Tucker and he's going to walk me through the subject's financial operations because a man like Price, well, the clue is in the name. He really loves his money. Ain't gonna sit with him if I begin intercepting his cash flows and such and then he will come out of the woodwork. In my experience his kind always do. Is that a schedule of events to which you'd find your good self amenable, doc?

Provisionally.

Wink's as good as a nudge doc.

Are you always like this?

Like how?

I suppose you would call it… down-home irrepressible?

Yes I am. I am from the South originally as you no doubt know.

I notice you and yours tend a little to the conservative in terms of formality in discussion and no doubt that's the better way at your level of enterprise but I am a small businessman and I have established a certain mode of being in the world that's memorable. No problem if someone don't like me so long as they remember me. That way when a thing needs doing that's in my wheelhouse I'm the one they call. No one objects to working with a fella they don't personally admire so long as that fella is competent and I am. Discovery doc is the key in the digital age.

I was concerned you might believe you were charming.

That brings us to my second question which was whether you would care to join me at a nearby watering hole and drink a refined cocktail sporting some sort of combination of fruit and umbrellas in celebration of this new friendship? I'm a coarse man, doc, but I have my virtues and among them is I know how to have fun and how to show a lady a good time. Hell I even can scrub up and wear a tie and under certain limited circumstances you might mistake me for a sophisticate.

I'm afraid I will have to pass on this occasion.

I can discuss the ballet quite persuasively doc. It surprises many people to learn that I am a positively Russian judge of the arabesque.

No. Thank you.

Well I can't say I am entirely surprised doc and surely I am not offended but you're a fine figure of a woman and you cannot blame a man for asking politely when he encounters a woman of substance and beauty.

No Mr Simons I do not but I find the conversation fatiguing and we both have matters to attend to. You may proceed about your business. I would advise against cocktails under any circumstances however for the next twenty-four hours as the anaesthetic I am about to give you does not react well with alcohol and it would be unfortunate if you were to die of white rum and pineapple before our business was concluded.

Wait what anaesthetic?

She's so fast. Cold needle in my neck. No time to count backwards. So fast and I'm gone.

On the sidewalk outside a diner. Car just dropped us off, rolled us right out onto the sidewalk like sticky Chinese food off a plastic platter.

Fuck you Jack get the fuck away from me I will fucking kill you I SWEAR TO GOD BASTARD! Get the FUCK AWAY!

Sarah would you mind lowering your voice I don't think this is entirely necessary.

Fuck you Jack.

I get that a lot.

Who are those people Jack?

Well that would be the doctor of the Seven Demons who is a very intelligent person but maybe not much of an investigator. Don't go home by the way, when she figures out what happened she will also realise that you chose not to tell her who I was and she will have you killed.

You said she'd have me killed if I did.

I sort of implied that but to be honest I have no idea. I am grateful that you interpreted what I was saying to mean that our interests were together.

So where do we go now?

I am going away. I don't know where you are going. I would strongly suggest out of town. Under another name. Or you could seek the protection of the authorities. I'm sure you have watched enough TV to understand how competent they are in that regard.

I thought you were in love with me?

Yes well I thought so too but as it transpires I just find you really attractive and it's entirely possible that in the context of a committed relationship I would actually fall in love with you but at this time and knowing as I do that I make you ashamed and dirty and you only did not turn me in because your principles are so deeply engraved on your identity that they completely override your common sense

I'm going to say I think that outcome is unlikely.

So that's it?

Yeah I guess. We're done. No client no lawyer. Not friends not allies not lovers. Two people in the street. Used to be we had a professional relationship but now you're terminated or you're no longer willing to be my representative. It really doesn't matter which way around we do it. I don't know what will happen to you and while I do care it's about the level of whether I catch next week's installment. That's just what it is.

Well that's fucking monstrous and so are you.

Sarah you pretty much killed Tucker and his entire family just now to save your own life and I'm just doing what I gotta do to save myself. Difference is I'm not pretending anything else and you're still telling yourself you're a good person in a bad place. You took my business and now here we are and now we're saying goodbye and that's all.

Sarah walks away from me down the street. She has very little money in her bag and she should probably go straight to an ATM and get as much as she can. If she does that in about half an hour, I reckon she'll die. I guess if she hides for a few days then all this will be over, one way or another. Maybe she'll have a life again. I think I have to acknowledge that it won't include me, but I guess it's pretty clear it never really did.

I am a walking business plan, is what it is. That's all.

Mount Caroline Emotional Health and Recovery Center for some reason they don't want to call it a hospital but that's what it is. Mint green hallway again and why would you ever use that colour? It crops up everywhere that expects hard wear and not a lot of cash inflow. Military surplus undercoat or some such. Maybe just a big fucking mixture of whatever they had, grey and yellow and white and blue. There is no way that colour is good for you. Fucking paint feels like lead too. Bet it's fucking full of lead. Maybe makes the people in this place more crazy than they were already. Or maybe it makes no difference and they're just people of unsound mind from way back. Almost all of them are nice. Almost none of them are dangerous. Crazy people get a bad rep because movies. Actual crazy people are just a little sad and they don't work unless you treat them or they fix themselves. Had a mad aunt a while. She was frightened all the time always, frightened of the most unlikely things. Said they spoke to her. Best you stayed with her, then she was sort of okay, you could tell her what was real and she mostly believed you.

Sure some crazy people do dangerous things because they think the world is doing dangerous things to them. That's pretty much what we all do when you think about it. It's rare you find someone who's just flat out murderous. That takes an especially poor combination of fucking bad luck. Even then you can mostly manage it with drugs.

Put on my best frost face like the doc's like hello agar jelly I regard you from on high. Whisper a few words to the mirror, find the voice. Saul Hart is a dickey ID: Brit pastor with myopia and a dusty medical degree, likes mandolin music, pale tea and cats. Footnote: when you go to a new physician people check the damn certificates. Anyone can use a printer.

I say: Hi I'm Saul Hart would you be Professor Langley?

Yes I would and I can't tell you Mr Hart how proud I am to know someone with this kind of dedication.

Well the Church of Saint Joseph is small but there are things we can do that make a real impact and these lost souls are His children after all.

When we put out our appeal every month we always hope someone will be brave enough to accept one of these cases because that's really the only way they have a hope of being stabilised in a family-type community environment but of course it mostly doesn't happen because it requires money and people with money just don't end up here.

Yes precisely and that is why Saint Joseph's exists because where there's love of course money is less of an issue. I say love I mean Caritas you appreciate or Agape not Eros.

No indeed Mr Hart of course.

Thank you Professor Langley.

Not at all Mr Hart. You appreciate we'll need to keep tabs on him for the first few weeks?

All understood. As I said on the phone I think it's best if we introduce him to the new lodgings. He may – they often do – turn them down and it's important for obvious reasons to allow him to return here if that's what he prefers but I have high hopes because the rooms we have at the moment are very fine, I mean not luxurious by any means but somehow filled with a positive energy. You won't often find a churchman speaking in those terms we don't care much about energy in the general way but I've spent some time in California and I've no doubt become corrupted. Can you hear it in my voice?

No sir to me I must say you sound entirely London.

Ah well very good. My sister tells me she can hear it in every word, she is quite scathing.

Ah well sisters.

You have one?

Sir I have four.

A wealth, Professor Langley.

A wealth of constructive criticism, Mr Hart.

Quite so quite so. Ah and is this our friend?

Yes, Mr Hart, this is Mr Crisp. Not his original name I'm afraid but we have a list and we choose a name for everyone and then of course if they recall their own they can revert.

Good day to you Mr Crisp. I hope we shall be fast friends.

Uhh.

I'm afraid he's a little shy Mr Hart.

Uhhhnnn.

That's quite all right Professor I do understand. Here my dear fellow lean on me, that's it. Now then you and I, we're going to be friends. I'm going to help you. Help you get everything you need and get you out in the world again, on your own two feet.

Uhh?

Yes.
Uh?
Yes.
Lucille?
Yes, my friend. Exactly. Lucille.
LUCILLE!
Yes. Let's get you settled in.

No point calling Tucker. He'll know what's coming down. He probably knew before I did. Likely Karenina called him, told him I was in the shit. Those two go back. Likely Tucker's breaking bread with the Seven Demons right now giving them all my shit he can. Part of the agreement. Reason he doesn't know everything I do. Safer for everyone if we don't trust.

Copy shop by the old picture house. The picture house closed last month. No more Bogart and Bacall late nights, no more Jaws or Jawas or jocks sitting through romcoms because they're actually in love. No more of any of that. Just a closed building and a copy shop where I left my case after meeting Linden, told them to scan what I took and dump it to a fresh email address. No way for Karenina to find that: like looking for a single piece of floating plastic in the Pacific trash vortex. What did I take from Linden's? Told you you weren't paying attention. Remember: there was that business with historical cinema and then I got a little physical and then – yeah you missed it again.

Look: I took the appointments diary off of Oliver's desk. Paper diary because an outfit like that they do not want a digital record that someone could maybe break into or email to themselves. Crypto all you like, password protect and partition or whatever the hell. Truth is that if you don't want something to get shared, you don't put that fucking thing on a local computer because computers are all about the sharing. That is not just how they are made it is what they are made of. Linden knows this so he has paper. Some temp every night must copy the appointments from the master into two more books:

Dorothy's and Oliver's. He or she sits up late in the library room they have in that place and does what they do and they get paid almost nothing and have no idea what any of those names mean and they get fired regularly so that they do not figure it out or get used to the rhythm of the place and you have to respect that. That is old school and it is wise.

Downside is that now I have stolen the book and they cannot take that back. They can change everything in the future but I do not care about that I only care about the past. This begins in the past and it begins recently. So who did Linden see this month? He saw... the Andersons, Jan and Don, about inheritances. He saw the Liebowicz kid about emancipation. He saw three corporates and blah blah blah my aching head Jesus this guy has a healthy practice and a varied clientele. Who did he see that might have an interest in Didi Fraser? Kinda no one. No one at all. So who did he see had no business being there?

Three names are tagged NC, new client. One of these, 90%, is my problem. Start there okay so: Sean Harper is a rich kid. Liz Crane is getting divorced. Father Roy Maxton who the hell knows why he's there it doesn't say, so you're gonna make some assumptions but it's just as likely he's got parking fines or he needs to get his church re-zoned. Who is Liz getting divorced from? What has Sean done and to whom? No idea. But it all adds. It doesn't add up yet but it adds.

The good father got no cash for the Seven Demons unless he's a lot higher in the church than you'd think. Search his name: no. Look at this fucking guy, he's Saint Francis without the Snow White birdies. Off the list. Why off the list? Because every real-life visit to people on this list increases the chance they figure where I am. Triage, people. Best is a single strike.

No Father Maxton leaves two.

Liz. Liz Crane is divorcing some huge fucker, not huge like physical he's actually kinda round and small but monetarily he's like a lead weight on a rubber sheet and all the money just rolls down on top of him. Liz doesn't mind all the money but she wants to bathe in it by herself now thank you. Liz is young and pretty, you look at her picture you're gonna say she's maybe Indian by way of ancestry like maybe Goan but that is a whole sackful of assumptions so my feeling would be don't. Tom Crane is not young and not pretty. Liz has served her time before the mast and wants her – actually I don't fucking know what she wants metaphorically speaking I don't know anything about ships or naval history. She wants to stop having sex with her blimp husband and move the fuck on. More power to Liz. Why would Liz want Didi dead? Is it possible that Didi is in some way a problem for Liz and her divorce? Like maybe Didi's great-grandson cleans the pool at Tom Crane's house and knows what Liz's O-face looks like from personal experience and proximity?

Gonna talk to Liz.

Sean. Look at Sean. Sean is a nice guy up to a point by which I mean that Sean inherited money but basically doesn't feel the need to make any more of it. Sean does work at a soup kitchen and puts those weird fucking cotton wraps in his hair all like different colours so he looks like a table mat. Sean does music therapy with kids. Sean saves whales. Fuck Sean and all his works. Fuck him so hard in the eye. Sean makes you ashamed until you remember that Sean has just under a billion dollars. Sean is Bruce Wayne and this charitable shit is his Batman. Lucky Sean. If maybe papa hadn't cut down half of a rainforest somewhere and found oil or whatever then maybe Sean could spend his time getting laid like any respectable young rich kid but there is some earned fucking guilt here is what there is. Gonna talk to Sean.

Liz, or Sean. Sean, or Liz. Toss a coin.

Short discussion with a limo guy. He ends up in the trunk under a blanket. I did offer him money it's not like I'm on a spree here but the negotiation did not proceed expeditiously to a reasonable conclusion. Dude seriously when a man is serious and you're not you just got to get out of the way. Next lifetime, yeah? His damn hat won't fit, whatever, improvise. Muss myself up, grab the phone from his pocket.

Yeah, he's really dead. I killed him for no better reason than I wanted ten minutes with his fare. It's not a thing. Feels kinda unartistic and redundant, but you can't make an omelette.

Hi Liz my name's Justin and I'll be your driver today.

Hi Justin.

Can I get an Aaaaargh! from you Liz? It is drive like a pirate day and I can give you a discount I realise it is not really cool in a limo but this is what my boss is saying and I gotta would you mind?

Aaaaargh Justin. Arrrrgh! Is that okay?

Yeah Liz that's just great. You give great pirate if I may say.

So do you Justin are those your real teeth?

Yes in fact they are. Well these are a little bit man-made obviously mostly some sorta ceramic but yeah these are my teeth I just had them put in some kind of 3D printing thing. A friend of mine did the design and then you just go right on in and they scan your mouth and zap that's it like a couple of hours they say I can eat steak later not that I do because I'm vegan. Can you do the pirate thing one more time I didn't get a great picture?

Aaaaaargh!

Thanks Liz.

That's okay Justin, you're kinda cute. I think I like making little noises for you.

Aw now Liz you're making me blush and you a married woman with a ring like that size.

Don't let the egg fool ya Justin I am washing that man right outta my hair, yes I am. He is gone. So let me just give you one more Aaaargh and then maybe we talk while we drive, Justin, cos I got places to be but maybe after I been there I might seriously want to find out what it's like to be a small seaside town mercilessly pillaged by buccaneers is what I'm saying.

Hell lady you can't say things like that when a man's getting out into the traffic, I near about killed that guy on the cycle.

Aw, Justin, don't tell me you're no fun.

Liz I can honestly say I am all kindsa fun.

So you gonna plunder my treasures, Captain?

Oh, hell yeah I am, but you gotta promise me there ain't no marque and reprisal happening on your coastline, you get me?

Uh…

Sorry yeah they made us read this dumb book on pirates is all. I mean is the husband really outta the picture? Because I can't afford to alienate no millionaire shipping magnate or nothing, they might send the British navy after me and hang me like Blackbeard.

Oh sugar he is gone like the wind. He is so much in the past tense. I got a lawyer and I'm gonna be not like Kardashian rich but I am never gonna work nor want again. I am moving this ass to Europe and I'm gonna camp out in Cartier's front room.

Man it's that easy?

Oh it was not easy there was some disgusting sex I went through to get here but trust me Justin you're going to be real pleased about that on account of the things I have been wanting to try out on a man who doesn't look like a Thanksgiving turkey in his underclothes. You got tattoos Justin?

No I do not.

That's good because that whole turkey thing is for real and right now tattoos make me think of poultry stamps.

Hey this neighbourhood we going to it's not far from a regular client of mine.

Does she talk like I do Justin? Am I gonna have to share you?

No ma'am she does not and she woulda made a fine accompaniment to your turkey husband I'm thinking on account of looking a great deal like chestnut stuffing at least what of her I ever saw which was you will understand not naked. She's dead now though. Didi Fraser her name was, lived just over yonder. You ever know her, ma'am, seeing this is your neighbourhood?

No, I didn't. What'd she die of?

She was murdered Liz, is what it is. Stone cold killed. Who'd do something like that?

Real-life pirates, I guess.

Yeah. I guess.

Justin I gotta tell you that is some mood killer you got there.

Yeah I'm just now realising that myself.

Listen you can just drop me off at the Museum, okay, and if I want you later I'll call the office.

It's my last fare, Liz, I'm sorry to say. You want to make one more Aaargh for me, just for the memories?

Honestly Justin I think maybe I won't. You've got the pictures and now suddenly it feels kinda weird.

It woulda been fun, Liz, but I'm thinking you'll get yourself a better class of man. You take care now.

Thanks, Justin.

Bye Liz.

And she's gone. Liz won't die because of me, and I won't have sex with her, which is kinda my penance for Justin the limo guy but also means she won't completely freak the fuck out when she finds out real Justin was stabbed in the heart and she took a drive with his murderer. You gotta do something for your fellow human beings occasionally when you can. Plus honestly: not that into her.

I'm going with my gut and say she didn't know Didi Fraser.

Dump the limo, put on a dayglo. Get down in the pipe in the park and find some stinking fucking mud. Walk the streets like that in a hard hat. Ain't no one wondering what you do for a living. Hitch a ride with a garbage crew for a few bucks: Sean Harper's street has garbage too. Everyone produces garbage except those weird zero impact fucks who can't figure out their mere existence in a city like this is an eco footprint the size of a village in the Andes. Whatevs.

Figure I was gonna bang on Sean's door and say we found something in the sewer with his name on it, like a letter, like a letter from Didi Fraser. Figure that was my plan, but maybe it wasn't. Don't need it anyway. Standing on the back of the truck in my dayglos, driver nearly flat runs over the doctor yes that doctor the doctor she of the amazing eyes and the anaesthetic walking with a Saluki answering to the name of Tycho. She's going into Sean's place, leaves the dog with the commissionaire. Swishes into the elevator. Saluki is perfect for her, says exactly what she is: she's refined and she's beautiful and she will chase you down but she has to see you first. Don't I know it. Swish swish. The doctor, she's got really remarkable legs, and I have to admit that talking to Liz like that while it was a professional choice was also not entirely unpleasant. Fight and flight and fucking all got their place in a person's head and they do on occasion get crossed over and confused, and I have killed and I have run like hell and there is some evolutionary part of me that's pretty sure I should breed now and breed plenty in order to secure my DNA and that woman there is strong and she is an alpha and that kind of thing is as close as you get to guarantees.

Elevator doors close. Bye doc. Hello Tycho. Aw, look at you, sorry man I hope it's okay just I love dogs. Where I grew up we're all kennel people you know? Not breeds refined like this one, this is a Saluki, but still. Dog like this needs taking care of for sure.

Yeah, well this one ain't yours.

That's true I don't got a dog right now not in the city, but I know – hey wait, he's got a little twinge there on the chest you see?

No I don't and you better—

Naw wait man I ain't screwin' around. That lady – hang on lemme just – yeah okay it's here. That's okay Tycho... there. Aw, shit.

What? He okay?

Well yes and no. I mean he's fine but he ain't okay. Dog like this you got to worry mostly about heart cancer.

The fuck?

Yeah, they get heart cancer would you believe thirty-one per cent of them? And this fella here he's got a little polyp there in the meat here that's not a good sign. You know the owner?

Nope. Jeez.

Listen I gotta go I got places to be but you see her, you tell her to get this dog to a veterinary specialist, like a cancer doctor. She's gotta be a rich woman she's in this building, owns this dog, and that's gonna save Tycho here because this kinda thing you catch it early and you get things right you can treat it now. It's like miraculous shit they can do. But you tell that woman for god's sake. Don't say some asshole in a dayglo right you say some vet came by gave you a number to call is what. In fact hang on yeah I know a guy, I did some work for him back six months ago, hang on—

And there you go. Walk away. Walk away now, down the street, stinking of pond shit and doing my good deed, saving that dog.

No there's no fucking tumour you can feel in his chest. What are you an infant?

Sean Harper is the client. 99.9%. Won't help now if I kill Sean. I mean I will kill Sean anyway but he's so far from the point right now it's almost sad. I'll kill him later for satisfaction and maybe I'll talk to him first to find out why all this happened.

But now I got a pin to stick in the map.

Plus later I'm gonna take the doctor's doggie for a walk.

Kong Fuzi said: you want to define the future you must study the past.

This is the kind of crap coffee traders tell one another, and one of the things that they do is they say Kong Fuzi rather than Confucius so they know they're smarter than you are.

Sitting on a park bench studying the past. Ancient history now. 95.

Back in 95 there was a guy. Supposed to be the best solo sniper in the world. Most any sniper gonna use a spotter if he can, this guy doesn't. Doesn't much use technology either. One of those Ukrainian log cabin motherfuckers like the original Kalashnikov, lives for the stag's hesitation and feels the wind changing in his piss. These are the guys who made Stalingrad the funfest that it was back in the day, and before that they sat under sheepskins and snow and they fucked Napoleon's shit right up as he tried to walk back from Moscow. Direct-line descendant of every awful wartime thing ever happened, is what I'm saying, and deep sniper magic from the Steppes. Don't believe in magic that's fine. Any sufficiently advanced terrifying murderous instinctual and acquired skillset is indistinguishable from magic is what. This guy was magic. They called him Volodya. Never had another name. It means Universal Ruler.

So for a while this guy ran the Seven Demons. Killed with them partied with them ate with them. Did not sleep with them because those people do not sleep. Then he hit fifty and he said that was enough. Retired with all the money in the world and never spent any of it because he never cared about it. Lives in a shack in the middle of nowhere. That is the thing you got to understand about these people. Sure they make money but they do not care about it, they care about being the Seven Demons, or about being that badass, or being able to kill whoever they like. The new Demons are the same. They got varied interests, but those interests are not money per se.

Just a historical point.

Make a few phone calls. Set up my dog-walking scheme. Send a guy to the warehouse district with a sewing kit and some very traditional men's hygiene products. Kinda thing I'm doing requires some fucking preparation is what. History is all very well but this is the modern world and I'm using a seven-stage cutout through the deep web plus two mobile relays a bunch of encrypted la la la. I could be on the moon is what I'm saying. Not that I won't get caught eventually. Just that it won't be now unless there's some mahoosive bad luck some coincident moment where I just walk right into one of them in the street on the crosstown whatever. There's a few months of digital effort in my comms even for someone brilliant and I don't have a few months because I'm not running I'm standing and Karenina will know that. Won't stop her from trying but by the time she cracks me – me not the system I will screw up and give her entry somehow because people inevitably do – and by the time I do something dumb and it gets her into my shit, it'll all be over anyway.

VoIP to a new casual tasking service LateToTheParty dot me. Talk fast, one pro to another: I need a pickup I'm going to be late for a client. It's a vet call so I really can't reschedule. I need you to say you're with the vet. Can you do that okay? Okay buddy I'll owe you… yeah just bring it right to the – yeah. Yeah. Okay cool beans man! Five stars in his service box, everyone likes a good rating. Al, that's his name. No point being stingy with Al, and he's good people anyway. But really no point bookmarking him either, sadly.

Okay. Okay okay. Got a little list, right.
  Johnny Cubano: check.
  And then:
  The doctor.
  The Finnish torture brothers.
  Karenina.
  Li Dong-ha the private mercenary guy.
  And Fred the PR sniper.
  Roll the dice man. Who's up?

Incoming call, familiar number. Don't take it. Move locations. Burn another shirtfront person. Cross off another credit line. Move to some shithouse apartment. Got great wifi though, seriously fast connection next door some kinda hacker commune or whatever, some high-grade cable coming out and an open-access ethos because they want you to beat the NSA. Power to the people man.
  Call back. Don't slip into Bob Simons.
  Hi Tucker.
  Hi Price.
  Tucker I'm going to assume I'm talking to a room full of Demons right now.
  That's a good assumption Price.
  They get you?
  I kinda got them if I'm honest.
  You went over?
  It's a dog-eat-dog world man.
  Oh I'm so glad you said that.
  What?
  Never mind man. Tell me what it is.

It's I'm taking all your money, Price, and I'm kinda giving these nice people everything I know.

Ain't much, Tucker.

More'n you think maybe.

Likely. Likely less than you think.

(It's really tempting to say something like Hi Sean but I don't because I am a professional and not a fucking angry teenager.)

Tucker laughs: sounds like someone getting his throat cut. Tucker has emphysema. Never fucking dies of it, but it never gets any better either.

Demon you there?

Yes, Mr Price.

You take care of Tucker, he gets windy if he has onions.

I have your friends, Mr Price.

Can't say I do.

The construction fellow is here too.

Billy's there? Dude are you there?

Fucksakes Price yes I'm fucking here! What the fuck you asshole?

Damn Billy that is a tough break. Demon that's a tough break you gonna kill Billy. That's pointless man. You know how fucking hard it is to find good scaffolding guys?

I understand you supply this man and his crew with cocaine.

I do but like on the understanding they'll be real sensitive in its application. Seriously, you're ever gonna do some construction in this hemisphere you're gonna want Billy and his guys.

William is this true?

Yeah man we're the best.

All your employees are competent? They have common sense and training? Not just you?

Yes of course man we're a team there's like two guys could do my job I—

Damnit Billy.

[Incoming video feed.]

[Decline.]

Oh now Mr Price come.

[Incoming video feed.]

[Decline.]

Don't think I give a crap man – what I call you anyway? I can't keep calling you Demon it's stupid.

Frederick.

Like Mr Frederick or just Frederick like some kind of Eurotrash in Italian leather slacks?

I do not wear leather Mr Price it is inhumane.

What?

I'm fucking with you Mr Price. Just Frederick will be fine. I'm going to kill your friend now. You were kind enough to try to save him and I really did respect your argument but by his own – excuse me (BANG) – by his own testimony he's (Mr Tucker I am sorry did I get that on you how regrettable) he has effectively trained his own replacement already (goodness he is a loud fellow roaring like a bull my goodness well it will be over soon). The orderly flow of the world will continue and of course they will now have metered access to a new product which affords a clarity of mind alongside the euphoria and rarely if ever triggers cardiac events in users. We call it Beyoncé because you just want to put your face in it.

Yeah that's hilarious man real classy.

Well I find that a little crass sexual innuendo sells very well among upper and middle class looking to titillate by transgressing the polite conventions of drug use and equally well among lower middle and working class who engage with the imagery in a more straightfor-wardly enthusiastic way.

[Incoming video feed.]

[Decline.]

Man I'm not gonna watch you do Billy and what all just so you can try to sneak Karenina into my phone that's bush league.

Disappointing. I had hoped for a streak of nobility but mankind is descending into barbarism so no doubt I should not be surprised.

So you killed Billy you gonna kill Tucker too? That'd just be a fucking waste.

No Mr Tucker is our friend now.

Get out of there Tuck. I don't see being their friend as a growth industry.

I figure to stick around some few hours at least, Price, maybe see you get yours. Nothing personal but it's more fun than pro sports.

You gonna make the pitch Tuck?

Sure if you like. You come in before they find Sarah or Charlie they maybe don't die.

I figured. Answer's no of course. But I got a counter-offer.

What's that Price?

If they just plain fuck off home and hide right now I'll probably only kill one or more two of them before I get bored looking and I won't even make it last. There ya go. Is that testosteroney enough for you? I gotta go see a man about – well never mind that now. Hey Frederick you want to finish Billy before I go or you just gonna get it done when you hear the click?

They don't answer. They just get to it. I listen because maybe there's something to learn. That and it never hurts to be reminded why you're doing something. Give them credit they don't take long over it. Billy has time to curse me a couple times and then he says please but not to me and then that's it.

I don't hang around for more banter. Pretty much seems we all know where we stand.

I will admit that I don't feel great about that. I would quite like to go and drink myself into the ground but if I do then I will miss my window on the dog-walking scheme and I will also probably die because if I get drunk I will misstep. Or I will get violent on a personal level and it is not time for that. I will get violent on a personal level when I am good and ready.

Not because Fred killed a perfectly good scaffolder just because a rich kid wanted me dead.

Not because – presumably – for some stupid reason of his own Sean Harper killed Didi Fraser.

Not because he sent men to my house to beat the shit out of me so I'd go away. (See this is an example of what I mean: am I looking for those guys right now? No. Why not? Because that is a fucking waste of resources man that would be petty. Those guys are just guys like Billy was just some guy, and they did a mostly professional and competent job on me and they did not severely injure me but they made the process of getting fucked up hurt and that is skilled labour right there. When I need someone fucked up just right I will need guys like those although I will have a discussion with them about appropriate masks because customer service is important. I'm guessing those particular guys had a relationship with Linden which means I can almost certainly hire them out from under because he is an asshole and no doubt he pays them scale.)

Not because of any of those things which are emotional things.

I will get violent when I am good and ready because that is when it is appropriate.

So I'm just going to cry a little bit for lost possibilities. Because I'm secure in my masculinity and it's sad when someone you know gets murdered. You should cry. You should cry even if all you really talked about was what really scary fucking place he most recently put his erection. You cry so I do. And then you get up and get on with your life because they may have left but the party is still going. I got things in motion, man. Cocktails to mix and playlists to cue.

I got bills due.

Tycho the Saluki arrives on time. Nice dog, Tycho. Little skittish but likely you would be as an animal being owned by a notorious illegal vivisectionist, like probably most of the time when she strokes Tycho he can smell cortisol and blood and bile and all manner of other things on her and that is his mama. Once there was an experiment, they trained monkeys to take a reward from a barbed-wire sculpture. Called it wire mother. The monkeys loved it even though it hurt them. Tycho's mama takes very good care of him. She loves him lots. But he has to know that the hands that run over his long mane are hands that crack open torsos. He's a dog. He can't fool himself about that shit. Mama is a predator, baby. Yes she is.

Tell you what though he loves his aniseed. Lots of sighthounds do. They will do anything for it. Carob? Tycho says you can fucking keep that shit, and we do not give a dog chocolate do we boys and girls not unless we want their hearts to explode, and I did not go to all this trouble to give Tycho a heart attack. Tycho'n me we're buddies now.

Tycho is flatulent, but who isn't?

He sits on the couch in my room and I can tell he's not allowed.

I say: good boy.

And he grins at me, doggy style.

Aw you little cutie.

I'm walking through downtown not far from where I've been operating and I come round a corner and there is fucking Li Dong-ha. Like right there like we nearly walk into one another. He's like five inches away. Eye contact. I know him and he sees that I know him. Just bad luck is all just wrong place wrong time.

Li Dong-ha doesn't quite get it but he knows something's off. He gives me his evil badass voice: Hello.

Bluff it: Oh sorry man – oh hey Tony? No I'm sorry you're not Tony. Sorry man you look like this guy I was at—

Good try but it's too late. Too slow and too late. He just motherfucking knows in his evil badass water that something just happened and he knows that I know it and now he's making the connection. Tick tick tick BOOM. There's recognition like zoom and pull focus, like shock cut, like the soundtrack is all screaming strings. Close up on the corpse.

Li Dong-ha grins like he's absolutely fucking delighted: Oh, you must be Jack Price.

Turn and run. Someone like Li Dong-ha you do not go to the mat with. Not if you're in your right mind. You'd know it even if you hadn't seen his resumé which I have. Fucking regimental unarmed combat champion, 707th Special Mission Battalion, no shit, the guy looks like Asian Thor. Only thing I've got going for me is he's as surprised as I am. He's totally thinking about having sex with Britney Spears, like Oops Britney not hairless Britney. Li Dong-ha lists this as an ambition. Creepy-ass fucker.

I get a few paces out ahead of him and then break round the corner. Sneakers on thank god, and he's in some fashion military boot item that's making fat fucking impact slaps on the sidewalk but he is faster than me and he's in better shape. Cut through traffic, nearly die, whatever. Across the street. Down another one. Right left whatever mad route, fucker can't catch me. Won't give up. Fucker can run two marathons at altitude and he knows it. Doesn't have to catch me, just has to stay with me. Smiling as he runs up the hill behind me, swear to god smiling like he's not sprinting like a top-grade football player. Fucking endurance hunting, hunting me.

Run run and keep going. One chance only. One chance.

Li Dong-ha picks up speed a little. Now I can hear him breathing over the slap slap of his €500 secret-brand combat boots. They've got little biplanes on them. Maybe dragons. Maybe vaginas. Something.

Brownout around the edges like the beating. Still not one hundred per cent because it's not like I've been resting up. Wouldn't matter if I was. I'm not this kind of supervillain.

Through the door into the warehouse space. If the fucker would just taunt me some, waste some time—

Flying.

Forward.

Pain.

Li Dong-ha just punched me in the back. Not the spine. Just the kidney. Probably the same kidney Sean Harper's goons fucked up but good. Fucking thing's paste now for sure. Piss and blood smell. Fuck I hope I'm smelling that because I pissed myself or it's in the air here and not because it's inside me.

Fucker's playing now. Now he's taunting me. Not even good dialogue just a list of bad shit that's coming my way. Fucker didn't even much like Johnny Cubano.

I crawl. He likes that. Crawl towards the far door.

There's a blue line painted on the floor. Fresh blue paint.

You cross that line I'll let you live another two minutes. Might make you wish I hadn't. You crawl that far Jack Price? You got that in you still? Yes you do go on. Yes you do.

Yeah fucker I got that in me.

I crawl. I'm not sure I do.

He kicks me up the ass. Coccyx agony. Vomiting. Piss and blood and vomit. Keep crawling.

Keep crawling.

Blue line.

Eheh.

Blue line fucker.

Yeah Price well done you crossed the blue line but I changed my mind.

Yeah I bet. Tell you what though.

What Price?

Should not have let me cross the line. Freeze frame, motherfucker. Freeze frame.

Freeze frame.

Here is one thing that I know: Li Dong-ha likes ribs. Likes mesquite ribs. There's a mesquite place a real good one two blocks over from here, they do this watermelon BBQ sauce and cilantro lime mayo turns chicken into something God eats when he's feeling a little blue. Cook is a new guy in town some guy from down in the delta and sure you may not go to heaven in a Ford V8 but it is just possible that the short rack he makes is some kind of key to the side door.

This morning I spent money. Ghost money through Poltergeist to PopupAccelerator dot com to two guys just guys looking for opportunity, and so they end up in the street talking real loud: gotta love those ribs man and that mayo. These two guys think they are guerrilla marketing for the ribs place, think that they're in on the ground floor of a new performative ad company which will be maybe incorporated tomorrow. They think they're looking at stock options so they are all in: You eat that mayo on the fries or you just dip the drumstick? You know they do a Sunday brunch with pulled pork like authentic man because it's whatever they cooked this week all stripped off and all fantastic?

Two guys just talking like buddies, talking as they're just walking along the road, just happens they're walking in front of this Asian guy who looks like Thor, just happens he's the head of this major investor and la la la.

And Li Dong-ha is all over that. He is so there. So then I watch the door and when he comes out I'm there like oops.

Oops man. You know he's gonna chase me down – gonna catch me – because what the fuck am I to running in the city? I am not Mo Farah and I am not Usain Bolt for sure. I am just some guy. This is his thing. So he will catch me. It's inevitable.

Yeah.

The point of being a disruptive player in an established business arena is there's shit you can do that no one thinks of. Your transactions are not like other people's transactions and what that means is they cannot bring all that power they have to bear upon the problem you create. In fact their weight and their strength become problems for them. That's what it means. Like Li Dong-ha is definitely gonna catch me and normally that would be me all done. But if you're let's say Osama bin Laden, you don't set out to perform an act of terrorism with direct leverage on political choices so much as you put on a show. Everyone got to know their lines and everything got to come together perfectly. It's theatre of death. That's what I saw when the towers came down. Some fucking awful piece of performance art that killed three thousand people and kicked off a bitch-ton of war and mortality and an economic crisis. Those unbelievable fucking assholes changed the world for the infinite worse with box cutters and lateral thinking. But what it really was was the most appalling theatre the world has ever seen.

My theatre is this room this space and the thing about it is that there is a cage in it and that cage comes down on that blue line and now Li Dong-ha and me we're on opposite sides of that line.

So now there is a noise like bong and that is the cage dropping and I am outside and he is not.

The cage doesn't look like a cage. It looks like some crates and a fork lift and some other crap. But it's still a cage. Or actually it's a lobster pot made of chainlink. Once you're in you can't get out. Not quickly. Not without cutters.

Eheh. Piss and vomit and blood but I am not in the box and Li Dong-ha is. Eheh. Keep crawling. Can't help but laugh. Comes out like fucking Tucker's emphysema.

What's funny dead man?

You got a gun there Li?

Of course I got a fucking gun. I got lots of guns. You're not getting out of here. I mean I love your little fortress hideout here I really do but in a second I'm gonna shoot you up the ass and then you know I'll maybe go find the other door and we can finish up.

I don't see your gun is all.

Sure it's in my coat Price. I don't wave it around when I don't need it.

Yeah well if you reach for it my friend's going to get real upset with you.

You got no friends Price everyone knows that. Tucker turned you in man we got millions of your money and you let Fred kill your buddy. You're a deadbeat man. You're nothing. One day soon we're gonna kill your girl too.

Not my girl. Made that clear.

Yeah well tell yourself whatever you need to man.

No she made that clear.

Oh well that's a fucking tough break for both of you man. I'm sympathetic.

Fuck you.

Just passing the time with a lonely asshole.

Your mama.

Oh fuck this Price I'm just gonna—

There's a noise I've never heard before. I think it's Li Dong-ha going for his gun. I've never heard it before because I'm pretty sure no one ever has. I know what it is but I still can't understand where the different horrible parts of it begin and end.

It's the sound of a man covered in razors standing up from a boxcrate and hitting another man in the face.

And then the guy covered in a homemade razor suit says:

LUCILLE!

Li Dong-ha is one helluva pugilist and he is strong like you have never even imagined a man could be. He is tough and he is mean and he is capable, but he is a guy in Armani bespoke being hugged by a delusional psychotic with enough of the Pale Peruvian Stallion in his bloodstream that he is right now seeing everything through a haze of bursting blood vessels. Li Dong-ha is a soldier and he has training, but no one trains for this. Lucille is mad as hell and whatever the fuck actually happened in his life that was so awful he is not going to keep that pain to himself any more.

Yeah. I took a crazy person who was not basically evil and I gave him mind-altering drugs and locked him in a warehouse in clothing covered in knives so that he would kill a monster for me and in doing so I have likely destroyed his chances of recovery forever. I do realise that is not a nice thing to do to a person and obviously – obviously I mean yeesh obviously – it's not like I do it all the time but necessity is what it is and also I mean he was right there and that's fucking destiny. That is fortune and glory calling out to him like calling his name if anyone actually knew what it was. Plus now at least he's not going to get thrown away like a broken toy. Now he's back on the board. He killed one of the Seven Demons and if he occasionally fugues out to Kenny Rogers well man when you're famous that's just a cool personality trait like a mutant power or something. So I guess what we're saying is that at a certain point let's assume Lucille is sufficiently in possession of his faculties that he understands what has happened here he's gonna want to discuss it and I will say man there is no need to thank me but you're welcome.

You're welcome man. I'm just glad I could be there.

Lucille's conversation with Li Dong-ha takes a surprisingly long time to be over and none of it is remotely pretty and a lot of it is barely even comprehensible. It's a fucking education I swear like one of those did you see that show where the guy turns dead people into plastic and then he cuts them into sections and he polishes their surfaces so they are like medical jewelry or architectural models that shit is amazing. My whole understanding of the interiority of the human body is changed by this experience – I'm talking about Lucille now not the other thing – and it is almost like a holy thing like transcendent. The body is this incredible organic machine and we should care for ourselves not just because every one of us is precious as a person with loves and hopes and a future but because we are art man. We are fucking art. And Lucille is fucking Monet or Basquiat or whatever. He's an art savant is what. Or maybe that's me and Lucille is my hammer and chisel with which I carve new shapes into the world. Wow man just wow. I feel I'm really part of something here.

When it is done I mail some video of the whole thing to Karenina with a bunch of puppy emojis. And then I go play with Tycho until the doctor calls to ask me to bring him home from the vet.

Ring ring: Yup.

Hullo is that Mr Kenton?

Hi doc.

Jack Price? For heaven's sake. Wrong number.

Ring ring: Yup.

Price?

Yeah it's me.

What the fuck are you doing at my vet?

I happened to intercept young Tycho here and I figured we'd be friends a while is all. You listening? Here Tycho say hi to the doc. (Arf arf arf.)

She doesn't speak for a while so I say: Hello?

Doc? You there? (Arf?) Go on Tycho you go play with your aniseed rag man I gotta talk to the doc. Doc?

Doc?

Fuck you Price.

Yeah no doc, come on, what the fuck do you think I am? The dog's fucking fine okay? Not like Billy I understand which is a fucking sin against reasonably priced manscaping by the way but I guess you do what you gotta do.

Yes.

Excepting this doc. Excepting this. I am not going to kill your dog. Your dog is gonna be completely fine. You see how that makes us different?

No.

Yeah okay fair point. They find Li yet?

Yes.

You see how that makes us different?

How does that make us different Mr Price?

Only one of us is having any fun doc.

Jesus Price.

Some kid I got nothing to do with'll be walking the dog in the park in an hour. For Christ's sake don't kill the kid okay? I mean that would just be unnecessary. I mean as far as I'm concerned you can kill the kid right but it would be kinda crappy behaviour and you don't strike me that way.

Okay.

Also seriously check the dog for cancer soon okay because he's sweet and Salukis really get that shit too much it's a breeding thing.

I know that Price I'm a fucking scientist.

But you got him anyway.

I liked him.

You gonna tell the other Demons we had this little chat?

Probably. Maybe not. It doesn't make any difference to what has to happen. Plus you did kidnap my dog Price it's not like you're a Good Samaritan.

I'm just drawing a line, doc.

Who isn't?

After that I go out of the city for a couple of days and fish by a lake. It's the weekend for fuck's sake. Nice local physician accepts small bundle of cash to believe my bullshit story I got set on by hoodlums over a lady's honour but they were her brothers and she's desperate the matter not go to the police. Nice physician says it's the best story she's heard in a while for this kind of crap. Says I better not be no meth dealer or nothing.

No ma'am I ain't.

Well then, says nice physician, you go down and have yourself a beer by the lake and sit still because you've been rescuing a few too many ladies recently and you're beat. You could lose that kidney you keep this up. It's maybe forty per cent luncheon meat right now but you're a lucky sonuvabitch – it ain't yet compromised.

I fish. Turns out I fucking hate fishing but maybe that's the whole point.

Change of pace: I get the barber in nice town to shave my head again because the stubble is itching. The stitches are out of my scalp and the internal glue is holding so I just look like someone drew Frankenstein shit all over me for a fancy dress party. Little bit of cover stick from nice beautician and it's all gone but the ripples. Tell you, make-up is freaking weird. It can change the way you look but entirely.

I put on a suit like an undertaker's and I drive up the coast for hours along the side roads town to town and wayside inn to boarding house, cash in hand and no ma'am, I was a mortician, but you see I am retired. I'm afraid I could not stomach all that death. Well now I'm a poet would you believe and I have an eye to find a small-holding and go back to the land yes ma'am.

This coast is not like any other place. It's not like Norway and it's not like Scotland whatever people tell you. It's not like anywhere in the real world. It's ghost country and it's full of spiders. There are spiders everywhere all year round: spiders eating bugs in the rafters and spiders making webs by the doorsteps. Leave your car parked too long and there are spiders on the wing mirrors and spiders in the fucking aircon. Get through that lot and you're by the sea and there are sand spiders and then you're in the water and you know what there are? Yes there are fucking sea spiders shooting little web bullets at the insects spiralling over the waves. When the fishing boats come in and vent their bilges into the harbours the bugs come down to eat and the spiders hide in the fishguts and they eat too. When the Russian cannery ships go past the trash drifts in behind them, the same thing happens. If you stand on the dock the spiders come and sit on you and look out to sea like they fucking know they're waiting.

I hate the northeast.

It's where I was born.

The old guy comes in by boat and he stands in the front end like that girl in Titanic except he has his arms by his sides and the boat is a tiny tinny piece of crap. It's got corrugated metal for a cabin roof and a bit of orange nylon string tied tight to the bit at the back that steers it through the water. I got no idea what this bit of string is for but I'm reasonably sure a boat with orange string on that bit is a cheap old piece of shit boat. There are crab baskets clumped around his feet and the engine makes a noise like GOGAGOGAGOGAGOG.

You Price?

Yeah.

You look like it.

Yeah.

But I should see the other guy, right?

Well yeah maybe. Figure you've got a strong stomach.

I do Price. I do. Come on. Come. What we can do is go and have a drink. I come all this way and you look like an American quilt.

Yeah I'm made of fucking unicorns is what.

I can see why everyone likes you Price! (But the way he says that it's like he actually does.)

I sit and he sits and that's all. Sometimes we drink. Mostly we just sit.

He's old. He's got thick hands because he does manual work, on a farm. He's got grey hair not white and he's wearing an old fisherman's sweater that smells of new lanolin. Got some of those smears on it you can never quite get out. Figure he kills his own food. Figure he guts it and cooks it and eats by himself. Or maybe not. Maybe he cooks for a lady. No reason why he wouldn't. Maybe he's got some special someone these days. Scars on his hands and no expression on his face, big broke nose so all the time he's elevatoring his glass and putting it down. He looks like a dipping bird toy.

I'm familiar with your situation Mr Price.

Yeah I imagine.

I cannot help you.

I think you can.

Nyeh. I cannot make peace between you and Demons. They have taken contract. Their reputation is on the line now also. You have inflicted some damages on them.

I guess I should have asked if that upset you.

Bah. You know it is a stupid question. I do not make transference, displacement activity. I am not big in denial. If I am upset I am emphatic. No. You know this. You are making nice. Is respectful. I like that. You want something from me, so you make respectful.

Yes.

Good for you. But I cannot help.

Right.

The way they manage their affairs is their business. If I have feelings about it I do not share them with my successors.

Would I have been able to do this to your Demons?

You would have died on the first day.

What I thought.

My Demons were more local. Maybe not good to take over a country, but to run a city from the underworld. Different approaches. These are now international.

Suppose I tell you I don't want to make peace.

… You got balls like ostrich eggs don't you?

Only the left one.

Come on then ostrich balls. Tell me what the fuck you do want and then we'll see.

If you're the invading Roman Empire confronting a proud barbarian culture and you don't want to be at war forever you have two options. You can kill them all or you can recruit them. If you want to recruit you start with bored young men in need of dick-affirmation. You find the bravest craziest asshole in the new generation and you show him hot and cold running pussy and booze and a gold cockring and you bet him he can't jump over a firepit and when he does you give him access to all that pussy and you call him a general and now he belongs to you.

I was gonna say that's crude but actually as I look at it I don't think it is. I think brave crazy horny assholes are crude.

Point being that you make your party more fun and basically more about screwing and getting drunk and being rich than the traditional party and once you've done that and literally every male from twelve to ninety wants a taste you go to the tribal elder with the most prominent boner and you say that obviously you always loved him most and would he maybe like to be cut in on all this action and all he has to do is bless the whole thing as in line with the holiest tradition and maybe the fulfilment of a secret prophecy he's always kept in a golden tube up his ass.

For some reason people are way more impressed by gold stuff.

And that's it. Job done.

The Seven Demons have got a little bit of your Roman game. They have recruited Tucker – to whatever point anyone ever has

Tucker's loyalty which is basically not far – and they caused Leo to defect albeit he just up and quit and then I fired his head from a grapefruit cannon into the Kenzo floral-print surface of Johnny Wexler-Cubano so they pretty much have to call that one a draw.

But now here we are like eight hours later in this nasty bar with the maroon leatherette and the fish smell and Volodya hasn't left. You get that's who we're talking about, yes? I am sitting here comparing scars with the last First Demon of the Seven, the former and now retired renowned Kalshnikov Ukrainian log cabin motherfucker, the marksman who can kill you from a mile away. Not that Volodya would ever fucking touch an AK which is the firearms equivalent of a haymaker punch or farting during a lapdance. The AK is famous because you can basically make one in any machine shop. You can make one at a village blacksmith's. And when you make it you can treat it badly and get it wet and dry it out and walk halfway across Asia with it and then pull the trigger and have a better than average chance it'll kill the guy in front of you and not blow up in your face.

These are not the qualities Volodya looks for in a gun. He's not a punk. He's a concert pianist. I know because he's been talking about his favourite guns in between the scar discussion and the business of how much I will owe him if he helps me (basically everything I have ever, because he is so magical and log cabin motherfuckingly amazing and he is not just a sniper and a farmer he is also a scholar and a lover of beautiful women). I am able to say with certainty that the best marksman's gun ever made throughout the universe, space and time is the customised limited edition Dragunov given to him when he retired from Ukrainian special forces.

Somewhere in the middle hours of this evening he has agreed to help me. I don't know if it was before or after I passed out in a toilet cubicle and woke up to him banging the chick from the next table against the hand basins. I do know that when he came back and she went and sat down with her friends looking mighty pleased with herself I explained that I don't want him to shoot anyone and now this whole discussion is tacitly about how I'm a decent enough guy for a kid with no history of hunting bears with a pocket knife but it has to be said that I'm a massive disappointment to log cabin motherfuckers everywhere.

Waking to the sound of Volodya's boat GOGAGOGing out into the blue-and-white water. Way past noon. Getting on for evening again. Thank god because I feel like shit now so Christ knows what this morning was like. I don't remember. Nasty little bar with the leatherette seats serves coffee like caulking what you call bootheel espresso. One step from being biodiesel. Drink it, drink it, hold it down, sit and eat dry bread wait wait and…

I'm alive. I can see colours. Okay.

Pretty sure that's a family of spiders at the bottom of the cup. Fuck it. Protein is where you find it right?

Back to the city. Things to do to the people I see.

Incoming call, old number. Bounced a lot. But not Fred. Fred uses the new number.

I say: Yeeeelllo?

Sarah says: I fucking hate you.

Yeah well that's actually fair.

I'm dead Price. I am fucking dead and everyone I know is dead.

Is anyone you know actually dead?

No. Shit. I don't know. Shit I don't know how the fuck do I find out?

Don't find out Sarah because if you go looking they will find you. Jesus are you calling me from your cell?

No the callbox outside my motel.

Did you pay for the room with a card?

Fuck, Price! Am I an idiot who's never seen a TV show? Or am I a fucking intelligent woman whose life has been fucked up by her interactions with the number one asshole in the country?

I wouldn't say I was the top really I mean maybe the worst but there are like politicians and judges and all that who are assholes who are way topper than I am.

I hate you Price.

Then why are you calling?

… Because maybe I want you to fix this. Can you fix this?

I am trying Sarah because that is also a precondition of my being alive.

Yeah well woot woot for the world. It's like heads I win tails you lose there.

Yeah well.

Fix it Price for Christ's sake fix it. They are going to find me and they will kill me and I don't even like you but they will kill me just in case it hurts you a little bit. A little tiny fucking bit, Price! That's right isn't it?

Yeah.

Will it?

Will it what?

Will it hurt you just a little bit?

Not really.

Fuck you Price.

What motel?

What?

What motel?

Why do you care?

I send a bag full of money and a couple guns to Sarah's motel, deep dark web distribution style. A new phone. Moderate risk to her but almost none to me because: Poltergeist. Fuck do I know, maybe she gets lucky and completely kills a Demon. Would be hilarious:

Hey you Sarah the Lawyer we are here to kill you!

No no you won't I am Sarah the Lawyer I don't even like that asshole and he doesn't like me!

Mwhahaha we do not care because evil! Now we crush you with our overwhelming criminality!

That's it asshole pew pew pew!

You got a gun? Fucksake lady! Pow pow!

Pew pew pow pow pew pew oh shit BOGGGA BOGGA BOGGA BOGGA BOGGA FWOOSH ZWINK ZWINK SPLODE you dead lady?

Pew!

Ack! I am killed by a fucking amateur! The shame!

Pew pew SPLODE oh alas I die but I never loved Jack Price and that's just bad judgement so I guess I had it coming. Eeeurgh.

Finis.

Man gotta keep his spirits up somehow under these trying fucking circumstances.

Fucking Seven Demons are putting their own coke on my streets! Man that is just fucking rude and they are calling it fucking Beyoncé which is I cannot I cannot fucking even. You better not mess with Beyoncé but oh yes they did and it's got a little Manga demon chick on the wrap with a little spangly top on like the cover of Dangerously in Love. What the fuck? I cannot have some zen hippy coke with a sex name running around turning heads in my neighbourhood. It's just rude is what it is and inconsiderate because they don't give a shit about coke and what if I come out of this alive? What if I don't and someone local wants to step in and step up? They've fucked up my business model is what and that is unreasonable I'm just trying to get by here in what is a dog-eat-dog world and this is pissing in the well is what. They're calling it a Metered Access Model. Metered access my ass! Fucking subscription service with all the risks that entails in terms of bookkeeping and regular payment schedules. It's fucking convenient for the client and it's fine if you don't plan to stay but it's an asshole infrastructurally topheavy model that's vulnerable to law enforcement penetration and backtrace and they know it, but they are not here for the long haul this is to dick me and it is dickery and yes I am offended because there is just no need. No need for this at all.

So obviously what you do is you buy a bunch of it and you cut that crap with some anthrax you happen to have lying around and then you put it right the fuck back into circulation. Put your face in that.

Yeah that's gonna sting man. Bottom line that's gonna sting.

Actually I did not have anthrax just lying around but you know what things are even the CDC people have mortgages and mistresses and once you reassure them it's a drug thing not an Islam thing they get all cosy and patriotic because people are racist man. Just fucking racist.

Anthrax, for fuck's sake. For the price of a mid-range executive compact.

Fucking society going to hell is what.

So once upon a time in Finland there were two brothers named Akilles and Tuukka and Tuukka was the eldest and he loved that his brother was called Akilles because: Achilles right, like the heel, like the mighty warrior who eventually died of being shot in the foot. How much fun is that when you're ten? Ooooh ooooh Akilles how is your foot? Did I tread on your foot? Will you die now? Oooooh don't smite me mighty hero or maybe I will tread on your foot!

Turns out Achilles was killed by a Trojan called Paris who has the distinction of being the guy whose entire fault the whole fall of Troy is and the best part is what was Achilles doing when he was shot? Imagine you're just giving a ten-year-old moose-eating farmboy fuckhead as much as you possibly can. Yes! Correct. Achilles was mourning the death of a guy some people say was his boooooy-frriiiiend. Right? Seriously fucking parents take note, right? I mean backwoods Finland in the early 90s? I'm gonna go right out on a limb here and say however enlightened your Nordic culture that was something to work with. And it turns out it was, at least enough so that one way and another Tuukka is the boss brother and Akilles is the one who follows him around and packs the cases and tidies up the torture chamber and books hotels. Akilles is the fucking organised one is what and he's smooth and smart and his brother is the madcap fuckhead who gets all the girls. Likes to steal Akilles' women too of course and pretend that's like a cool brother thing. Like that. These guys are tight like forever but only because they are locked together with all the batshit id and ego brother crap and there's no place else for them to go. Brothers is their identity. Always has been.

Whatever. You want to understand how this goes you look at a map of Europe. Russia is just huge. It's six and a half million square miles. The contiguous United States with all its enormous deserts and prairies is three million. Russia is continentally big. It's got a lot of borders and the countries with those borders are pretty nervous about it because Russia periodically reverse prolapses and then they're not countries any more. Finland has had to be pretty tough about it. You know how big Finland is? Finland is one hundred and thirty thousand square miles and it has been independent for one hundred years. Stalin never got Finland. Got all those others like Latvia and Estonia right but not Finland. Finland leaned on a fucking giant stuffed polar bear and picked its teeth with a bolt action and was like: Yeah Joe was there something you wanted to say? I'm sorry pencildick I can't hear you over the sound of the arctic wind.

Log cabin motherfuckers, see. Remind you of anyone?

So Volodya says to me: Akilles.

You sure?

You got doubt?

Nope.

Nope I also nope.

Got no doubt. Akilles is the one we talk to because you know what, if Akilles could have another identity where he was the boss, would that be interesting to him? No no of course not that's just an awful thing to say! You bet your sweet fucking ass it would and all he'd have to do is turn on the person he loves and hates most in the world and that right there is a fucking coin toss. Also narratively: one brother kills the other and assumes his position? That is fucking Seven Demons PR gold man it's not like Fred will be pissed about that if this goes his way right? PR gold. And Akilles has to know that deep down, has to have thought about it because brothers know those things.

Yeah you're not the younger one then.

Roman Empire man. Recruit the barbarians. Volodya is a tribal elder, he's a spiritual authority to the Seven Demons. He's taking lunch with Akilles, got a little microphone doodad so I'm listening like I'm right there at the table not sitting in this crappy diner down the street. You know what they do, Finns and Ukrainians? At least the log cabin motherfuckers which these men are? They go for an early lunch they put a bottle of vodka on the table and when they take the lid off they throw it the fuck away. I know I can hear the cork hit the floor. Clink slurp hiss. Now to business.

I am Volodya you have heard my name.

Yes Volodya I have. It is a pleasure to meet you.

I was the first of the Demons in my time.

This is known Volodya you were the only one of us to ever retire.

No! Before me was Maxim the Bomber and before him was Miss Pan. They also retired.

I did not know this.

It is not known. People would still seek them out. For revenge.

Do they seek you out?

Of course but my house is in my mountains where I can hear them coming.

And then?

And then I hide Akilles. They come and they find an empty place and they go.

You do not kill them?

Of course I do. I follow them home and do it there and it is never known that they found me so the number who come is very small.

(I'm really glad now I asked him to meet me rather than knocking on his door.)

You are Volodya the Sniper.

Yes. That is why when I kill them I do not use a gun. In this way I am invisible.

(For Akilles this is like church.)

But you are here. We are speaking.

Yes Akilles because you are like me. You also are a thinking man. You are tidy. It is a great pleasure to speak to a tidy man. I have passion Akilles but I am tidy. It is a matter of discipline. It is training. It is my nature. Also yours. We are passionate men who can hold that passion within. We love women and we let them go. We kill when it is appropriate not when it is not. We are fire in a forge not making the forest to ash. For this reason we are sometimes misunderstood. It is sometimes necessary to correct an impression of gentleness. Yes?

Yes.

Then I can speak to you of this history and I know that it will go no further. So I do because I want you to know this about us. That you are like me.

I am not the First Demon.

No today you are not. It is Frederick. He is also a sniper. It pleases me that he is a sniper. Not so much he is a PR guy.

He is a good leader.

That also pleases me. It is good to follow a good leader.

It is.

(I've got the bud in my ear and I'm like Volodya are you fucking with me now? But he is not. That what just happened? That was smooth as glass seduction, log cabin stylee.)

Now Akilles tell me of your brother.

Tuukka?

Of course.

What do you wish to know?

I have a venture in mind.

Tuukka is very skilled.

Can he lead men?

Yes.

You say that as if you are not sure.

I am sure.

That also. Yet you follow him.

I follow Frederick.

Nyeh! This is problem. You do not follow your brother because he is what I need. You follow him because he is ahead of you. That is all.

No I – he is my brother it has always been this way.

That is not a reason that it should be so forever. That is habit. Sometimes Akilles it is good that the order of things is turned upon its head. But this presents me with problem Akilles I need a man for a contract job and I thought it would be Tuukka. Maybe instead you. Can you also lead men?

I have never tried.

Can you organise and instruct?

Yes this I can do.

That is all. These are professional men. I think also you will show them that fire in you and they also will burn as you do in your light. That is leadership too.

I do not know.

But I do.

When is the contract?

Immediately.

That is a problem. I am engaged.

I have heard this. Also I have heard that it is not well.

It is imperfect.

I hear where there is a man you cannot beat.

That is not the case. It is temporary.

What does your brother say?

He says we will be the ones. He is hunting. It is what he does.

What is he hunting? A fucking deer in the financial district?

He says he can catch the scent of a man's spirit in the air.

What do you say?

I say it is amazing how often he catches that scent when I have spent a week following the money.

Hah!

Eheh!

HA! DRINK!

And so and so and so it goes and it is fucking endless but you can see it already. You can see what's happening. Elder Volodya is getting under this guy's skin.

That's when I almost die.

I'm laughing my sophisticated ass off about Tuukka smelling a man's spirit in the air of this city – not in any city fucker, but this one there are so many things in the air spirits and ghosts and haunts and what all else and then there's life man there's coffee and jasmine tea and pizzas and the stink of buses and there's men wearing too much cologne to hide the musk of that hard thirty minutes with the woman they carpool with. There's professors smoking weed and comedians burning joss to hide how they don't and everywhere musicians and rosin and dry ice and the sea carrying freight and seagull shit and there is a whole damn living world in this air and there is just no way Tuukka is smelling me.

And then I see the fucker walking down the street and I know. I just know he is looking for me.

That is impossible.

He is looking. For. Me.

Tuukka doesn't even know his brother is here. He's not looking that way, not not looking that way. Doesn't look towards Volodya, then does, still doesn't really see him. Not looking for Elder Volodya. Looking for me. Got my description in his hunter's head, my picture maybe because you know the doc has that kind of mind that gives a really good description to an artist. He's seeing the line of me and the heft and height and he is fucking looking for me.

Fuck am I paranoid?

Fuck is that the point? Am I supposed to run and then Tuukka's gonna see me? Or if I stay here is he gonna just walk up and come into this place and see me? What the fuck?

Fucking manhunter. What the fuck?

Here's Tuukka: better than six foot tall, got that rangy Nordic thing, like he skis and shoots and he can do that all day and still make the hot tub a real special place for a group of inclined ladies and then get up the next morning eat a bear for breakfast and log cabin motherfucker his way up Everest or what the fuck you want. Got that rangy, loose walk like his bones are heavy iron and his muscles are all plingy elastic and fuck it fuck it how is he here? Walking curved like straight towards me not like he knows like he can fucking feel me.

Scent the spirit my ass but he is.

Motherfucker.

That is not possible.

Any sufficiently advanced mojo is indistinguishable from science remember.

There. Look at that son of a bitch. See that? He is touching his gut like it's talking to him. That is not his gut there is something under there. That is a direction belt: sequence of pads strapped to the skin, pad vibrates it means THIS WAY. Fucker is homing in on me, getting a signal from something. From what?

Fuck.

FUCK.

Karenina is up in my shit. Did the impossible. Backtraced my phone somehow. Fucking Tsutomu Shimomura'd me. Fuck. I bet that's exactly what she did fucking blunt force infrastructural approach: flooded the fucking city with detector wagons, got lucky when Fred called me to gloat over Billy. She got the pattern of my secure login, my telegrapher's fist. You know what that means: fist? Turns out the rhythm and pacing of your interaction with your technology is unique to you like the way an old-time radio operator could recognise another one's style of Morse. True story. Fist now is a little less distinct, why I'm not dead yet. It's seventy, eighty per cent is all. Lots of false positives. Lots of dead people who use their thumbs like me maybe. Tracing and tracking ever since and now she's got lucky. Lucky enough. How good's the triangulation? Ten metres maybe not good with elevations. Fucking fuckedy fuck. I'm being fisted and that is not the title of a porn movie I mean clearly it is but not fucking today.

Cut and run. Leave the phone running, kill the data – one touch. Should have had one made with a self-destruct, might have taken someone out. Next time. Next time. Although it's a bit dicey walking around with a bomb against your head. Not sure I like that. Plus what if you drop your phone? Plus definite no-fly material. But there are use cases I mean now I mean—

Shut up shut up. Look around there's an exit by the kitchen. Less than a minute. Leave the phone? Tuukka will know I was here will know I ran. Will know to follow me. Will report. Will know Volodya was here with Akilles. Busted. Either Volodya turns me in to protect himself or he assumes that when they catch me I'll turn on him. Either way I get to add him to the list of people trying to kill me.

Forty seconds until Tuukka walks in that door.

Woman buys a sandwich. Walks out. Should have put the phone in her pocket. Too slow. Too far. Thirty seconds. Frozen. Bunny frozen. Dead bunny frozen. Look around: no one else leaving. Someone has to. Make someone leave. Pay them. Scare them. Can't do either. Too slow. Why would you leave? A fire? A robbery? No good no good. Twenty-five seconds.

DUDE DID THAT BITCH JUST LIFT YOUR WALLET? (No I did, same time I gave you my phone, same time I put my hand on your shoulder. See how that works?)

What the fuck man what Jesus she was never even close to me—

But he's already on his feet going out, running after her HEY LADY WHAT THE FUCK?

Tuukka sees him go running past. Hand comes up hits the guy just right just fucking perfect never seen anything like that, twisting sweeping the guy off his feet like Keaton like Chaplin but there's no crashmat. Guy hits the ground head first and he's gone like switching a light off you can see it even here. Tuukka looks shocked: oh hey mister god that's terrible are you okay? Blood and brain in the gutter. Woman who doesn't have the wallet never looks round. Tuukka pats the guy down. Phone's just a phone. No wallet. Everyday story man she got his cash and he just ran and tripped I never saw anything like it I am from Finland we do not have street crime it's not fucking Denmark you know.

Walk out slowly like I'm window shopping. No rush but don't oversell it. Walk like I'm going somewhere. Walk. Check the reflection: Tuukka taps his gut. No dice. This is the phone, but it's not the phone he was looking for. Dead guy on the ground is just some guy with a fist like my fist. Shame. He had a good feeling about this one.

He chooses my direction, and I have to step back a little to let him by. Big Finnish guy, lots of masculinity. Used to making his own space.

And he's gone.

I need to pee real bad.

And after that it's really time I killed the everliving fuck out of someone again or I'm gonna lose my momentum.

So there's this Australian guy in some band and it turns out what Australian rock drummers really like to do when they're on tour in this city is buy a big sack of coke wholesale so they don't run out during whatever belly-shot groupie bath they're having which would be like Pee-wee Herman-grade uncool. And so this guy goes ahead and does this and because he is totally on trend and on point there's really only one branded substance he's going to want and he's going to want that substance and he's going to snort it off the tits of Miss Nebraska who is in no way averse to this so long as she also gets to jump his bones and make a sex tape and that is what they do. They do things that are definitely illegal in Texas and then they do those things a couple more times in ways that require some sort of trapeze which they improvise using hotel furniture and bath robes, which I have to admit is some pretty fucking impressive cocaine DIY although I gather the management is not entirely cool with it. And their sex tape is basically like three days of sex between gigs and there are all kinds of people there like producers and hackers and a couple critics from *The New York Times* drop by and talk Kierkegaard real quickly for four hours while Red Kat Bonanza – this being this guy's actual name apparently because Australia – does something naked and ejaculatory in the background with Miss Nebraska. It's a real scene like Warhol like Studio 54 like this club I went to in London one time where you ate strawberries off of Italian women while they sang opera. Or Italian men if that was your bag but those fuckers were made like Pavarotti and it was real hard to find the strawberries because manscaping was still kinduva niche thing back then and anyway not part of the mood.

Like that.

So here is Red Kat Bonanza and he is hoovering it up like a dugong and boning and on and on and then suddenly he is really not well at all. And this is where you have to acknowledge the existence of God right like I have to raise my voice to the reverberate hills and sing hallelujah like Jeff Buckley who Red Kat in no way shape or form resembles because Jeff had talent coming out his ass and Red Kat is successful sort of because he has none and this makes him angry and his anger kinda resonates with the same kind of particular miserable underpaid fuckhead.

Because it seems that Miss Nebraska is not merely the owner-operator of some of the nation's finest bazooms she is also a fucking trained expert in bioweapons from the US Marine Corps and she takes one look at Red Kat and she calls her old boss who is now at CDC and she quarantines that motherfucker and she puts the hotel in lockdown and now that motherfucking Beyoncé cocaine is the single least wanted commodity in the criminal world like toxic fucking waste is more desirable and so also the Seven Demons are maybe a little toxic by association and if there is one thing that will maybe shake their altogether cosy financial and fear-based relationship with the city's powers that be it is the sudden and pissed off arrival of pretty much every Homeland Security agent in the entire world ever with the biggest killboner that very erectile organisation has ever seen.

Funny story about anthrax: there are worser things can happen to a body and there are several kindsa anthrax that are actually perfectly okay to get so long as you treat them smartly and this is one of those kinds. It's pretty hard to catch and hard to transmit and it is not real durable because I am not and have never been a total fucking idiot but it is also real hard to distinguish from another kind of anthrax which basically is what bioweapons people go to bed at night praying they never meet and by comparison to which an Ebola outbreak or a fucking zombie apocalypse would be vastly and irretrievably preferable. So when someone has this kind of anthrax it pretty much guarantees a most hostile overreaction and that is what we get. For like a week there is literally nothing you can do if you are a criminal except drink and go shopping because sure as fuck no sort of illegal activity is a great idea. And during that period of course the whole sorry story about a new criminal element comes out like how I'm this ordinary professional felon (identity unknown) doing ordinary orderly professional felon shit and then into this respectable fucking environment where rich people and the scaffolding community are served with high-quality coke and no one at all ever suffers by it and maybe even a few cops have been known to get some of their substances through this incredibly genteel and cost-effective service, into this happy situation comes this fucking punk rock military asshole machine making waves and serving up dead people and anthrax to the masses. Farewell to the Pale Peruvian Stallion and hello to Beyoncé and that shit is not so good for you and maybe comes from some sophisticated anti-American scheme like in all those movies where someone does ruin to our great nation with sub-standard adulterated or dangerous narcotics.

Rumour is that Beyoncé herself is majorly pissed and you can so entirely see why. Here is a self-made woman with opinions and success who has lived through some shit and is a fucking survivor and she is also this terrific artist and now not only is some human dumpster fire abusing her intellectual property and her personal brand by trading a fucking illegal drug under her name but they are poisoning those drugs and attacking these United States. She is pissed like Capone pissed like Captain America punching out Hitler.

Like she is going to come to this city and get shit done is what, and actually maybe I should just stop here and let Beyoncé fuck up the Seven Demons and their whole damn lives. Because you know she totally could do that. And if she did do that it would be like eight minutes from there to President Beyoncé and again I say to you that Jack Price is a man who affects the world in positive motherfucking ways because: President fucking Beyoncé. Yeah you better vote.

So yeah I'm in a hot tub at a love hotel in the garment district with a new phone thinking about sex because that is what the words President Beyoncé should damn well do to anyone.

Incoming text message. Like SMS. Who even sends those any more?

Also: who sends them to a number no one even fucking has? Well other than marketing. This is not marketing.

HEY PRICE.

Who has this number? Oh: Hi Sarah.

Hi Price. YOU DISMAL FUCK.

You got the money and stuff.

Yeah nice tx

Ok

What are you doing?

Whut?

Im bored. This is shit.

Yeah I guess

Fuck you Price

You said that.

I'm afraid and I'm alone and I can't believe I'm bored. How am I possibly bored? People will kill me if I go outside.

Probably not smart to text too much.

What are you doing?

Taking 5.

Anthrax thing was you wasn't it?

I couldn't say.

Thought so.

Sarah I don't know what to tell you. This is shit for you but it is what it is and to be honest you were pretty clear about your take on me so.

I have Stockholm Syndrome.

You're thinking of going to the Demons? They will kill you.

Yeah now you want to talk.

No if you go you go that's your choice but you'll die.

Or you will.

What can you give them about me that they don't have?

Fucking nothing. Except maybe me.

Yeah that ship is on the water.

So you say.

Yes.

What are you doing?

What does that even mean?

Shall I tell you what I'm doing?

Yeah sure

Accept multimedia image: y/n?

I shouldn't open that, Sarah, you might be compromised.

O believe me Price I am compromising the hell out of myself here.

Did you just send me a nekkid selfie?

Open it and find out.

I don't think so.

Yeah well your loss Price.

Yeah.

Stockholm Syndrome Price.

Yeah. Bye Sarah.

Fuck you Price.

Accept multimedia image: y/n?

n

Accept multimedia image: y/n?

n n n n n n n n n n n n n n n n n n n n n not y y y but n n n and FUCK IT.

n

Sarah's right. Being on the run is shit, even when there's a hot tub.

It's midmorning and the vodka is open and there's black bread on the table and pickles. Also some kind of nameless ham. The tea house has black walls and old oak tables and someone's smoking in the corner, blue smoke like dye in water.

Hey Price! You don't eat ham?

I'm all about the ham Volodya just not today.

Is great ham. I make it myself.

Yeah I figured.

You don't trust my ham?

Before it was ham did it drive a Hilux up the wrong dirt track in Newfoundland and knock on your door with a bad attitude?

Fuck Price that is nasty.

Man gotta ask.

Fuck you are nasty that is the most nasty thing I ever heard. Is goat for fuck's sake. Perfectly ordinary mountain goat like maybe height of your thigh. Curing very difficult. Real touch and go process okay because you don't want too much smoke but if not enough then obviously problems with preservation. It is a proud skill for me okay Price not some bullshit trophy thing like Stalingrad.

I was thinking of Stalingrad.

Fuck Price don't do that okay? Everyone where I was born is fucking obsessed with Stalingrad it's like Elvis in Mississippi. One of the best reasons to never go back there: never have to talk about if I am better than Zaytsev ever again. Of course I am fucking better than Zaytsev that asshole made up his entire shit. No König no fucking duel in the ruins no fucking whatever the fuck. Fuck Zaytsev is what I'm saying okay? Eat some fucking ham. Is goat.

Okay.

Okay.

It's good ham.

Should be that asshole ate at Joël Robuchon's place every day for a month before he flew to Newfoundland... I kid Price seriously don't spit the ham okay? Damn you believe some appalling shit about people.

You are an evil old fuck.

Yes that actually I am. Come on! We drink! Akilles is on the knife edge.

Yeah no doubt. What's he going to do?

Do? Oh fuck Price that asshole is weak as shit. What you think he will do? He will come tell me politely to go fuck myself. But he also is not going to tell anyone about our conversations because he knows they will know he had some hesitation in this decision.

Yeah.

We still good?

We are still good.

Ham is goat Price okay? Jesus.

Okay.

Not so many cops on the streets now. Anthrax scare is getting a little bit less scary now it's clear there wasn't all that much of it. Not that anyone's going to want that fucking impostor coke any more that is not happening. They'll maybe try again but they've got to understand there are lines now and that right there is already me winning because the Seven Demons are not supposed to acknowledge lines and I have made them forget that. Of course if they kill me that lesson is kinda academic so best not to crack the Dom just yet.

Miss Nebraska has a talk radio deal. Whatever man.

Red Kat Bonanza is recovering well and is under about fifty different kinds of arrest for possession of everything and also sex with a groupie who turns out to have been seventeen. I'm shocked I tell you shocked to discover that seventeen-year-old girls fuck rock musicians. We must put a stop to this madness or our whole society will end in nuclear fire because as we know this is what female teenage orgasms inevitably lead to.

So the city is waking up again and this means it's time to boogie.

Hi there is that Marla? Hi it's Rufus Agincourt yeah I emailed yeah exactly I just wanted to sort out some details?

Well hi Rufus I am so delighted to talk to you today and Loving Sky Celebrations is so delighted to work with you on your proposal plans.

Thank you Marla I so really very much want him to say yes do you think I'm putting too much pressure on him doing it this way?

No no Rufus I think this is just a romantic gesture like romantic as anything and the way you tell it he is all but shouting out that he wants a ring on that finger.

That's what I think but you know what if I'm misreading the whole thing?

You're so not sweetie it's gonna be fine he's gonna love this. That letter he wrote you when you were away in Paraguay that is one of the most heartbreaking things I have ever seen in twenty years as a planner. And I just think you all are made for one another.

Okay Marla let's get to it!

Okay! Well okay! You said you wanted this to be big and loud and exciting am I right?

Yes I did I want the world to be watching when he says yes.

Then Rufus the first thing we need to do is talk confetti okay because exactly what kind of confetti a couple wants that's the best barometer for all kinds of style choices. Now I know that your partner – what is his name again?

Tuukka. He's from Finland.

I just love that and I picture him riding this sled with dogs pulling it and whisking you away through the snow!

That is what it's like Marla every damn day is a dog-sled ride.

Awwww shucks so Tuukka isn't part of this conversation OBVIOUSLY as it is a surprise but tell me some of his favourite colours okay?

Well he likes aqua and what is that other blue that is like azure but more like I think it begins with an S?

Indigo?

No like it begins with an S?

Cyan?

No that's not it longer like more poetic I can't—

I'm going out on a limb Rufus and I'm gonna say you're thinking of cerulean?

Yes that's it! He loves that. He wanted to paint the living room that colour in his old apartment but the landlord was heavily into his minimalist whites.

Well okay do you think just lots of amazing tints of blue or do you want maybe some orange or some gold in there to make a contrast?

Oh I think that would be amazing we went to this jazz bar one time and it was all blue and gold and that would be perfect.

Well I can definitely do that for you for sure.

That's great of you, thank you. Now there is one thing can I maybe get some little pieces of poetry in there like I will write them on little pieces of paper and like my love will be raining down on him in the middle of all that colour and light?

Oh Rufus that is so nice hang on let me... Hmm okay Rufus that's more of a problem because we don't have the capability to pack our own unless you don't mind working with our vendor which you can. We have a very good relationship with a firm over by the river mouth and they will pack anything for you but I'm afraid there's an extra cost.

Well Marla I don't care about the cost I just want him to be showered in my words you know like Zeus came to his lovers in a shower of gold I mean oh gosh that sounds a little porno doesn't it. God how I mean wow that's so NOT where I was going!

Rufus that's fine sweetie. I knew exactly what you meant and I'm a grown-up girl okay there's no cause for alarm. Listen you call this number I'm emailing you now and you talk to Matt there. He is kinda gruff but he's actually a real star and he will take you through the whole process and I think they even have this DIY option where they spec the whole thing for you and you can buy propellant online and just put whatever you like in the main delivery space so in the worst case you know get all your friends round and cut up some crêpe paper and so on and shove it in but don't overstuff it okay because you don't want to fire a little paper cannonball at your partner right?

No Marla that would be just terrible as he recently lost a family member to cannon fire I mean that would be awful.

Oh gosh I can't believe I said that I didn't even know there were still cannons in the world was he like in Europe?

No no he was one of those re-enactment people they have in the South? Tuukka's family is a little odd maybe but you know it's not them I'm marrying.

Right no of course but I mean gosh.

Yes absolutely.

I'm so—

No Marla please don't worry at all it was silly of me to mention it. I'm going to talk to Matt and then come back to you with credit cards and all that and we'll go from there okay?

Okay! And I'll have the boys polish up the gold-plate drones for you so they are just completely shining and when that confetti comes out of the sky honey and you're down on one knee. That's gonna be the single most important moment of his life.

Yes Marla I truly think it might be.

Okay guy so have you done molecular gastronomy before?

Yeah Mr Cobb I have but you know more modest I'm looking to take this to the next level.

Just Cobb man just Cobb.

Oh okay gotcha Cobb it is. But yeah anyway yeah I've done a little but small scale.

Right okay because not everyone is suited to this kind of cooking right because it's real scientific.

Yeah I get that I mean I am a research chemist so you know—

Oh right good because that was the next thing I was gonna say to you like you really have to be aware that this stuff is not just cold like ice it's cold like you have to treat it like a mixture of napalm and a chainsaw right because it will basically just take off any part of your body it touches right. I mean it's not fucking Woodstock with his tongue on an ice cube man, it's like amputation and then if you were to allow it to come in contact with something real hot like boiling fat or whatever I don't even want to consider what the fuck that would look like but if you're a chemist you're presumably all au fait and stuff.

Yeah I am Cobb that is exactly it. I am au fait. Like for a while I had to do an aluminium and iron oxide reaction on a semi-regular basis you know what that is?

Yessir I surely do that is one seriously motherfucking exothermic motherfucker.

Column of white fire Cobb. The military call that stuff thermite.

Yes indeed.

So I am au fait.

I can confidently say that you are Dr Agincourt.

Please call me Rufus.

So how much this liquid nitrogen you wanting?

Probably not that much I just need to do some scrambled egg ice cream right but I'm gonna need to practise you know?

Right okay I'm gonna put you down for two separate pints and I'm guessing you'll want some safety gear and so forth? We got these silver space mitts they're pretty agile and obviously tongs and so on.

Yeah that's great and I'll need one of those high-grade thermos things so I can have the stuff standing by the table without taking the edge off of the chill.

That's okay man that's how we transport. Okay look I gotta warn you this whole shebang ain't inexpensive.

That is fine Cobb I'm pretty sure it's gonna be worth it.

Hi, Charlie, you there?

Hi boss I am entirely here.

Tell me you are in like Nova Scotia or some shit.

Or some shit boss yeah.

Nova Scotia would be ideal.

Yeah no but yeah but no.

Okay well Charlie there is a thing that I need.

Name it.

It will not be simple Charlie and it is not safe.

Boss answer me one question.

Yeah.

Was the anthrax thing you?

Yes.

Goddam boss that is cold. All right wait I have another question.

Okay Charlie what is your other question.

There's a couple like in a chain.

Okay.

Will I get paid?

Yes.

Will someone die?

Yes.

Will it be like fucking atrociously awesome?

Yes.

When this is all over will I be able to talk about it?

Sure Charlie always presuming that it ends with me not dying and that you do not have your discussions with representatives of law enforcement per our usual agreements on that topic sure.

Then I am so in man I can't believe you had to ask.

Well you know it's been a trying time.

Yeah boss totally. What do you need?

I need you to do some real offensive artwork and then I need you to break into a secure computer system remotely. Put that artwork in every corner like everywhere and then dick around. No need for any serious penetration just so you're really annoying. Fuck up the clock and delete the printer driver. As much dick as possible to no reasonable or respectable end. Embarrass yourself. When you know you've gone too far do more of that until you come out the other side and then start again.

How secure?

Like totally. Front end of a relay that probably uses Poltergeist at the back.

Uh boss no can do that shit is locked up tight man.

No serious stuff no data collection just to mess with superficials.

Can you get me a local node?

I do not know what that is.

Like a phone that's connected whatever.

Yes I can get that.

Weeeeelll okay maybe if I just could maybe fire in a—

(La la la I have no idea what Charlie is saying now because it has words like hex and porting and la la la. Magic.)

So that would help?

That would help but—

It's Karenina and she's gonna be stretched real thin in a few hours.

The Russian bitch who totally turned on you? Oh shit yeah boss now I have a chaos boner.

And that's good right?

Just get me the phone. I am all fucking kinds of strong in the Force for this motherfucker.

You want to find Tuukka you only have to follow Akilles of course and now I pretty much always know where he is because he and Volodya are having this intense platonic log cabin motherfucker negotiation which Volodya says is going nowhere. So there goes Tuukka the huntsman and he really loves his gymnasium oh yes. There he is doing some kind of crazy flying pressup plank thing and there he is benchpressing an aircraft carrier and my gosh isn't he strong and la la la. It is possible that weights talk is the only talk on earth more boring than coke talk.

And gosh oh look here we are at the south end of the square and there is Marla and here am I and there is Tuukka by the market at the north end and she knows because she has seen our anniversary photos. Time for the most romantic moment! Tuukka sees me and he is running towards me and I am running towards him and slo mo! Oh gosh how amazing and there is Marla's video crew because you would not wish this kind of private moment to be lost to YouTube that would just be wrong.

Tuukka is slowing down dead in the middle by the fountain because what the actual fuck am I thinking and I'm shouting I LOVE YOU at the top of my voice and the guy on the vegetable stand is clapping and there's a little crowd. It is a real twenty-first-century iconic moment.

Oh yes it fucking is.

Right on time there's the drone like a little robot cupid and the band strikes up over on my left because of course I had to have a band I mean what's romance without music and because we are modern and cool and ironic I figured the most romantic thing would be a swing version of Gangnam Style and so that is what Tuukka hears when he should be hearing the little rotors getting closer.

Now everyone's clapping because this is a thing that happens in the city. This thing of performance marriage proposals and even if Tuukka has absolutely no fucking idea what these people are on, he knows they are not assuming he's going to shoot me in the head, and he also knows because here I am that I'm also not. And he rightly regards that as extremely fucking suspicious but here is the thing: Tuukka is a hunter. He has a particular mindset and it is not a prey mindset. He knows about taking precautions but once he has begun his kill run he has real trouble imagining there might be a fucking pit full of stakes under those leaves.

So he stops and I get down on my knees and Marla hits the button to shower him in confetti and—

At last Tuukka hears the drones and the left one is all blue and gold confetti just like a goddam half time show and the second one is—

He is so. Fucking. Fast.

I tell you you gotta see it I mean wow like superhero fast like jumpcut fast. Instead of getting a facefull of liquid nitrogen he gets his head entirely out of the way and it splashes on his leg and makes a hole in his left hand like a chunk of ice, about right for whisky if you're a fucking philistine who takes ice, falls out of his palm and onto the ground BLOP and the whole square is quiet for just that instant like when you say clitoris to the guy next to you at a dinner party with your boss's southern evangelical wife just as her teenage daughter brings in the trifle not that I have ever done that and specifically not at the Hendersons' in 1998 that was a huge misunderstanding.

BLOP.

These are city people and they see some pretty intense shit but they have never seen anything like this and they are staring because you do when that kind of fucking insanity happens right in front of you. They just stare and then someone says damn. But damn like when you mean it and have never meant anything so much before in your life.

Tuukka does not scream.

Motherfucker does not scream in fact he looks pissed and looks at his leg and tries to stand on it and come and fuck me the fuck up. Fortunately his leg is not fully functional because—

BLOPBLOP.

That is a large part of his quadricep. Tuukka's muscle days are going to be on hold a while until he gets some expensive fucking corpse nerve-and-muscle transplant therapy and yes really that is a real thing. I'm saying six months until he can chase me down the street and nine until he can actually catch me but Tuukka still isn't screaming even though there's like Tuukkacicle all over the flagstones and a fucking pigeon is pecking at it. Tuukka is pissed.

I hit him with a plank. You always bring a plank to a drone fight.

He goes down hard and there's the phone and I need that so I go for it and that is a mistake because Tuukka is not just nitrogen proof he is plank proof also and seriously what? Is that fucker getting up?

Colour me just a little impressed right now. I mean sure I have basically shot him with a cauterising death squirter and so he's not bleeding out but even so man holy shit that's gotta sting. I hit him with the plank again. BONK. He goes down. I give him one more in the head and figure that should do it and the cops are seriously on their way at this point so fuck it catch you later and I run and Tuukka the log cabin motherfucker will. Not. Stay. Down. I should have just shot him but hey hindsight you try being me and see if you last long enough to piss on your own balls.

Motherfucker. Actually thinks he can still do something here. Face looks like a broken egg from when I hit him with the plank. Motherfucker cannot see. Cannot run. What the fuck does he think he's about?

Pistol out and Marla still has the drone remote in her hands. Tuukka turns and fires: Zen archery log cabin motherfuckery. BLAMBLAM! Marla is lucky today: Tuukka's leg is wobbling and he just clips her, bullet catches the meat on one arm. She goes down screaming and that's roughly when the band leave their oompah and just take the fuck off through the west gate and I go south as fast as my little feet can carry me because there are bullets like everywhere. Gun sounds like it's a machine pistol that's how fast he can pull the trigger and how the fuck many shots are there in a gun these days like fifteen? And no he does not hit me and I run and I hear one of those fucking shells and it has gone past me by the time I hear it and I know because the guy selling ice cream just fucking explodes like his neck is gone and he's a PEZ dispenser and then I look back and Tuukka is WALKING. What the fuck is this guy on? He's using his leg like a fucking prosthetic like just locked in place and tied off with his belt around the knee and my plank for fuck's sake and he's hobbling and it folds under him and his other leg moves fast enough that he catches himself and keeps coming like a half-crushed fucking spider. Scuttle scuttle drag drag round the fountain past the fucking in memoriam benches Stan We Will Always Love You and This Is Where He Proposed To Me. Tuukka does not stop to take in these happy memories of dead boomers he's just scuttle scuttle drag drag and all the time fucking pointing that damn gun at me like it's on a string tied to my fucking face. Six foot but bent down to four and a half and he's fucking crushed spider running now with his gun out ahead of him and he's reloading on the fucking move.

What. The. Actual.

Yeah okay you gotta say this guy belongs in post man. Like for realz.

He shoots my wallet in my left coat pocket like I feel it tug and there's just a hole and that could just as easily have been my fucking kidney.

And then I'm out of the line of fire and in the subway and then out and up and over and gone. And running and running and still running because that is what you do when the monster is after you. Run and run until you can't and then run some more as soon as you can. Round and down and away because everyone in the city is looking for your geostrata Frankenstein motherfucker face.

And well shit.

Well we'll call that one a draw.

Oh that was no fun at all and I feel like shit and I am sweating like what—

Oh son of a bitch there is just a little bit missing there on the left side of my stomach hey. Huh. Well that is inconvenient.

And turns out that it hurts.

Probably it's not gonna kill me. I'm not a doctor but it looks actually it's fucking disgusting and there's blood.

Be good to stop the bleeding definitely. That's fine. There's a plan for that. I got a place I can go. Be good if I could just sit down a while though.

That would be good.

Wake up or die motherfucker that's right I'm talking to you. You better open your fucking eyes.

Whozat?

It's you dumbass. I'm like your inner smarter you.

Oh right.

You are Jack fucking Price and this is indulgent shit you cannot afford falling asleep in a fucking alley in a bed of trashcans you will die dumbass. Get up.

Yeah yeah ina minute.

No now like right now.

Okay I'm up.

Nope. Nope you're not. Here tell you what let me just—

Blindwhiteagony like nothing Jesus... sitting on my balls... finger in a door... tonguebite... beatdown... someone screaming like a steer on the cutting block.

Okay motherfucker you awake now?

Just gonna puke hang on then I will fuck your shit up.

Yeah anything goes soldier so long as you get the fuck off the ground.

I'm an asshole.

Yeah. Now get gone.

Yeah I hear ya.

One foot in front of the other, and eventually you're gonna get somewhere.

Get some off-book medical attention courtesy of Poltergeist. Get some cash get a new place get clean. Get a jacuzzi get a jazz bar choose a new suit new look. No more dives. That's it. If I'm gonna die I'm gonna die five star.

Order a coffin in my size get it sent to a place. Fucking red satin motherfucker. Fucking guns and naked chicks on the scrollwork fucking disgraceful thing no one should even consider. Fucking coffee machine in there and a fucking bell: ring for coffee service. Because good taste can go fuck itself. When I go there will be weeping and wailing. There will be a party. There will be fear and shame and mountains of fucking free coke is what. People will say my name. They will put me on T-shirts like Hendrix and Guevara. They will name rock bands after me and the girl your mama is terrified you'll end up with will have a tramp stamp with my face on her perfect roses-and-cream ass. That's fucking immortality right there: a million pornstars and strippers and groupies and emos and hipster chicks and rock and roll rebels for generations to come will lie face down and ask for the needle just so they can be touched by my ghost mouth by my soul in the ink.

When I go.

But not today.

Because there is business and you know I take that kind of thing real seriously.

VoIP outgoing: location scrambled encryption through a Swiss system called Vielleicht and then back through Poltergeist and then la la la and if you try to backtrace you get digital fucking herpes which Karenina seriously isn't going to care about right now because—

Price? Is that you you fucking asshole?

Hi Karenina are we not friends any more?

Price this is fucking bush league.

Oh you got my message.

You fuck! You have fucked with me like to make me look bad. You know how CHILDISH that fucking is how fucking weak-ass? I have to explain is all you can do. You just have spite is what. Is unprofessional is RUDE to make me look bad in new gig. No other reason! Is for shit okay? Fuck you old friend just fuck you!

Yeah no I mean I wanted to make a point to your Seven Demon friends wait how are we dealing with that now because I mean shit there definitely were seven and now it's what four and a half if we include you? How's the probationary period coming by the way? Is it working out?

You know very well how you pigfucking shitmonkey is not good because there is bullshit in my system from you and your fucking childish bitch. I know is Charlie okay I know! No need for this Price we are friends and we are enemies but was not necessary that we hold one another in contempt is what I'm saying just no fucking need for that at all. Can be enemies maybe there is a resolution then friends again but now not. Now no way. Now it is fucking I am on your ass is what, okay Price?

(Charlie sent me a little file and I have to say she has excelled herself here and I can completely see why Karenina is a little miffed because all over her screens and in all the connected devices there are images which are basically a little NSFW. Every time the Seven Demons turn on their phones right now they get a picture of their little cute manga devil getting Chuck Tingled by a white horse in Peruvian military uniform and this apparently is not sitting well with their systems engineer who feels it reflects poorly on her professional competence. Which it does but that's kinduv unfair because it's about all we can do. Apart from fuck with the printer settings which I gather Karenina is less pissed about although I'm guessing it's not really softening her mood that the LaserJet is running self-tests every fifteen to twenty seconds in a slowly accelerating loop which Charlie says is arrhythmical for maximal annoyance.)

I think you're just a little jealous because she's like under thirty and she can kick some digital ass and get laid at the same time is what.

… I beg your pardon?

You heard.

Price listen you may want to take a step back okay. Just step the fuck back from me and listen to yourself. Right now this far I am not in your face right? I nearly got you the other day with Tuukka and today you nearly got him congratulations right? But we both know that you can fight this war only so long. You got money and if I am upset with you and crazy enough I can do something about that. Seven Demons can. They don't know this so they don't propose it but you don't wash your fucking mouth out and get down ON YOUR FUCKING KNEES RIGHT NOW YOU LITTLE SHIT I WILL FUCK YOU IN THE EYES SO HARD YOUR MAMA WILL GET HEMORRHOIDS OKAY? OKAY PRICE YOU MISERABLE LITTLE FUCK? DO YOU HEAR ME YOU BEG ME RIGHT NOW OR I WILL MAKE YOU—

Yeah yeah.

Price what the fuck is that noise?

That's me farting on my handset you lonely crone. You know why we're friends? Because you look at me and see someone you would have fucked in your glory days when you were hot. That's it. I'm like a trophy. So fine whatever. You're right that would have been awesome back then except I was five so you know never happened. But let's not pretend okay?

… You're done Price. Is over for you.

Bring it, Karenina. I double dutch dare ya. Plus tell Tuukka I said hi and his brother's probably dead by now.

Silence on the line.

Once upon a time there were two Finnish brothers. They were brothers. Not like friends or whatever and not the kind of brothers you get in places where the snow is less than six feet high four months of the year. They were brothers the way people used to be, like rock and ice and night and day and they were brothers. Akilles could talk to Volodya all he liked about taking Tuukka's place but never was he going to betray him and for sure never was he going to kill him. Not never no how, no more than Tuukka would ever take something he thought his brother really wanted be it a job or a girl. Like Tuukka okay: you know in the end that guy would walk in front of a train before he fucked his brother's wife or whatever. All Akilles ever had to do was say no man that is not okay that is my girl my true desire and Tuukka would treat that woman with so much respect it would break your heart like blown glass falling on stone and they both knew it. The party girls who shared them knew it. Everyone knew it.

Volodya knew it. And I knew it.

So we didn't set out to recruit Akilles. We just wanted him to think so. We wanted him to talk to Volodya the sniper, the great tribal elder, and get to know him. We wanted Akilles to have this big secret like a magic evil demon daddy and keep it to himself just for a while and then after he had made a real relationship there obviously what he was going to do was bring Volodya to his brother to have that same experience. A gift to his brother in the language they both spoke.

Volodya the sniper, with that long case on his back.

A man who kills with his hands, with a gun, with a knife. The kind of icon you can admire if you're a halfmad Finnish murder junkie with a hyperviolent profession living in the shadow of your brother.

The kind of man you drink with because he might stab you over the waitress and he might kill you for honour and he might shoot you in a fair fight but he's never going to drop tetrodotoxin in the vodka luge just as you put your mouth under it. Never going to look into your eyes as it hits and tell you you're just dizzy. Never carry you back to your table while your lungs stop working and prop you up with his arm around you. Never tell you Jack Price says hi and there was never a friendship, just a ruse of war. Never break your heart while you die.

Except if it was professional. If the job required it, Volodya would do any of those things and more.

I gave him a very great deal of money and other suitable considerations. It was a contract.

Seven Demons, man. Nothing personal.

Incoming text message: Hey Price.

Sarah.

Hi Price it's me.

Yeah Sarah it's maybe not the time.

Why not I see you did another fucking appalling thing.

What thing?

Price a guy was attacked in the middle of the street by a wedding confetti death drone full of liquid nitrogen and you think I'm not going to recognise the style? You think that doesn't scream Oh! Look it's the same mad motherfucker who shot a man with a severed head last week?

Yeah okay I grant you there is some continuity of ethos.

There is some continuity of fucking ethos Price.

Yeah.

You okay Price?

I got shot. Not much but a little. It hurts. No big deal.

No big deal?

Well okay it's a huge deal because I got shot and it hurts. But it hurts like you know a sprained ankle or whatever it's fucking awful but it'll pass. I'll get better.

Can you move?

Yes. It hurts.

Poor baby.

What now?

Shall I put on a nurse's outfit?

Yeah sure if it makes you happy.

No point though because you can't tell me where you are.

Nope.

So I could put one on but you'd never see it. Unless you opened my pictures.

Yeah.

Unless you did that.

Sarah I do not understand what is going on here.

Sure you do. I'm alone in the world and I'm afraid of dying and I know you like me. Want me. You've been good to me in your fucked up way and I know what you want even if you're saying you don't. The psychology isn't all that complex.

No I guess not.

It's not and it pisses me off but that doesn't stop it working okay?

Okay.

Say something.

I wish I could take advantage of your obvious sexual need.

I wish you could too.

… Fuck.

Yes please.

Fuck.

Yes. Say it again. Say fuck.

No.

Bastard.

This is all kinds of no.

Say fuck again and I'll take off my clothes.

Don't.

What?

… Don't take them off. Leave them right where they are.

Okay.

Now send me a picture.

Of what?

Whatever the fuck you like. You've got about ten seconds before I change my mind.

Accept multimedia image: y/n?

y

It takes a second to download because MMS not email. And then it takes me a moment longer to understand what I'm seeing. It's a wrist. I recognise the watch, one of those little chainlink things, dial the size of a dime. Sarah's watch. Slim wrist, brown and strong. Muscle on the bone. The top half of the hand visible, not quite as far as the knuckle. A rippling V of denim and zipper, a line of black lace just below the iliac crest. The barest whisper of close-trimmed hair. The outline of fingers pressing down.

You like that Price?

I do.

Then say fuck again and let's see.

No.

Come on. Say it.

No.

Seriously?

Yeah.

You're out of your damn mind you know that? Out of your damn mind. You wanted this and I'm right here. Right here and now you're what you're all shy? Stupid typical man bullshit. Chase what you can't have don't want what you can.

Yes. I'm going now.

Jesus yeah okay you go. Jesus.

Sometimes you just have an instinct. I get up and walk out. Don't hang around to see who comes. Probably nothing. Probably just Sarah with Stockholm Syndrome like she said. And Karenina's busy right now you know that. She is busy. She is angry and she is doing something huge and stupid. No time to sweat the small stuff, like hunter killer malware searching random SMS exchanges for my name. After all, over ninety per cent of SMS is marketing and automated sales offers, and all that shit says 'half price'.

But sometimes you just have an instinct. Something wrong. Get gone.

part three

Part three

MORNING IN THE CITY, sun coming in sideways and bouncing off the architecture. The weird transformation of natural light into artificial making every scene an interior. Who the fuck wants to live here really? In this place clamped over nature like a steel plate jammed over a missing eye?

Incoming VoIP call: number listed as the fucking Tokyo police. Like excuse me what now?

Hello Mister Price?

What the actual fuck?

Mister Price?

Yeah this is Price. Who the hell is this? No one has this number.

Actually I have this number because it is cut into the face of a dead woman with a knife Mister Price and I therefore also want to know what the actual fuck.

What the actual fuck?

Yes I also want to know that. Who are you please?

I'm a professional criminal but not like Mafia like modernised and digitally distributed and disruptive but not in Tokyo I got no interest in Japan whatsoever except that I went once and it was really nice. Like I would go back to see the city but just as a holiday right strictly no business. It's not my area and you guys have a perfectly good criminal system of your own.

Also good law enforcement I assure you.

Yeah that too although I read where a lot of criminals pretty much just hand themselves in like it's cultural. Is that so?

Well it is to a certain extent but you got to have a look at these other individuals we must deal with Mister Price they are quite entirely serious and have almost their own historical culture and sense of position in society and they do not do that.

Yeah that figures. Whatchacallit like an embedded criminal stratum?

That is not something I would say near a politician in this city. They do not like that idea at all despite knowing it is perfectly true. Honne and tatemae, although I do not myself subscribe to the school of thought which places that discrepancy at the heart of our culture.

Yeah okay I hear you. So all right just to reiterate I am – wait this dead lady was she by any chance a postdoc in some kind of mathematical discipline?

That is a most interesting speculation.

I'm taking that as a yes.

I could not possibly comment on the matter to a foreign lawbreaker.

I get you that would be way inappropriate.

Yes Mister Price. Way inappropriate. I hope you will not draw any conclusions from my admission that I find your guess interesting. That would be a grave embarrassment to me.

I completely missed that.

How convenient for me.

You mind I ask your name?

I am Inspector Ando of the Public Security Bureau. Watashi no namae wa Ando Hideaki desu. That is like a cross between the FBI and the NYPD counter-terror unit.

Okay Inspector Ando look I don't see why we shouldn't have a perfectly cordial conversation here because we got no direct conflict in our interests because you work inside Japan and I got no intention of ever doing that. Are we going to discuss this without reference to the obvious polarities of my position vis-à-vis the local criminal code?

Yes I believe I can do that.

What I figured. So a little while ago is what it is the lady lived downstairs from me got shot execution style. I don't like that because it's my building not like I own it but I live there. That kind of thing makes me nervous you see?

I do.

Well okay so I ask a couple questions in my off time. I'm usually a high-end cocaine dealer, modern small operation, almost no consequences of any kind except occasionally a scaffolder gets a little high and drops a pole which obviously freaks the shit out of everyone.

Scaffolder?

Construction worker. Metal rods for working on the outside of buildings?

Oh here they are very insistent those are tubes.

Yeah – really is that like an international union or – nevermind. Okay so that's my thing and it's quiet and profitable okay not like the movies just everyone gets on with it and the worst thing happens is manscaping. Yeah no you don't need to hear that part.

Thank god.

Oh yes. Anyway okay it turns out then that for whatever reason some rich kid hires the Seven Demons to take me out.

Chikusho fuck a duck.

I – what?

Japanese does not have a wide lexicon of obscene expressions for expressing surprise and dismay. For example there is no equivalent to your motherfucker that really works for me.

Chikusho fuck a duck?

It is imperfect but it gets the job done. Please proceed.

So you know the Seven Demons.

I am PSB Mister Price of course I know of them just like you know that if you came to Tokyo and tried to run your schemes I would be up your ass inside a day.

And you know it wouldn't be that simple but okay. So here are the Seven Demons and they are all over making a ruckus and I have been maybe a little flamboyant in my response to this situation and maybe they're getting fractionally extreme now.

Extreme? Getting extreme? Forgive me I thought extreme was the defining characteristic of that group.

Yeah well it is but at this point they may be a little emotional?

Because you are still alive I take it.

That and it turns out that someone shot Johnny Cubano in the chest with a severed head and since then Li Dong-ha fell in a human blender and Akilles Mäkinen was poisoned by a daddy surrogate. While all of that was happening I put a pretty tame strain of anthrax in some of their cocaine so no one wants it and I freezeburned Tuukka Mäkinen's left hand and quadricep which I'm calling a draw because the fucker also shot me a little, and then I got a friend of mine to put a picture on all of their phone screensavers of a cartoon horse cornholing their logo. So you know right now I'm saying they're not in their happy place.

Chikusho fuck a duck.

You said that.

Yes but last time I only thought I knew what it meant. Don't get me wrong Mister Price I admire what you have achieved but if you ever come to my country I will arrange to have you hit by a goods vehicle before you arrive at your hotel. I am making a note now.

I really wanted to come and sit in a hot spring with those little bathing apes.

That is in any case not possible because it is a nature conservancy and they would bite your face off.

Yeah probably they would at that.

Also strictly they are monkeys.

Yes okay anyway I am guessing the dead lady was a postdoc with a cryptography sideline who went by the online name of LuciferousYesterGirl and some of the Demons just dropped by your place and tortured the shit out of her for all and any information pertaining to the setup of an Icelandic dark web service name of Poltergeist.

Why?

Because that is how I get money without having stash houses and the Demons are tired of my having money and doing bad things to them.

And why did they not do this straight away?

Because there are quite a lot of people use Poltergeist and maybe it's not the smartest thing for even the Seven Demons to be seen to try to compromise it like really not smart at all but I guess after a certain point Karenina didn't give a fuck about that and she maybe didn't entirely explain to her friends quite how ill-advised it would be to cross that line after I called her a washed-up old lady with no prospect of getting laid ever again.

… You are quite a spectacularly awful person Mister Price.

Clausewitz grade.

Unbelievable. So they killed this woman in my house to get to you?

I guess.

And they left your number—

So that you would call me and tell me and I would know I am about to get dead.

This Karenina I have not heard of.

Naw she's a tryout. Old friend of mine actually which is why there's maybe a little additional friction there.

Why do I get the feeling you like all this?

Well Inspector like you said I am an asshole. The Demons this is a contract for them but for me it's something of a holy calling and I'm happier than I've ever been in my life.

That is sad.

… Yeah I guess it probably is.

Thank you Mister Price.

You're welcome.

Don't come to Japan Mister Price.

Understood Inspector. You're always welcome at my place though because there's just not that many people I meet I can really talk to.

Chikusho fuck a duck.

Yeah well so long I guess.

Goodbye Mister Price. I think I should not wish you good luck but somehow I do.

Thanks man.

Coffee but not from Sunby because you do not go back to where you were. I'm waiting for a delivery, guessing it's my last Poltergeist so I made it a big one. I can feel the jitters in the network already. There are local services that have gone offline, been taken down. Local providers who are missing. That's just prep work to let me know how fucked I am. Flying time from Japan to Iceland, travel time by air from Reykjavik to the middle north, time for digging, torture and cracking a database, dehashing whatever blah blah I should still be safe right now but not after this. I'll need a new source of funds. Poltergeist is going down for a while or at least I have to assume so. That means no more digital hijinks: it's all analogue now.

Local news: there's a crazy, bent-over muscular murderer wandering the streets of the city apparently, guy with his leg all strapped up and like an actual hole in his hand and he is killing people who used to work at some office in downtown some tower place with a lot of international connections. Got five of them so far and still clearly looking for fun.

Yeah that would be my old office.

Those would be my colleagues from back in the day.

And yeah I'm guessing that's Tuukka just crab-crawling around throwing them under trains and off of buildings and setting them on fire. Man's a fucking nightmare is what. Fred's gonna have to wind that boy in. Wind him right the fuck in you can do this crap in backwoods Bogotá and sure in fucking Sanaa on a Monday night but you cannot do it here. That is just straight up uncivilised is what and it's inappropriate. Is it supposed to impress me? Why the fuck should I care? Why the fuck do I give a damn I never liked those guys even when I worked with them. I mean that's the whole point right testosterone and victory and there's no I in Team but there's a whole lot of it in me.

Never liked any of them but most particularly not that asshole who didn't take the elevator. So this all is fucking inappropriate is what. Just noise and waste and making a damn mess. Typical of this situation. I'm just a guy trying to get along. It's not affecting me. It's rude but okay if that's what you want to do it's fine. Fine.

It's fine. I'm fine.

Later, in a vacant lot, dropping credit cards and phones and all my clothes into a stinking vat of something chemical. New clothes in a hurry, in the cold and the semi-dark of a sump corner tented and tarped. Now walk Jack. Duffel bag. Go to a crappy hotel out by the airport where no one spots new faces. Low on cash. No flow. Something of a pinchpoint coming going to have to do something about that. There are fifty places here where no one stays more than a single night and no one has a name. They won't even spot me if I come back to one I've done before. No one cares: transit clients leaving at all hours, international hub. There's a flight to Tokyo at midnight. Could get a passport and just go. Fred the demon PR guy might not even follow. Gotta be wishing he hadn't bothered with me by now. It's been fun but what's the endgame? More of the same?

But Ando was pretty clear about that. Gotta figure he's not a stupid man. He likes me but he has strong opinions about my suitability as a neighbour.

Gotta feel there's a generally applicable truth there.

Crappy TV in my room in my crappy hotel and oh look Iceland is in the news. There's something you don't see every day because Iceland. Basically it's Björk and volcanos and if you're nostalgic then yeah way back when it was like the party flight to London but now not so much. It takes some serious shit going down in Iceland to get above the fold. When Reykjavik was the impact zone for the financial crisis that was just about enough to get our media to spell it right but not actually send someone over.

Now though.

Now Iceland's got explosions and gangsters and that is all kinds of mediapathic so there are actual boots on the ground.

Seems like someone went over there with a bad attitude, some Russian grandmother with no sense of humour and this guy with a voice like a really white James Earl Jones, and these two have been exerting some entropic negativity on the general Icelandic hacker buzz. There have been deaths and things going splode and a great deal of screaming. Iceland has a population of fewer than four hundred thousand and they are not as a rule a hugely criminal bunch. Most people there have different jobs depending on the season. Like when I was there I took a tour with an undertaker who was also a guide and a hunter and among other things he showed me a maximum-security prison about the size of a hayloft with eighty inmates. Most of them had killed no more than one person and then in some kind of drunken jealous rage. Not saying that Iceland has no crooks just that the talent pool is relatively small and the number of eligible sociopaths with applicable physical skills is relatively low. I'm guessing they outsource that when they need to.

And then yesterday the backwoods began to explode. I cannot imagine how fucking cool that must have been and I am sad I was not there. Millions of euros of secret hardware in liquid-cooled sub-glacial server farms exploding up through the sheet ice and down into lava flows like fucking napalm in the morning like *Apocalypse Now* under a midnight sun. Men and women in privacy bunkers working for offshore corporations dragged out by this angry Rus grandma and thrown into the path of boiling volcano steam eruptions from the actual fucking molten core of the earth: bisected by a force somewhere between a tidal wave and a laser.

Karenina is definitely acting out and I got to admit I do feel a little twinge of discomfort in my testicles. She is kicking the world so hard there's some kind of psychic scrotal resonance effect. Got to respect that.

Hands are shaking. Should have taken the elevator.

It's fine. Take a breath. It's fine.

Just feeling a little unloved is all like unwelcome in Tokyo and hunted in Iceland and you know. No one to talk to really. Just me all by myself.

It's fine. Take a breath. I'm fine.

Should have taken the elevator.

Putting on a suit to meet a man. White shirt black suit. Real cufflinks. Haven't worn a suit like this since I was in coffee. Expensive suit and

I paid in cash of course counting out the bundles. You want to get your spending under control you carry your money in a bag and know that when it's gone it's gone. That is a real sobering fucking moment of realisation. Much better than fucking numbers on a screen. That is your whole life right there.

Of course that is part of the point of my meeting with Mr Driskol. I am looking to secure a revenue stream. Mr Driskol was on the list of appointments I stole from Linden's office. He is a very rich fairly evil old dude. Family money, slave money originally, then Depression finance and more recently arms and oil. I learned a few things from scrutinising Mr Driskol, mostly that people get by with fucking twentieth-century security paradigms until some asshole like me comes along. Driskol works with Mr Linden because occasionally he has to fend off suits from communist environmentalist anti-American conspiracy theory pressure groups in countries like Venezuela who have the nerve to object to one of his fossil fuel enterprises burning down a village or two although of course he is never personally involved in that sort of thing. In private life he gives out a lot of scholarships to young women who fit a very particular physical type many of whom he then dates for a few months on or after graduation. In short Mr Driskol is like Daddy Warbucks if Daddy Warbucks was an on-again-off-again genocidal maniac with a fondness for girlfriend farming which now that I consider it nevermind.

Big black car comes to pick me up because Mr Driskol is a traditional man. Thing's got cigars in a humidor built in the door. Maybach, top marque, very expensive. Nice. Long journey so I'm talking to the driver.

Hi man I'm Price.

Hello Mr Price.

(Voice like knocking on a castle door. Cute.)

You work for Mr Driskol a long time?

Almost all my life.

He a nice guy?

I couldn't say. He is a man of moods.

Moods?

Moods and parts and opinions. I believe that rich men generally are.

Yeah.

May I ask what is your business with Mr Driskol?

Proposition for him. Kinda complex. Import export.

Would it be illegal sir?

Whatever gives you that idea?

This is the illegal business car sir. For legal business Mr Driskol has another car. It is teal sir. This is the black car for illegal business. Occasionally there is a mix-up.

Not today.

As I thought sir.

So he does illegal business?

He does business sir. He does not greatly value the laws of man.

He a religious person then?

I believe he has a spiritual sensibility but not in the conventional sense no.

And he doesn't mind you asking this stuff?

I would say not sir.

You're Driskol aren't you?

What gave me away Mr Price?

I don't know Mr Driskol I guess I was just lucky is what.

Shall we sit and talk Mr Price? I own a property just around this corner where we can speak without interruptions.

Yes let's.

(Little tiny gun called a pepperpot just against the back of his head.)

What are you doing Mr Price?

Regrettably Mr Driskol the nature of our business is somewhat different from what I led you to believe.

Mr Price if you assassinate me you will assuredly get very little of my fortune. A hundred thousand in emergency petty cash in the house. Perhaps one million if you can extract from me some of my banking details but it is hardly cost effective when we could make considerably more. Add to that the fact that I will be missed within a week and it seems an exercise in futility.

Yes sadly I don't take on partners and I have a temporary crisis of liquidity so a hundred thousand and short-term access to your home and identity plus this lovely vehicle will actually do fine. Plus I think you overestimate your profile Mr Driskol. You've been very careful to disappear from the world and your life is arranged through a series of cutouts so I think I could be you for months before it was noticed but to be honest I doubt I'll even need a week. Daddy Warbucks.

You are a moralist Mr Price. How depressing.

(If it makes you feel better let's pretend I lock him in the basement with whisky and some porn and let him out later. But let's not imagine that is what I actually do.)

On the TV it seems like there's an epidemic of fucking commodities guys falling from buildings now and YouTube spots in which they scream. It's really not that many. Not even double figures maybe. It's just they play the same clips over and over and you can hear them all the way down. Can't go anywhere without hearing people talking about it. Can't go to bars can't turn on the TV.

My hands shake all the time.

Fucking Fred is after my mind is what.

Fuck you Fred.

Fuck.

You.

I need coffee is all. Bar of the Regent Heights they have a roast so strong and rich it shows you the future and thanks to Driskol I can get a suite.

Incoming SMS message.

Hey Price you pointless asshole.

Hi Sarah.

What are you doing?

I'm wearing a dead man's suit and drinking prophecy from a cup the size of your mouth.

You want to come round here and just drink from my mouth?

Yes.

You want that?

Yes I do. Fuck it. Let's go. Tell me where.

Are you serious Price?

I said I was.

Fuck.

Yes that's the plan.

You better fucking show up or I will come for you.

One way or another that's gonna happen.

… Fuck yes.

Tell me where you are.

Fuck now I don't know if that's really you what if it's them.

You've always known I wanted this and you've always pretended you didn't and you actually don't want it now but you also do because all of a sudden up is down and you're hoping maybe down is also up. You want to know before you open the door that I'm not going to be a lazy asshole because if you do this if you basically defile your soul you want it to be fucking spine-crackingly good so that when you tell your grandkids you once fucked a multiple murdering drug dealer in the middle of a crime war you can say it was unequivocally great sex.

Sarah says: You arrogant prick it is you.

She tells me where to find her. I take Driskol's car in case we need it for a bed.

Townhouse apartments, lateral spread. Very high-end. How the fuck did she get here? Sarah got some game maybe.

Put the car under the house in a space.

There's an elevator up to the ground floor. Big elevator, lots of nice design. Mirrors. I can see me from the 90s reflected. 90s me on my phone selling coffee. 90s me on my phone saying:

Take the elevator.

It's possible I may be a little wired and a little stressed out.

This is a bad idea this meeting but it's only a fairly bad idea. It's what Fred's trying for, trying to shake me out of my pattern because my pattern is working. Ideally I should just get on with my thing. But I am a human being. Sooner or later you just need to see someone smile because of you and you need to be touched by a real person. You can't just shrug it off and if you try the crazy gets inside you and then you make more and worse mistakes than this. So you choose a way to break the rules that won't hurt you and then you get back on track. This probably won't hurt me. Unless Fred gets lucky or Tuukka can smell my scent. Unless Karenina's got her groove back.

Fuck you Fred.

Better yet fuck Sarah then kill Fred.

Prophecy bean in my blood. Heat and anger and fear and lust.

Coffee sex here I come.

I should have told her to drink some before I left.

First apartment on the first floor. Gold-plated rails high ceilings in the common parts. Like a museum or a Vatican-themed whorehouse or something in-between. Deep rugs on the floors wood panels cut in Deco shapes or maybe a little earlier maybe Art Nouveau. Like elves from those movies about elves.

This is the door. Wooden door like real expensive real traditional real cool. Sexy. I can smell wood polish. Picture Sarah polishing the wood. Hands working over the flat brown surface. Hands working. Cheek pressed against the wood.

I grip the brass knocker and use it. Knock knock Sarah.

Door opens a crack. I can see skin. An eye, big and very wide. Brief flick of a nipple as she moves away: silver pink and very tight. Paler than you'd think. Flicker of a black lace gown. That watch. Door swinging open.

Step through. Hear it close. Look up.

The doctor says: look at your hand.

I look at my hand. Weird blue print like printing ink on the palm. Shit. She rigged the knocker.

Doctor says: that is a suspension of—

Do I need to know what it's called?

I was going to enjoy saying it. But no.

It's going to kill me?

Eventually, if I allow it, yes.

I don't understand.

Yes you do.

I—

If you kill me Mr Price – if you do anything I do not ultimately approve – you will be consumed from within by an agony that passes your present understanding. That is now inescapable. On the other hand I do not propose that this thing should come to pass. It is merely my insurance for this meeting.

Where's Sarah?

SLAP. Right in the face. Watching her do it is beautiful: torsion and twisting, the power in her. Blood in my mouth, cheek stinging. What a woman.

Rude Jack. Very rude. Sarah's gone. I got her phone of course. I loved our correspondence but it was frustrating. I nearly told you it was me so many times. What would you have done?

No idea.

Look at me Price.

I look. The doctor is beautiful. I take a step closer and she smiles, turning ever so slightly as if I may run past her to the window and she will have to catch me. She presses her chest forward just a little, lets the movement shift her body. It's a very good look.

Price you have not been talking to Sarah on your phone. Not since Fred tried to take her and she was not here. You have been talking to me. And I have been talking to you.

Oh.

Yes.

Why?

Because you please me. Your mind possesses an aesthetic. You did not kill my dog. Why not?

He's a nice dog.

Fred would have killed the dog. You killed your cop friend and you fired his head into Johnny Cubano. What happened to Li Dong-ha is one of the worst things I have ever seen but it was even worse for your assassin. You have broken him probably permanently.

I actually don't feel great about that.

Exactly. You are not a sociopath. You experience the world like a normal person but at the same time there is no limit on your behaviour. Just as there is no limit on mine.

None?

None at all. I am interested in you. You are anomalous. You are attractive. It is not a common combination.

Her arms circle around my neck. I can feel her hips against mine, her body all the way up and down me. One hand on the mark on my face, stroking, loving the stamp of her anger. My mouth is watering. I feel her breath on my neck and make a noise that is not a word.

Oh, yes, she says. Exactly that.

Do you drink coffee?

All day every day Price.

Lips on mine. Thin lips that open into something that can't be real, a mouth that understands and has no restraint at all: come in. Come in. Come come come in. Now.

She steps back and takes my hands, moves them up and down. Holds them on her breasts and then away, around behind her. I elevator her up and she climbs on me, bearing down, gasps when my fingers find her, ripples against me, then growls and breaks free.

She leads me into her bedroom.

The bed is vast and there are no covers on it just a wide soft sheet, soft cotton not silk. There are no personal effects, no clothes. This is a room with one purpose only.

The doctor stands at the foot of the bed and slips out of her gown. I kneel down behind her and press my mouth against the small of her back, my hands on her hips. I feel her tilt towards me and I can smell her body. I can feel her on my fingertips. I use my teeth and she hisses, presses into the bite.

Stop.

Okay.

From beneath the bed she withdraws a steel travel case. Click clack. It opens.

Put this on me – here.

It is a one-inch square of white adhesive-backed plastic. She takes my hand and folds my arm around her body, brushing it down her stomach, then back around as she bends forward, tabletop. Index finger on the coccyx.

Here.

I do.

Now take off your clothes and turn around.

I step out of my clothes and she watches. I'm still bandaged and she tuts. Tuukka you asshole. I feel the scratch of the plastic down my spine, the brief pressure as it sticks. Her hands trace my balls, clasp and release. Maddening.

Don't worry Price. I promise. Do you trust me?

No.

I don't mean in theory. Of course not. I mean now. Here. In this room. Do you trust me?

Why should I?

Why didn't you kill my dog?

Why didn't I?

Because you knew that in one way or another we were coming here, to this point.

I wanted to recruit you.

She laughs. It's the dirtiest sound I've ever heard in my life. Good. Recruit me. I need to be recruited. Really. Recruited. Again and again. And. Again. Recruit me until I can't take it. Any. More.

She laughs again, then scrambles up the bed and finds a thin silver wire. Plug me in.

What?

Plug me in Price.

Is this experiment sex?

Oh believe me I know exactly how this works. So: do you trust me?

Yes.

I clip the wire to the white adhesive patch.

Turn around.

I do. I feel a tug as she closes the clip. Nothing more.

Step away Price. Good.

She does something with the case. I hear a whistle, a dynamo spinning.

Now. Touch me.

Will I die?

How much do you care?

She arches her back.

Not that much actually. I step forward and extend my hand.

I feel a fizz like being washed in Coca-Cola in a straw. Blue light arcs to her from the tips of my fingers and she gasps, then grins.

Yes Price.

Fuck you crazy bitch.

Yes. Move your hand.

I do. Lightning rolls up and down her stomach and she writhes.

Yes. Up.

The lightning traces her ribcage, her breasts. Up to her lips. She grins like a boxer.

Yeah. You gonna kiss me Price or you too chicken?

I lean down and feel it build in my mouth. The stubble on my chin stands on end.

From my mouth to hers: lightning. I can see her pupils go wide and then close at each flash. My lips are burning like I've been in the sun for a week.

Closer. Just your mouth. Now.

My lips on hers and the lightning goes and something else happens something like madness or magnetism or frenzy. I hear the whine again and I can't stop. I'm drowning in her. I can't breathe because it's all the kiss and nothing else. She's killing me.

We break apart.

Gotta be careful Price this stuff'll kill ya. Do it again.

I shake my head and step back and she growls until I play both of my hands up and down her, two inches above her skin. Mouth and shoulders. Neck. All the way down.

Oh bastard. Bastard. Bastard yes. I will O. O. I will fucking. I will GET you for this Price. Fucking. Get. You come here right the fuck now come HERE.

She drives her hand into a spot dead in the middle of the bed, between her knees. I do as I'm told.

The doctor looks at me, lip between her teeth. Breathing hard. I've never seen anything scarier in my entire life. Nor more beautiful.

Fuck. I'm in love.

There will be pain, the doctor says. There will be pain and then – you will see. Trust me. Now. Slowly. Come here.

I do.

When I wake I am alone. My whole body feels like I fell asleep in a tanning bed. The mark on my hand is gone but there are other marks now that are not medical or scientific. My neck and shoulders are a map of her teeth. My back is raw.

I want to do it all again. Now.

But I've got places to be.

In the elevator on the way down I keep waiting for my hands to shake. But they don't. I guess this whole thing doesn't bode well for my relationship with my former lawyer but you know what they say: when God closes a door he opens an electrosexed unethical medical-experimenting international murder queen window.

I think about my asshole friend who took the stairs. It sucks but it is not like a yawning fall from a great height. It is just my asshole friend and he is dead. I say his name. His name was Peter and I disliked him sometimes. Mostly not. Huh.

Electroshock therapy. Go figure.

Time to be up and doing.

Remember Billy who was big and made a living putting tubes up buildings whilst ripped to the tits on the Pale Peruvian and then Fred went and killed him in a total gesture of disrespect to artisanal construction? Yeah that Billy. Well I need a big favour from his brother so it's time to do a little pastoral care. That's his brother Rex who does demolition likewise pepped on the Devil's Dandruff which you know holy shit but whatever. I guess you can't stop people from being people.

Ringadingaling.

Hey Rex it's Jack Price man yeah. I am so sorry. Your brother was a great – no I don't got – well maybe actually I have one or two bags somewhere – yeah I do as it – yeah as it happens yeah. Your brother was a great man Rex and – yeah I mean I know you gotta be feeling the bite of the world a little without that you got some of the Pale Peruvian to tide you over during this difficult time yeah. I will bring it Rex. Bring it personally. Well no actually it won't be me but you'll know it's from me because right exactly. But I mean Billy man I am so sorry. I haven't been to see the guys at Without Friction. Right I just can't because I can't because – honestly because also too what the fuck man how do you express your deep and abiding grief to a guy got his balls in a bowl of warm wax? Yes Rex I will just bike it the fuck over man no screwing around today yeah listen there's one thing could I just ask you? Yeah no I'll give you details later just tell me again about the views from your rooftop at the Triangle. I hear they're like amazing? I got this special someone I really want to impress man and I think yeah you got me. Okay man thank you look out for the bike bye.

Look at me makin' plans like a kid.

Take a moment man. Take a moment and stand on the harbour

front and look past the great ships that carry cargos of life to places you cannot imagine with smells and sounds that at the simplest level of humanity you have not tasted and that entail a perception of the world of colour of existence that is not like your own. Smell the burning hydrocarbons and recognise paleolithic ghosts in the engines of those great machines and pain and slavery under an industry that exists to rip the earth's blood from the ground. Smell the water and know that dry land is rare on this planet. Look up at the endless sky and know that planets are rare in the universe vastly separate from one another and walled off by laws no criminal can break not even Einstein and beyond that our universe is just a fucking bubble in a foam of universes. Even when there is so much appalling shit going on, take that moment. This is your life and it is amazing. Even when everything is all fucked up you are a bundle of cells and electricity in a sack that walks and talks and you experience in a way that the raw matter around you which is already the ejaculate of suns cannot and that is stupendous man it is—

Jesus fuck doctor what in the fuck did you do to my brain?

Portside coffee thick like sump oil. Tastes about the same: slum beans discarded by coffee kings in Lima and Nairobi, mis-picked too young from the tree, sold cheap and baked hard in industrial ovens so it gets a false adulthood before it dies. Ain't that the fucking state of the world? Red plastic tabletop with a metal rim and it's the shift change I can hear the whistle. Shift change. What's Fred doing I wonder? Karenina's bringing him my money now. My ghost money ripped from Poltergeist and Panama and Grand Cayman. Still doesn't quite get it: if I need something I can steal it. There's a hundred Driskols out there. Global bastardry is in oversupply. Don't need more than I have in my pocket to be a problem. Don't need anything at all to disappear. It's a big world Karenina and I'm not you. I got no overheads I'm an idea not a corporation. If we're talking reputation here I've already won. I'm the guy who took out three of the Seven Demons. I'm the man shot Johnny Cubano with a severed head. I know you're not gonna give up but you got to realise I broke your toys.

Karenina, Tuukka, Fred, and then there's the doctor and who the fuck knows what she's up to but she's playing her own game now.

Where's Sarah? Does Fred really have her like the doctor said or is she in the wind?

Well yeah I may have slightly forgotten about her during the amazing sex with a medico-criminal nutjob and so on but I got to ask if she's okay. Just because she puts me on a level with street gum – which you know I mean that is fair by her lights right – that does not entail I got no regard for her. In the end it's Sarah. I care about her as much as I care about anyone.

We're coming to the end now. Coming to it. Things are happening. All the balls are in the air. All the balls except mine which are still a little bit electrified thank you for asking.

Mist on the inside of the window. Whistle blowing for shift change. Bad coffee.

And now I'm not alone at my table.

Man got a face like a first sketch. All the features are there and in the right place but they're not what you'd call delicate. Steel brush hair like in a Schwarzenegger movie from the 80s from the Commando period. Don't look entirely approving I have to say not like he's one hundred per cent on board with my charm and my elective lifestyle at all. More like he has a few choice things in mind to say and figures to say them in a fair but emphatic way. Against that he's got a tiny little fucking coffee like in a thimble and he elevators it between thumb and finger like his firstborn and sniffs at it then downs it and sighs and says, which I got to agree with:

That is disappointing.

He's got a voice like the Swedish Chef if the Swedish Chef had had his throat cut one time by murder clowns. I say:

Yeah it's not great.

Mr Bates would you please go and oversee the next batch? There is some Civet in my case.

Yes Mr Friday.

Mr Bates?

Mr Friday?

Please purge the machine thoroughly with clean water. So you would be Jonathan Morgenstern Price.

Mr Bates is a small guy but not a guy I would instinctively send for coffee. These two are friends not colleagues but that does not mean they are not also professionals with relevant skills. I do not ask how they found me. I say: And you would be Mr Friday.

Really Morgenstern?

Yes.

I have a brother-in-law in Oslo with that name.

I wonder if we're related.

Genetically speaking we are all close family I suppose.

You want to introduce me to your group?

Yes of course. You have heard me refer to Mr Bates. Then the wide fellow there is Mr Overlook. The two persons just keeping an eye on the door are Ms Quint and Mr Dory.

I look around. Overlook is Friday's lateral twin. Quint is a narrow old bird with that eternal Nordic thing going on – she could be fifty or eighty. She looks like Didi Fraser if Didi had lived without make-up and eaten raw bear from the moment she gave up the nipple. She's a reasonably disturbing sort of person in the first place but for emphasis and to avoid the possibility of being mistaken for a tourist she is carrying over one shoulder an open aluminium gaffing hook of the sort used by fishermen to impale the brains of troublesome sharks. It is quite a statement and not really in tune with this year's pastel woodland colours but it certainly has its own energy. Then there's Dory. Dory has a lot of hair. He's basically a really disturbing version of those little trolls that have giant gaping assholes into which schoolkids are for some reason encouraged to insert pencils like that's not gonna provoke some seriously weird psychosexual architecture.

I say: Oh yeah that's very clever. I get it.

I'm glad.

Bates like motel Overlook like hotel Friday like the thirteenth Quint like *Jaws* and Dory like in *Finding Nemo*.

You don't see an issue with Dory's inclusion in that list Mr Price?

Fuck no are you kidding me? Two thousand children get eaten with their mother in the first scene and then their father who has appalling PTSD goes looking for the last kid he has left in a trek through this cannibalistic wilderness in the company of a dementia-suffering love interest and everyone laughs at them for ninety minutes. It is the darkest most fucked up thing I have ever seen in my entire life.

Mr Dory spreads his hands like: I fucking told you so.

Mr Friday says: Mr Dory I am not sure that being in the same mental and emotional perceptual space as Mr Price is a victory of any kind.

So what can I do for you good people?

We actually are good people Mr Price.

Never said otherwise.

Well you know that it's important we clarify this matter because you are accustomed to dealing with really pretty bad people.

Yup that is true.

And of course you are a bad person also yourself.

Yeah I guess. No yeah I definitely am. I kinda wish I wasn't sometimes but I guess everyone's the morally conflicted hero of their own narrative am I right?

No, Mr Price you believe that because your cinematic lexicon is limited to unambiguous pap produced in Hollywood whereas in our part of the world there is a rich tradition of interiority and self-examination in film which creates a far more healthy understanding of identity.

Yeah okay that's... well I feel that is not why you came to see me.

This is true. In fact I personally did not come to see you at all.

No?

No.

I'm a little used to being the centre of attention right now so that's kind of a relief.

In fact my only purpose in being here is to provide emotional support to Ms Quint who has recently suffered a family tragedy.

I'm very sorry to hear that.

Yes. Ms Quint does not speak English. That is the other reason I am here. I will tell her you are sorry but I doubt very much that she will believe you. She is a little cynical about your actions in this context Mr Price.

But she's not here for me.

No. She is not. You are very much just her pathway to the discussion she wishes to have. Her door into this world.

That suits me fine I'm basically in the first instance a facilitator that's my absolute thing I would be delighted to assist in any way.

In fact that is untrue you are a very particular kind of narcissistic high-functioning sociopath. I would love to scan your brain during decision making under pressure it would be a great benefit to the study of abnormal cognitive process. Would you consent to this?

I know someone who'd really love to do that on your behalf although in fact she does not concur with your assessment regarding my being a nutbar.

You are referring to the doctor Mr Price. I believe one must consider her perspective on horrible criminal insanity as unique albeit also uniquely informed.

Plus also we recently made it so she is not objective not like scientifically.

I do not think that I would accept data that had passed through her hands in any case. I am sure it would be completely accurate but there are lines.

So I hear.

Mr Price I have known Ms Quint for all of my life. We grew up together in the same town and I knew her husband before he returned to his place of birth to die. I am godfather to her son.

You're real close.

We are indeed although I was not godfather to her other child as my own wife was at that time pregnant and we did not wish to create an ambiguous context for our family. If I had been perhaps certain things would now be different and we would not be having this conversation.

What line of work are you in Mr Friday?

I am an advocate of individual rights Mr Price. I am an entrepreneur of deeply private things.

Ms Quint comes over to the table and sits down. Mr Bates brings four short coffees. They're too hot to drink so we sit there and look at them. Ms Quint takes from her left pocket a small chemical photograph of a pretty European Japanese girl holding a graduation scroll. For a moment I don't recognise her without my number cut into her forehead but then I do: LuciferousYesterGirl.

Mr Friday says: I am Poltergeist Mr Price. We all are.

Oh Karenina. I knew in some form there would be blowback. I knew if you got really pissed off you would overstep and someone would come. I knew you'd get into it with Poltergeist because it was the wall between me and you. But I figured you'd be at least a little bit careful.

I figured it would be the mob who got pissed. One of the mobs. Or maybe even the FSB or some international shit.

Because here is the thing: Poltergeist is a tool. It is neutral. It exists and continues to exist because it is willed by all sorts of people around the world on all sides of politics and law. It is where whisteblowers hide from companies and companies hide from taxmen and politicians hide from newspapers and journalists hide from dictators. It is where spies go dark and where Al Capone leaves his bookkeeping. It is infrastructure. You do not simply walk into Mordor and switch off the aircon.

But Karenina, Jesus. I figured even hating me and full of rage you'd be circumspect enough. I figured you'd make sure who you were cutting on.

Oh honey I really thought. I figured to give you trouble to distract you, take down Fred and then we'd see. But you went all the way. You could have grabbed someone else. Could have left her alive. Could have left the body unsigned. If all you'd done was blow up hardware this would be a different thing. A sternly worded note.

But you didn't.

And now here we are.

Mr Price you haven't touched your coffee.

No Mr Friday I haven't I figure I owe your friend here an explanation.

Yes.

Will you – okay wait you said I'm a high-functioning sociopath do you even care what I say next like if I say I'm sad and this isn't what I expected does that matter to you or would you just like the facts and then you'll kill me anyway?

You may say whatever you wish. I cannot speak to how it will affect us emotionally that is tea leaf reading.

Okay will you translate what I'm saying to Ms Quint like directly?

I would advise you to be most cautious. None of us would take it well if you were to upset her.

(Dude the fuck? You think I'm a fucking idiot she has in her carry-on a gaffing hook, three guys look like murderpuppets and a yeti. She's not someone you piss off I get that.)

Yeah I get that.

Then yes.

Ms Quint I am responsible for what happened to your daughter. I goaded a woman named Karenina. I know her and I used that knowledge to be as unkind as I possibly could. I wanted her angry so that she would make a mistake and she did. I did not imagine the magnitude of the mistake she would make. I assumed she would inflict commercial damage on your organisation and attack the server farms. It did not cross my mind that she would do what she did but it should have. It should have. I could have known if I had considered it because what I said to her was to wound her in the heart. She was my friend, and I knew just what to say.

Friday makes Nordic sounds. It's like the weather forecast at half speed. Quint listens and her face does not change at all. After a while she speaks. More weather.

Friday: she says that in an international legal context as for example say the Geneva Conventions on war crimes it would indeed be possible to make a case against you for not knowing something that you could have chosen to know if you were in a position of leadership but that since you did not control the actions of this woman you cannot be considered responsible for what happened except in what you might call a contributing sense like a culture of violence but that is neither unique to you nor sufficient to merit her adverse notice or she would kill the world.

Weather continues bad. Storms off Helsinki. Friday listens some more.

Friday: which she has considered very seriously but it is obviously not proportionate rationally speaking, and she is aware of that, which is why she has rejected this option. I must add we would have argued against it quite strenuously.

Weather.

Friday: Ms Quint wishes to know why you sought to wound the woman Karenina in this fashion.

Well she recently took a position in a small independent firm and that firm was by coincidence hired to negotiate my withdrawal from a particular discussion. Their position was what you might call definite with regards to my continued vitality so I took exception. I figured she would incur the displeasure of one of your meatier clients like maybe an aggressive intelligence service and I would have time to work around her.

Friday: you are a user of our service.

Yes of course.

So to recap this Karenina who is also a user of our service in pursuit of ends dictated by a commercial entity and with the intention of depriving you of your life sought to circumvent the protections which Poltergeist exists to provide by torturing and murdering Ms Quint's child.

Well—

You need not answer Mr Price the situation is quite clear.

Ms Quint: interrogative weather.

Friday: expositional weather.

Ms Quint: the actual fuck weather.

Friday: yeah that's about the size of it weather.

Ms Quint: fucking Valkyrie Grendel's mother screaming harpy weather.

Friday: hugs.

Ms Quint: sad.

Friday: silence.

In fact pretty much the whole place is quiet now because the coffee machine has stopped. Out in the bay there's a big ship doing some kind of slow turn BOGGABOGGABOG. There's a seagull who's pissed about something but they always are. And that's it. As close to silence as you get in this place while Ms Quint empties her gagging, shuddering tears into her big friend's shoulder. Mr Bates and Mr Overlook look like furniture. Mr Dory looks like topiary. None of them looks like anyone you'd want to fuck with at all.

Eventually she stops and she goes back to sitting exactly where she was and then she speaks.

Friday: Mr Price she wants to know if this Karenina is still trying to kill you.

Yeah she is. Her friends too.

Friday: Ms Quint is not interested in her friends this is a matter between two women.

Well yeah they all are anyway I mean that's kind of their whole thing at this point and I have to admit I'm also trying to kill them.

Friday: then Ms Quint says she would like you please to expose yourself.

Uh—

Ms Quint: stern.

Friday: embarrassed.

Ms Quint: get on with it.

Friday: sorry that was not good English I meant not nudity but that you should reveal yourself to the woman Karenina.

Okay.

You will do this and when she comes for you she and Ms Quint will be able to discuss this matter freely.

Is this a restorative justice type deal I mean are they going to hug and then Karenina will just shoot me in the face?

Friday: query.

Ms Quint: gaffing hook.

(Silence. A gaffing hook is a very expressive object. We all look at it for a while. Finally I figure it's time someone said something.)

Yeah okay no translation necessary Friday okay I will do this thing but would you maybe do something for me too?

Mr Price it seems we will in any case be saving your life.

Small favour. Like professional courtesy.

Go ahead.

Can you make a building disappear?

Outgoing SMS message:

Hey.

You there?

Knock knock.

Yeah Price what?

Is that you?

It's me. What do you want?

Just checking up on my lawyer.

You remember who you're talking to right?

Yeah this is my lawyer's phone so—

Oh right I get you. Okay fine Hi Price it's me Sarah! Gosh fauns and ponies and yoghurt every day.

Like I say just checking up on my lawyer.

That's sweet.

It's not sweet.

It is sweet look at you with your little crush.

It's not a crush.

Yoghurt. Every. Day. Wheatgerm and sage brush to cleanse the apartment. A biodegradable yoga mat Price.

It's not a crush let's call it a residual sense like of some kind of obligation.

You got obligations now? When the hell did that happen?

Shit I don't know what the hell it is let's just say it doesn't mean anything it's like some kind of loose chip in my brain and I just got to ask.

Well fine if you want to know I – I Sarah your lawyer whose phone this is – I went out the door just ahead of the bad guys man no one knows where I am not even that bitch doctor with the exceptional body. You see how hot that woman was Price? That woman was way hotter than me. It's kind of intimidating actually to know that she exists in the same universe as me and the idea that I might have imagined I was you know the same species as someone like that it's a little weird.

Right okay.

I'm probably halfway to Australia by now Price if I'm any kind of smart at all do you think I'm smart?

Yes.

You better fucking hope I am. You know just as I disappear from your life forever on my way to Australia you mind I give you a little life advice just like randomly in passing?

Please do.

If hypothetically you were to have sex with someone who wasn't me-Sarah-who-is-your-lawyer-with-the-biodegradable-yoga-mat you might should avoid asking that person what they think about my situation as if you care in case they took exception to that on the basis of common courtesy and devoted some time to determining my precise location. Especially if that person was oh I don't know insanely hot and really fucking dangerous for example.

Yeah that would be real unfortunate I'll remember that. You mind I ask you a professional question?

Why the fuck not.

So here's a hypothetical legal scenario for you to contemplate. You personally so, you know, contemplate it closely because I really want your reaction and no one else's. Let's say someone with whom you have recently had a probing legal discussion during which you have really got down to it and uncovered some really remarkable and interesting things, and that person is about to seek some kind of resolution on a pre-existing matter regarding some recent overseas transactions. And let's say your colleagues might have opinions on this and your interlocutor with whom you were just a short while ago locked in some pretty involved and let's be honest mutually satisfactory negotiation was of the opinion that you might want to look out from what you might call a more removed vantage for any operations in the hours to come because that might be preferable in like a holistic sense. Would that present you with an ethical dilemma?

You there?

Hello?

Hello?

No Price it would not.

Wait now I don't know what that means. You still there?

All. The sirens. In. The world. Coming. After. Me. Coming down on me. Cops like rain like fucking Hurricane Katrina like nightfall. Coming down on me in my car. I like driving in my car. Shit strong coffee in a crisis fucking Nordic civet fuck. Vapour trails is what. Drive away drive away drive drive the cops are coming.

And by that I think I mean all of them.

In. The world.

This is what happens when a Nordic woman with a gaffing hook asks you to expose yourself and you say yes.

Down the underpass. Feels safe because underpass because

they have a fucking helicopter up there can you even? A helicopter for Christ's sake. Likely more than one. Just unnecessary. All of this shit man it's unnecessary like a tremendous waste of everyone's time there's just no call for all this negativity. I mean what did I ever do?

Underpass feels like walls and a fortress but you can't stay there you gotta come out and when you do there are just more and more cops. Man it's like a convention or one of those scenes in movies that these days they do with computers and everything's just a little too perfect. Underpass takes no time. No time at all. Flicker of shadow then gone like zip. Count to three and see the first cops coming out behind me.

Jesus fuck they have a lot of guns and they are pissed.

I did what Poltergeist asked me. I made an order through a supposedly safe server they knew Karenina had compromised.

And she pointed at me and she said:

ANTHRAX.

Which I mean on one level is completely unfair because I was so careful about what strain and that may have looked like a terror attack but it was totally a targeted strike and a ruse but well you gotta put your hand up sometimes and say okay that actually was my bad.

All the cops in the world, loaded for bear, and me in a little tiny car waaaay out in front and hoping like hell I am not about to get real fucked up. Grey road and white lines I am all about the white lines but not this kind. Holy shit I'm in a car. I'm in a car driving like pursuit like a real bad guy and I am horrible at it. Horrible. This is not my environment man this is a complex skillset you hire this the fuck in. What do I know about high-speed driving? Like twenty minutes on Grand Theft Auto before it pissed me off (INTERSEC-TION FUCK FUCK F— I'm alive but fuck.)

In among the narrow streets now like crazy narrow single lane one direction boyband traffic flow motherfucker like alleys and places where they hang washing over the damn road and you can shake hands from one fire escape to the next. Buildings going by so

fast it's like vertigo like falling like I should have taken the damn—
no. No no. It's okay. Okay. Just drive in a straight line. Just drive.

Walls are closing in. Little import fits between. Cop cars are
bigger, gonna lose some paint but they're coming anyway and not
just this alley but all of them five alleys side by side behind me like
a fucking tsunami of cops like fucking Hokusai got a career in law
enforcement.

This isn't gonna work. They are spreading out around me using
their numbers they are putting me in a box. Little box on a screen.
They are putting me in a box and the box is getting smaller all the
time. They will get me and I'm gonna die and they'll make a fucking
internet meme about it. The Ballad of Jack. Foot like lead, nerves
like steel, going up to glory riding an affordable Korean hatchback
with a NOS booster and environmentally friendly 15" wheels. Yeah,
you better run, old Italian lady with your damn olive oil in a can.
This here is a hostile context for pedestrian traffic now.

Jack be motherfucking nimble. Check behind me. (DO NOT
CHECK BEHIND YOU.) I can see the Triangle on the skyline like
big dumb tower architecture but way impressive somehow and in
front of it like motherfuck like cops and robbers man. So many
damn cops. Way in the back there I'm pretty sure that is fucking
Tuukka on a motorbike and next to him in a fucking sidecar that
is no doubt Fred with a long case across his back and no doubt he
has a view to a kill here, in case Karenina goes soft and he just has
to pop out that old Barrett and put one through my eye. Yeah okay
that is fucking motivational. Foot back on the accelerator pedal. Yes.
Yes but no but yes.

I'm not Steve McQueen I mean I can hit the accelerator and
the break and on roads in this country you can expect your tires
to screech at like ten miles an hour but this is different this is like
holy shit. Thank fucking Christ this thing takes corners like a pole
dancer. (OH SHIT BUS OH SHIT I'm fine I'm fine.)

Gotta put your hand up for that too for Southeast Asian design
philosophy right. Put my hand up for that and for having released
a pretty relaxed and comparatively uninfectious anthrax on the

population. I mean not that anyone's caught it except Red Kat Bonanza and I read where he's fine but still.

But if I put my hand up right now someone will take it the fuck off because even without Fred man these cops are serious these are not your daddy's donutmunchers. These are today's version and they have a tank and a fucking fifty cal and they are looking to make the news cycle tonight. They are fucking everywhere with their air support and technology up the wazoo. I'm just a guy in a car.

There's the fucking superturbozoomrocket button on the dash and I'm absolutely not to push that right now but it's looking better and better every second.

Okay hard right and we're on two fucking wheels now but that's okay that's okay. Jesus this is not okay. If I go down they'll give me more years for this than the murders man than for all the coke. This is downright fucking antisocial even for me.

Wonder where the doc is. Is she seeing this? Come on doc this has to be some kind of attractive. Just a little. This kind of flat-out insane has to be doing it for you.

Wonder if that fucked-up sex was some kind of Rubicon for her too.

Wonder if she wants to do that all again.

Focus Jack. Focus. Follow instructions and it'll all be fine.

Follow instructions? You got any idea how long it's been since I followed anything wasn't wearing a silver microdress and heels with fish in them?

Big red brick coming up, turn left, then we're back on the big industrial roads. Wide and straight like an airstrip. Red brick's got words on it like painted advertising. Michael's. Michael's canning and preserving. Mom-and-pop, folded circa 1932. Still got the signage but now it's a warehouse and that's all. That's the punch point. Doc are you watching? I'd really like to think you are. I feel we got unfinished business.

Follow instructions Jack.

That's the punch point. That's the punch point. Jesus fuck. Five. Follow instructions Jack.

Four.

Objects in the mirror are closer than they appear.

Three.

Follow instructions. Follow instructions. Two.

Follow instructions. Say hi to Mike the canner in heaven or hell. One.

Follow instructions. Follow instructions.

I do.

Someone explodes a bomb in my asshole. Tiny Korean car is now a fighter jet.

Out of NOS and out of sight. Breathing space maybe a minute. Heel the car over. We're where we should be. Time to jump the fences. Suspect on foot and the good guys are closing in man.

Breathe. Wait. Wait until they see you wait—

STAY WHERE YOU ARE JACK PRICE YOU ARE UNDER—

That's French for run Jack run.

Truth is you can't run and you can't hide. There's just nowhere to go. You see those shows where they follow someone with a helicopter and a bunch of cars and that? Well that is the bare minimum of what they can do and they are doing the max now. And I'm one guy on foot. I am done.

Should be done. If there was any justice in the world. Should be.

Zoom out and pretend you're a satellite. See the world as a bright blue marble. Get the overview effect. Now zoom in and see the city, then this district, then these streets. Now you're seeing me the way command and control sees me. The way Karenina sees me. You notice something?

Yeah. The map ain't the territory. In fact it's not even close.

Somehow the main system is getting little bits of bad information. Some of it is flat-out wrong, sometimes just a little too slow with the good stuff. Tip line's busted up and corner cameras and ATMs are all giving them bullshit answers. It's fog of war man I mean you bring highly complex gear in a stress situation and it's gonna throw some artefacts. That's just how it is. Don't matter if you're in Fallujah or right here at home, you need air cover. The helo is the best friend a girl has. Best friend Karenina has. It's top of the line it's got fucking satellite realtime uplinks and broadband live connections and frequency-shifting comms and—

And if she was thinking she'd know that when you wire your equipment like that, then someone like her or Charlie can maybe get up in your shit, but okay you harden it and you make sure they can't and that's fine, that'll work. You make your gear tough enough that you can't crack it and you know that means it can't be cracked. You call someone who is like hacker Kryptonite like that's even that person's handle like Crypto-nite see what he did there?

But you know who you call to do that?

You call Mr Dory.

So right now Karenina is tracking me and she is doing it but good. She has my number. She has me on satellite heat camera and live ambient surveillance. She is running the show from her command car and she is treating me like a mouse in a maze. She closes streets like a wizard waving a wand and she has her machine make the box I can move in smaller and smaller all the time and I can actually feel it happening. I can see my options going away and it is scary as fuck. Down into the subway or off along the street this way that way I can see cops and they have guns and Karenina is coming and I gotta admit she is gonna get me.

Would get me.

Oh Karenina. You screwed up.

Dory owns the city now. My box is getting smaller but as it does the walls are getting thinner and going away. There's reports of a riot kicking off by the power station and half the task force is breaking away to deal with it. A bunch more just got snarled up in the maintenance work round Independence Plaza. Steam pipes is what I hear maybe gas. Karenina's bleeding support and she can't feel it. And when she chose where she was gonna run me down, she also didn't know that there was construction by the local crosstown – just somehow wasn't on the map. Data entry lag right? Talk about your systemic failures. I guess someone in the permit department didn't get to work on time today. But that weight limit on the temporary bridge is for real and that means the tank can't get over – but the command car can so Karenina is all thunder and fire. She checks the data on her screens and she can see that everyone's coming with her. The tank checks in: alternative route found, ETA nominal. Except the tank crew are getting a hold order. Which they obey.

On she goes because she still has all the cops in the world right there with her. She can see them on her screen.

Back by the crosstown Fred and Tuukka have ditched their bike and they're walking. Fred's got his long case like a pool cue. They're in no hurry. They're chatting. They can see she's got it. She's running me down. They're not concerned. This is how it is to be a Demon, pointing at things and making them die, commanding armies and standing in a pile of the dead. This is what it's supposed to be. They're back in charge now. And when they fill the gaps in their roster, people will forget there were ever four Demons, and the name of Jack Price will be a lesson in humility.

I know this because I can see it all happening on my phone. Which Karenina does not know I have.

Which is invisible to her, like so much else. Like me as I walk down the street singing my little song. Mm mm mm hmm hmm hmm hmm. Kind of an anthem now. Mr Linden's office phone. Got a kind of Imperial March feel. Kinda like it.

She's living in Dory's magic kingdom now and nothing is real. She's got facial recognition running and it's telling her I'm way over the other side of the box hiding under the counter in a Hungarian deli place. She's leaving more and more cops behind but her transponder is telling her they're all still right there, just seconds away. She's the tip of a spear and she's jamming herself down my whole neck all the way to my ass. She's got an impact team from SWAT right up ahead to make the hard entry.

Except Karenina. Oh honey they don't exist. Ain't no spear darling there's just you in that command car and everyone else turned left at Albuquerque. Even the helo's gone. Got a system failure, engine trouble, the whole damn nine but somehow she hasn't got that message. Somehow she's still getting the feed. If she wasn't so deadset focused on me she'd know that. She'd miss the sound of it in the air. She'd look up and see an empty black sky.

It's just her now, right out ahead and all alone. Just her and one driver heading into the narrow streets.

Five.

Four.

Three.

Two.

Dory kills the lights.

He kills power in this whole eastern half of the city.

He kills phone traffic and emergency service comms.

We're in a dark so deep it's like we fell back four hundred years. Out on the water the ships light up, emergency power. There's a coastguard launch hailing, looking for answers. Nobody has any.

Two miles back, Fred and Tuukka know something's up and they start to run: Struwwelpeter and his sea-troll friend, far too far away to make any difference now, even if they knew where the hell they were going.

Here we are in the tuna cannery. Smells like cheap orange breath-mints. Seriously. Who knew? Big dark empty place looks like a giant men's room except with weird robot stuff hanging off the ceiling so like a men's room where they do alien autopsies so I guess not like a men's room at all. Like an autopsy room for aliens that smells like Tic Tacs.

You'd think the whole place would smell of rotting fish right and sure no doubt it used to but this place is clean like antiseptic clean like it's almost frightening. It's purpose-made. The whole floor and all the workspace is a single piece of vacuum-formed plastic. When they finish for the night they close all the doors and push a button and orange-scented industrial bleach comes down and gets every inch of every surface and then there's a rinse and that's it. Slurry runs off to be strained and reclaimed as chemicals and the whole workspace is like new.

I figure there's gonna be some conversation. That was how it was when Ms Quint and her friends caught up with me. There was conversation, I mean even maybe a little more than you'd actually want. It's the same scene except that Dory isn't here because he's working and I am because obviously. Mr Bates is playing butler, Mr Friday is here to translate. Ms Quint is standing in the middle of the room. There's obviously going to be some discussion of what's happened and some angry weather and then maybe some crying and hugging. I'm a little concerned actually what if Ms Quint comes over all Scandinavian and they form some kind of a bond? I mean I am all for restorative justice but you know not in this precise context not right now.

In comes Karenina with her driver all torch and handgun cool because they know there's a SWAT team in here ahead of them and it's all clear and they know the entire damn cavalry is coming up behind. Because on their gear all of those things are still true. Even the helo is still up there, though they don't have radio since they came inside.

Bates shakes hands with the driver. Hey you get the guy? Naw man we ain't seen shit is what. Fucking ghost town.

Karenina makes her way into the room. Doesn't see me. Light in her eyes and Quint's in charge because all of Poltergeist is waiting on her and it shows.

Karenina looks at Quint. Quint looks at Karenina. Long silence.

And Karenina doesn't have the slightest fucking idea who she is. Nothing passes between them. No spark of recognition. Nothing happens.

She looks around, sees me.

Price? You want to get down on your knees and fucking beg you fucking miserable—

Quint sighs and puts the gaffing hook straight into the side of her head. No conversation at all.

Karenina goes away.

Quint looks down at what's left behind and shrugs. Looks at Friday: weather.

Friday: Yes well I imagine it will be something to look back on at least.

We walk out in a line. Bates shuts the door and presses a green button marked:

CLEAN

part four

QUINT MAKES ME A PRESENT of her gaffing hook. At least I think it's a present she may just be saying I should dispose of the murder weapon because Friday is out of the room and you can't really tell a lot from her face. Anyway she pushes the hook into my hands like here this is your thing now and I take it because my hands are monkey hands and that is what monkey hands do. She looks at me for a while. I look at her. The hook still has some small but presumably vital working parts of Karenina's interior experience on the western slope where it's scratched. Figure it was scratched by generations of sharks or whatever not by a bit of skull but honestly there's no way to know for sure. Maybe the doc would know wherever she is.

Friday comes in and there's weather of course because these people cannot do anything without talking about it and you get the feeling that there's probably some Ingmar Bergman in there or some Tarkovsky. I don't understand a fucking word so I'm just guessing.

Quint: rain coming bring the sheep in from the upper meadow.

Friday: yes I will do that but one of the rams has an erection.

Quint: he's a ram he always has an erection do it anyway there's fog on the west hills that means precipitation is probable before the bear farts.

Friday (to me): Quint says that you are a thin man and she is sad.

Right okay well I guess I am a little—

No. She means that your life is thin. There is nothing in it except you. It does not really touch the world and if you go out of your life almost no one will notice and this is a sadness to her. You are a thin man and she says it would be better for you to grow a little fat.

Yeah I had a plan in that regard like there was this girl but it turns out she doesn't like me very much and in fact she's probably dead now. Leastways I thought I was getting messages from her but – never mind that okay I'm thin I get it.

Quint says that there is an empty sack in you that you must fill up with love and children. She has traveled all the roads there are in the world and she knows sorrow and she knows joy and now she has killed a woman and it was not a great matter after all. The universe will not notice. Only we will notice. She says not to let the same thing apply to you.

She said all that?

No.

What?

No. She was asking me about the taxi to the airport. But I thought you could use to hear it and you are the kind of man who takes advice better in translation. It was in a self-help book that I read once.

What?

Mr Price: it does not matter where these words come from. Perhaps they are from a great poet of my country. Perhaps they are things that were said once to me. Perhaps they are a motivational poster that my sister's son has on his wall next to a portrait of Chris Hemsworth in his underclothing. It does not matter where they come from only if you think they are true.

Sure okay but—

Why are you holding a gaffing hook covered in your friend's brain?

Is that like part of the profound thing?

No I am genuinely a little confused.

You and me both brother. You and me both.

And that's it. They're gone. Sensible car comes and takes them to the airport and that's it. Goodbye Poltergeist. But also hello Poltergeist because the machines are running again retasked in some other place. Nordic digital resistance is strong and somehow they've pretty much always believed they were in a war.

Seven Demons came to town one time, took a contract. Must have been halfway to being a try-out for their newest recruit. Had no idea who they were fucking with.

Yeah well I didn't either.

Three Demons left now and one of them walks like a crab. One of them is scary as hell and one of them is a sniper.

Three Demons and me.

I'm cleaning my friend's brain off a gaffing hook. Quint was right to give it to me.

This is all my own work.

Almost all.

Almost.

So you put one foot in front of the other is what you do. You put one foot in front of the other because if you stay still you die and how does that help anyone?

You put one foot in front of the other. But that's not being alive that's just not being dead. You want to win this you gotta feel it you gotta love what you're living so you don't just put one foot in front of the other you look in the mirror and you see your own face and you grin that grin. You put on your suit. You put on your Italian calfskin boots and then my friend then you put one foot in front of the other. This is your life and you're earning it one step at a time.

You put one foot in front of the other and you do it with style.

So here I am, with style, and here are the bright and the glad, the rich and the pretty. Hot people partying basically partying without great attention to good taste which is the best parties. Gold and mirrors and light that makes you think about sex. Ambient music just right. Dance floor over there kinda shuttered off so it's dark enough. Place is called Inhibition which of course is what it sets out to destroy which is why the logo has a line though. Very ha ha. This is a bar where you can drink drinks that are rare and expensive but not very good. It's where Sean Harper spends the bulk of his evening leisure time which is basically every evening. He has a regular table. He entertains here, courts here, seduces here. He solicits donations to his pet causes in one private dining room, gives speeches in another, then comes back in here and relaxes like he's Sinatra back in the day. But he's got that look. That thin look. Like he's thinner than I am by a mile.

Do we remember Sean yes we do. Sean owns that place where I first met the doctor's dog. Sean is the little pissant who for some ungodly reason hired the Seven Demons and I took it amiss and here we all are. But somehow or other Sean is a sideshow.

And that is the whole point. That's what this is about.

Because here is Sean right and he is this wealthy kid who does charity stuff and throws money around and he has never had to reach for anything but it dropped in his lap or basically right onto his dick. And yet at the same time he cannot do anything that matters.

Sean Harper didn't kill Didi Fraser for a reason at all. He noticed her because she cussed him out but that isn't why he killed her. He killed her because it suddenly occurred to him that it would be cool. It was something he'd never done before and he thought he might like to. Are you following me? He killed her because it was the only thing he could possibly do that might actually have consequences and then it did have consequences and those consequences were me. Then when that scared him he had to double down. He got it in his head to hire the Seven Demons because he thought he'd try being a bigtime villain and then it would be about something other than just his own littleness. Ultimately he's a fucking insignificant little prick and he knows it and that's why he wanted to do a murder and that's why when it went sideways he decided that was gonna be like his defining moment like When Sean Went Bad. Didi Fraser wasn't part of some bigger plan. She was part of a plan to get bigger that just made Sean smaller and smaller and here we are.

There's his driver outside. Man can't wait to go off shift go home to his family. There's the doorman. That guy just arrived all clean and spruce and lots of energy. Imagine what either one of them would make of Sean Harper's life. Hell, imagine what Didi Fraser would have done with it. She'd have bought a megaphone the size of a stadium and cussed out the moon.

But Sean...

I came here to kill him but there's hardly any point. He's barely alive as it is. He's a man of no consequence whatsoever and everything he's done with his life amounts to exactly this: the international mercenary assassins he hired to kill me have forgotten he's their employer and so has he.

Fucking Swedish arthouse levels of futility happening here.

But that's what it is I guess.

Outside I got two guys with a big wooden tea crate and some packing stuff think this is an intervention. Which it is in a way.

I'll make a permanent decision later.

So a snitch walks into a funeral and the priest says, Hey Buddy you're early but there's really no point in you going home.

Yeah just think about it for a second you'll get there.

Anyway this is me walking into a funeral except it's actually a wake like a memorial and it's a week after they put my man Billy in the ground but the whole place is still all deathy and full of sad people because the guy who died was family and he was great fun. And that right there is one of my couriers dropping off a parcel for Billy's brother Rex because cocaine never sleeps.

This is Billy's house: crazy pale house all generic and fake historic like you can build anything you want you're gonna make a fake period house like why man why? But that's my boy no taste in architecture I guess. Those are Billy's kids over there crying a little and then laughing and feeling bad about it because what the fuck you do with grief and mortality when you're eight. And that is Billy's wife, sweet and sexy but just as weird and bewildered as he was, long slender legs and waisted cowboy shirts and she pretends she doesn't know about the strippers because boys will be boys or maybe you just shouldn't talk about that shit on these occasions I got no idea what real people do.

This is weird. I can't help it I just assume every man I see here has perfectly trimmed body hair, and it really doesn't help me fit in with the mood.

Billy's wife says: Hey, Jack, thanks for coming I'm still just so sad.

Hi Laurie. I got no idea what to say do we know what happened?

They're saying it was terrorists Jack and honestly I just don't know.

So I hug Laurie and I go over to the peanuts. You will always find Rex by the peanuts. Even if the Rex I am looking for is not in the building or the city there is always a Rex just grazing on the peanuts and looking like a guy who knows he should have stopped eating like five mouthfuls back but now he can't he's locked into salt fat beer salt fat beer and so on. He's going home with all kinds of digestive distress.

Hey Rex.

Hey Price.

Sorry about Billy.

Yeah well that's the world man.

It is the world, but it is also assholes.

Yes. My whole job for this year just came to a halt this morning. They lost the fucking paperwork. Now I'm just holding my dick waiting for the word. They say a week at least, and what am I supposed to do in the meantime just sit on my ass?

Rex there's a parcel for you on the hall table which might ease your pain it's maybe not ideal for you to open it in company it's more a private sort of thing a professional matter for you at your office you get me?

Yeah man I read you loud and clear. Thanks man that's actually gonna help my boys a whole lot maybe let off some steam.

No problem listen Rex let's say this one is on the house but you recall there's something I need from you too sort of a quid pro quo by which I mean a favour for a favour.

Yeah man I know what that is but of course.

I might need more than just a little access is what I'm saying.

Well what more we talking?

Well Rex we're talking I need to borrow some stuff of yours and to be entirely honest you might not get all of it back.

Shee-it Price that is a serious fucking quid for my quo.

I know man but it's a good cause. I'll be straight with you because I trust you. It has relevance to this sad occasion.

Man the terrorists? You're going to do something about that?

Am I going to do something about that? I have done things about that which our people will remember in songs for hundreds of years, Rex. From here to Mexico man from here to fucking Abbottabad they can hear the echoes of what I have already done. And what I'm going to do will be like a California fire. It will burn and burn until there is nothing left. You know I was talking to a guy from the Japanese FBI yesterday, okay? I been dealing with heavy-as-lead motherfuckers from your Scandawegian commercial intelligence sector and just these last few days some very international bad people. Yesterday I saw a lady who was a chief suspect in collusion with others – and not from here man – take a gaffing hook in the motor cortex. She is now residing in the sump of a fishworks by the water. She actually fucking sleeps with the fishes, man. So I am going to do something about that. For Billy and for my country I am.

Wow man.

Yes Rex.

Wow man that is awesome man that is like patriotic is what that is.

I believe that it is Rex I believe this is the great patriotic fight of our time. We are the fucking colonial marines facing the redcoats and the fucking aliens from space and whatever else this hostile universe is going to throw at us. And we are showing them what it means to. Mess. With. The. WRONG. Son-of-a-bitch. Is what.

(Rex does this kinda yodel thing like a warcry which I could not pull off but on him it kinda works because he is this huge ugly fuck who smells of peanuts and beer but at the same time obviously this is kinda not the time and so a lot of people look at us and Rex says: Sorry.)

I say: Primal screaming therapy man. It's the best for grief and it's totally making a resurgence on the West Coast. Rex, man, call me. There are things we need to do.

OK Jack. Hey Jack you mind I call you Captain?

No Rex that would be fine although you want in on a secret my actual rank in the Resistance is Colonel. By the way can I borrow a hand detonator like right now? I'll send you a list for the rest, but I don't need anything else today. Just the clicky red light part that scares the crap outta people.

Oh shit man okay yeah of course. Thank you, sir Colonel Price.

At ease Rex. This is a democracy.

Outgoing SMS:

Hi doc.

Price.

Seems like a bad thing happened.

Yes it does.

And you were not there.

No I had something else to be getting on with.

You know I can't tell when you do that whether you're like arms folded and pissed or all melty and come hither?

What do you want?

Like to have a grown-up discussion.

Oh god we're not eighteen please tell me this is not about—

No for god's sake doc no this is about professional matters.

Fine. Go ahead.

First I need to know if you're wearing clothes.

Of course I'm wearing clothes Price it's the middle of the day.

You're not even slightly naked and sitting in a fake execution chamber pretending you're about to go under and getting real excited?

What? No. Price that's just warped. Also I'm at work.

I just figure that's how you spend your free time.

I go to movies and eat sushi. I like books but not non-fiction. I have a great sense of humour but most people don't really get me.

Really because I have that same exact thing.

Price. Please.

Okay I want to meet and discuss something.

Anything you want to say you can say to me here.

Doc I don't wish to be in any way rude or diminishing of your personal importance in my life but it ain't you I want to be discussing with.

You're not serious.

Yes, doc, I am. I want to sit down with Fred and say my piece. I even bought him a present.

You're out of your mind.

He's a sniper so I got him a watermelon. Snipers love water-melons right it's a whole thing?

See above.

That I think is well-established fact by now but that don't change that it's hurtful you would say it like it's a bad thing. Come on doc humour me.

... Fine. I'm sending you an address. One hour.

And for Christ's sake get some clothes on I'm a fucking respect-able guy.

Fuck you Price.

Fuck you too doc.

... Fuck you.

Fuck. You.

Fuck. You. Right. Back.

Arms definitely folded and definitely not naked in a freaky sex room. Doc waiting outside the restaurant and you need to hear me saying that word with all its parts: rest-oh-ront because that is emphatically what this place is. It has grown-up style coming out of its plucked Italian buckskin ass. Too new to be an old favourite and too old to be the new thing. It's just right here and I musta seen it a bajillion times and never been in. Not my kind of place but the more I look I realise it's no one's kind of place. It exists for meetings between people who don't want to meet. It's got calm in the green-and-gold decor and the fat-handled cutlery and icy detente woven into the thick velvet curtains between the booths. This is where you bring your wife after the divorce. This is where you come with your mistress to meet her baby. Probably where the guys from the UN go when someone invades Afghanistan and that's how it stays open. This is a place where you can yell and pretty much only the sommelier can hear you.

For really fucked-up situations like this one they got private dining.

Tuukka waiting in the car. Not welcome at the party I said on account when I see him I think of that godawful noise his frozen leg made when he tried to walk on it and shit fell out and that is not conducive to enjoying the fucking terrine is what. Doc wrote it all down because she is very precise.

Fred. Hi Fred.

Mr Price.

Fred does not look the way Fred should look not when you get close. You're hoping for some kind of physiological indication of the man's deep and primal nature like he should have this big dramatic scar or smoke coming out his nose. Fred is the First Demon after all and that kind of thing should leave its mark on a man but no. Fred looks a little bit dull and a little bit irritable like I've made him late for his daughter's tuba recital and Fred is pissed because he really secretly wanted to miss that tuba recital but he'd resigned himself to going and was in that place where parents got to go to where they love every blarting hoot of a tuba recital with biological fucking certainty and now he resents the everliving shit out of life that he cannot go.

Look I got you this melon.

What?

It's a melon. For you like as a gift.

Why do I want a melon?

I thought what with you being a sniper – no never mind I'll keep it – Jesus no one's into the classics any more. Listen Fred I need your attention for some preliminaries okay just so we don't have any embarrassments?

Proceed.

Fred what the fuck is proceed for god's sake? Okay, never mind, look at this object here in my hand do you know what this is?

That is a remote detonator for an explosive device of some sort.

Yeah only it ain't all that remote at this precise moment is what. This is my insurance. I press this every so often and nothing happens. I press it in a particular fashion and something does happen. So my plan is that you and I walk out of here at the same time. You pick your exit and that way there are no regrettable but shortlived disagreements between us. You get me?

If I attempt to kill you at this time you will have the option to kill us all.

Plus if you succeed I don't push the thingy and—

Yes I understand—

Boom.

Thank you for explaining that to me.

I figured it was best to let you know in advance of whatever appalling shit you were considering.

Yes, I do see. A strategy of Mutual Assured Destruction, of course, very much an artefact of the 1970s in which you were born.

I'm a child of my time Fred. We are the Radiation Generation. You know I grew up outside the city? Turns out there was one hellacious power plant out there and when I was in school they showed us a Geiger counter and the two most radioactive objects in the room were my chemistry teacher's old watch that his daddy gave him and also me. And apparently I read where people from my area when we're buried we're technically toxic waste.

Is that so?

No Fred that is bullshit but I had you going.

Oh, indeed. May I, in turn, make an observation, Mr Price?

Be my guest.

Thank you. I was curious to meet you today, Mr Price. Curious because you are fascinating to me. I did not intend you any harm. There is time enough for that tomorrow.

What's happening tomorrow?

You will die. Anyway, as I was saying: I was curious to know whether you would be the man I had envisaged. Which you are, of course.

Not following you Fred.

Then allow me to elaborate, Jack Price. You have referred to me occasionally in the course of this remarkable affair as a PR guy. That is, in fact, not strictly accurate. I have worked in public relations, as well as serving in the military both as a solo sniper and as a psychological operations officer, but my training is in behavioural economics and abnormal psychology. That is to say I am a scientist whose field of study is a combination of the way in which people make economic decisions and the functioning of the mind and the brain in cases where someone's mentation – that's to say their thinking – is outside the normal societal range. For a while, I even worked with – though not at – the Federal Bureau's noted profiler unit at Quantico. I very much enjoyed profiling serial killers, I must say. Although tragically it has to be acknowledged that what you might think of as gut profiling – qualitative and symbolic judgement as is most often depicted in film and television – is vastly less accurate than brute data modeling. Although at the sharp end of the model is a small group of very intelligent persons who must apply the right guesses and turn knowledge of the general population into theories of the specific.

Fred when I said I wasn't following I did not mean please do more of the same with more bullshit.

Yes, it pleases you to affect foolishness. Yet your actual functional level of intelligence is very high. You're an extremely intelligent man with almost no restraints or inhibitions at all. And I believe you characterise yourself as quite without emotional attachment either to objects, possessions, your profession, your home or to the things most people value such as pets, friends and family. You blame the aftermath of your curious dislocated and vicarious encounter with a terrorist outrage but although that was genuinely traumatising for you it was not the root but rather the moment at which you allowed your bad genii out of the bottle. It was an excuse, if you like, to be who you have always wanted to be – and we were the next one. We allowed you to cut loose your residual empathy and behave like a monster while feeling that you had no choice. But you have always had a choice, and you have always had emotional attachments. You know this, however much you fight it. Thus you are doomed. In the end, you will act the hero because you must. It is who you are and who you have always been underneath. You are a man who needs excuses, Mr Price. You need reasons to suppress your compunction and you have found them. But in the process you have also taken steps to protect the people for whom you care and those people have become fewer and more obvious. I think you have learned that love is still in you. Humanity is still in you. And I think that in learning that you have become ever so much more vulnerable to someone like me. So whatever you wanted to say to me, here is what I came to say to you: when you go to sleep tonight it will be the last time you ever do. Tomorrow I will call you and I will make you an offer which you will accept. You will choose to give up your quite empty if colourful life in exchange for an end to the suffering of those you care about. You will do this because beneath it all you possess compunction and you know that I do not.

Well gosh Fred.

Mr Price.

Is it my go now or is there more where that came from?

Please, take your turn.

Well okay Fred you know that you all were hired to kill me because Sean Harper murdered a mad old lady who looked like an explosion in an ugly elderly paint factory?

I am aware of Didi Fraser's death.

Okay well so the whole point of that exercise completely fucking escapes all of us right? I mean can we agree that this whole thing between us is way past the point where it has anything to do with Didi?

Agreed.

But it is your technical reason for being here. Like I know that even if Sean called you off you'd obviously still want to disembowel me with a lemon squeezer but technically you work for him?

Quite so.

Well so Fred here is what it is. You forgot about Sean and I didn't. I never gave a crap about him either, but I at least understand compunction – even if I got no idea whether it's still in me or not if I'm honest. But I get the logic by which the world works and here it is. Either you stand up now and take off all your clothes and walk out into the street and you shout JACK PRICE KICKED MY BALLS UP OVER MY HEAD or else when you call me tomorrow I will shoot Sean once in the face and twice in the – wait that's backwards isn't it. You definitely want to start with the chest right, and then pop pop? Fuck it. You get the idea. I will kill Sean boringly but effectively. And I know you won't care on a personal level but I figure I've pretty much demolished your personal brand already. But if I kill your client now, you're finished. You can rebuild the Seven from here it's not impossible but if Sean dies ain't no one going to have any respect for you. Seven Demons will be finished until someone takes them from you and they will Fred they will. I hear where Volodya the Sniper is in town already sniffing around. Hell even Tuukka might think it was time for some new management he has to be carrying some dissatisfaction in his heart. Even the doc here she might reckon to say goodbye to your boring condescending ass in your grey suit. She's got her a wild streak behind the eyes. But you will be done. So why don't you just start to strip. Fred.

Mr Price, I'm not sure I understand what I get out of this deal, as you put it. You seem to have left me disgraced either way.

Oh shit Fred did I? Dang you're right. Oopsies. What can I say I'm not a smooth polished professional like you. Oh, on that subject, I went down to the harbour and picked this up. I'm pretty sure it's Karenina but you know it's real hard to tell from just a femur. But I figured it'd be good for you to have something to remember her by.

Price...

Yeah Fred look at that. You got a temper too, just like me. So let me just make one thing clear: you came here with Seven Demons. Now you got two and a half. You know what that is Fred? That is the Price you pay. THAT IS THE PRICE YOU PAY YOU WEAK MOTHERFUCKER. Are we clear?

I will speak to you tomorrow, Mr Price. Sleep well.

Yeah you too. Oh wait that was like a death reference right and I completely trod on your cool exit line? Sorry man.

Outgoing VoIP encrypted call:

Hey Rex?

Colonel is that you?

Yeah Rex it is. Looks like we're on buddy. You good?

Yes sir. I am.

And the right people know?

Yes sir they do. Word is out, sir.

Rex this is going to be some tough fucking action. There will be consequences Rex I ain't gonna lie.

No sir I know. But the Tree of Liberty sir.

God bless you Rex.

God bless you Colonel.

Incoming SMS message:

Well that was big and loud and masculine.

You loved it.

You've actually weaponised being an asshole.

I know right?

It's fascinating.

So are you in your freaky naked murder room now?

I am not in any kind of freaky murder room now.

I see what you did there. Doc whose side are you on?

I'm very pissed off with you Price.

How so?

Because you came and did something really ridiculously fucking stupid and obnoxious and mentally unsound right in front of me and then you just left.

Well I figured I had to do what Fred said and go treasure my last night's sleep on Earth.

You got twelve hours left and what you want to do is sleep? Who the fuck are you and what have you done with Price?

Now that you say that no. But you didn't answer me.

Tell me something instead.

Shoot.

What was the detonator attached to?

What was the blue mark on my hand?

Biodegradable microfilm suspension of a modified CRISPR-Cas9 genetic modification tool.

I'm guessing that would not have been good for me.

No. What was the detonator attached to?

Nothing.

You're an idiot.

Fuck you.

Oh at last.

I'm not playing games doc.

Nor am I. The next sound you hear will be the doorbell Price and you better fucking open it or I will kick it down.

I'll shoot you.

You really want to spend your last night alone in some cheap bed with a dead woman who only wanted to have sex with you lying on the floor in the hall?

Wait is that a thing?

Open the fucking door Price. I can smell you. Come and breathe in.

This is crazy. Okay I'm here.

Breathe. Softly. You won't notice it at first but your body will know I'm here. You'll get flashbacks because scent is closely associated with memory.

Nothing's happening.

Yes it is.

No it's... Fuck.

Yes Price.

Fuck.

I am going to have sex with you now.

You can break in here and ravish me but you can't make me enjoy it.

As a matter of fact I can. Open the fucking door.

Sitting in some place. Diner. Espresso bar. Whatever. Morning on the last day, one way or another. Coffee and sex instead of sleep. The doctor knows things. How do I feel? I feel alive. Vulnerable. Clean like I've had a shower which I haven't. Fresh like I've been swimming in the lake. New born like I'm baptised. Walking down a wide avenue with green trees all up and down it like it's hardly the city at all. The fuck am I gonna tell you I'm happy like a happy normal person not just like a man uncorked and allowed to do terrible shit. Seems like Fred has a point. Maybe I have grown as a person in these days like I've rediscovered something human inside me through electroshock sex and Scandawegian gaffing hook parties. I've been on the run. I've been declared a dead man by the Demons and I'm still here. Maybe I understand this whole place a little better now. Maybe I made some kind of transition from saying goodbye to the old city every day to living in the new one. Maybe I've come home.

Yeah, I'm surprised too.

Crosstalk on the news: Hey buddy turn it up what's that?

Home invasion it's on all the channels.

New show like that makeover thing where they—

Naw man it's real. There's been this citywide thing like people being dragged out in the street. Just ordinary people dragged outta their houses onto the street. Poor folks rich folks whatever.

Perpetrator comes out of nowhere for no reason.

And then what?

He fucks them up. Cracked a guy's head open, eyeball hangin' right out. Bad things man. A bunch of them died like ten like twenty no one knows. Maybe more. I heard it was hundreds but who knows. It is fucked up man. They're all connected to this one woman. This lawyer.

Shit.

What's that?

Nothing man just old-fashioned. I do not like to see a lady in distress.

(Can't have been hundreds. There hasn't been time. Figure I talk to Fred, then at least half an hour to evolve the plan, ten minutes average per victim including travel which is if they all live close together and they don't so figure... Sixty maybe. Sixty-five, tops. Even so that is some classic appallingly monstrous playbook shit that I have to take my hat off to. You do not see that in this city in this day and age that is old-school bespoke murder is what that is. These Demons they just do not care. And where are the cops? Regular citizens got a right to expect some assistance from the cops. Fucking failure of command and control infrastructure is what. Compromise of basic capability by an external operator. Man heads are gonna roll.)

Picture of Sarah on the screen. Her professional portrait.

Yeah. It is kicking off.

Fifty-seven people. Motherfucker has dragged fifty-seven individual people out of their homes into the street and killed them in public. Sure they're framing me for it of course they are but that is not the point. That is just housekeeping. This is performance, for Sarah.

Hi, Fred. I see you there.

Fred is not doing that for my benefit because he knows I don't give a shit. I never will. I can like people perfectly well. Maybe I can even be in love but when you get right down to it there's me and there is everything else on the face of the earth. The doc is exactly the same. She can have whatever it is we have and still if she has to she will shoot me in the face. She'll be sad later maybe for a while. She'll remember me what do you call it fondly.

But she will shoot me in the face because that is who we are. Myself I'd probably shoot her in the throat because memories but honestly I'm not really a gun person so who the fuck knows how that would play out. I'd probably blow off one of her ears or something and have to try again. But I would is what I'm saying.

God the sex is great. I'm thinking about it now. The curve of her, the clench of her. Plus she has this chart. They should hang that thing in schools. It is—

Anyway where was I? Oh right yes Sarah.

Sarah.

Sarah gives a shit which is why she in the end hates me and thinks I am a monster because she does care. If you tell Sarah that she has a choice? That she can come to you or you kill her clients and then her colleagues and then move on to her family unless she comes to find you? Doesn't matter where she is. If she hears that, she is coming back. And if I show up they can let her go I mean after they have me she's worthless she's just some woman in the street.

If I don't come they can still kill her after being polite.

You know in my present mood I got this weird instinct to sit down and think about this. Weigh things in the balance but that's not it. That's not it at all.

There is a perceptual issue here is what.

Yeah a perceptual issue. Another one.

The Seven Demons are the untouchable bastards of the whole entire criminal universe and world and this is how they roll. They go into a place to do a job and they do horrible shit until the job is done. If the job is not done they escalate. They do shit that is more and more horrible. They do shit that torturers and murderers and monsters everywhere think is totally fucking excessive and then they do it again to make the point that the first time was not an accident and then again because they want to practice and they've got time before happy hour. For sure, the thing that never happens is that someone reaches out and does horrible shit to them.

Except now show me where on the doll Uncle Jack put Leo's head. The untouchable people have been touched and that is horrible for their brand, which is part of the point, but now it also begins to be a problem for me in terms of you might call career progression. My whole white-collar do-no-harm coke dealer to the financial aristocracy thing is pretty much burned. It was burned when I killed Johnny Cubano right in the Kenzo and since then it has only gotten more so and when I launched an anthrax attack on my home nation and evaded a city-wide manhunt... leave us say I cannot exactly just go back to what I was doing.

Problem is what you call in personal branding the heroic narrative. The narrative has to satisfy. Most specifically it has to end in a new stable state. You got your criminal news consumers out there in a vast economy of badness. You got bandits and pirates and slavers and drug runners, and traditional gangsters and new money gangsters and brigand aristocrats, and corporate evildoers and private military combines, and terrorists and intelligence agencies and sicarios of just about every church and state, and there is some vicarious fucking satisfaction here in what I have done for every aspiring professional bastard on earth – but it has to end high. What I do next has to be unequivocally bigger and scarier than where I started otherwise somehow despite everything I will have showed a soft belly and then I am D E A D dead. Unless I can produce a new normal in which everyone knows exactly their place and that there is no room for tumultuous realignments of this kind to continue, there will be points scored by the first jackass who jacks Jack's ass, and I do not propose to spend the next decade hiding in Guam. Don't get me wrong I love Guam, but I'm not in the end a Guam guy.

That means it is not enough to win. I have to win epic. And that means a measure of risk.

Incoming SMS message:

Price?

Yeah.

They have your lawyer.

Yeah I figured.

They have the girl too the computer girl who pissed Karenina off so much.

Wait they have Charlie?

Yes Fred has been working on your hinge points Price.

Price?

Price?

Price has he found them?

Outgoing VoIP call.

I say: Doc I bought that man a melon out of the sheer goodness of my heart.

It's a fucking melon Price.

Yeah but I bought him a gift and I honestly did offer him a way out of this.

Price for fuck's sake what the fuck does he care?

Not what he cares doc it's me I care. I bought that man a present and this is how he responds? Fuck him doc fuck him. Jesus I had just plain forgotten, owing to your fine company and your ladyparts, just exactly how much I hate that asshole. Do you know what is appropriate in this context doc? Do you? Because I fucking do, and you do not want to be in my way. There's been this kinda nice ambiguity in our relationship to this point and I have something of an addiction to your presence and I don't care that one day you're gonna kill me with some rare moth venom or maybe I will see it coming and have you fired into space in one of those really unreliable private space rockets and that way I could look up at the stars every night and think of your perfect body frozen and orbiting me forever. But you got to understand I'm going to finish this now. And if you get in the way I will kill you and I won't have time to make it poetic. You got to choose doc. We've gone about as far down this foes-with-benefits thing as we can. I'm gonna call another meeting with Fred and this time it's going down. High noon doc cowboy time. Just fucking guns everywhere and bombs and shit and whoever doesn't get blown the fuck to pieces is the winner. I don't fucking care. I'm taking him down.

Doc you there?

Doc please do not say that I'm making you hot right now because that is not where I'm going with this. You gotta choose.

Okay doc, here's what it is. If you go in my coat pocket right now by the door you're gonna find a note. And if you look in it, you'll know where to find me and what I'm gonna do. You're either in or you're out but—

I have already come to a decision Price.

Cold. Cold so cold.

She has beautiful eyes, the doctor, clear and sharp like a hard goodbye. Mouth just a little tight like there's something she's forgotten at home as she pulls the hood out of her pocket. Slow motion and fireworks and glockenspiel music and the cold so cold and the taste of mulled wine and I remember the way she looked at me when she said there will be pain I remember that so clearly.

Count backwards from I'm dead.

Wake up and I'm a man in a hood. Certain curious arrangements. Okay. Start talkin'. Jack Price is what. So I talk.

Hey Fred what's good? I'm guessing you're around.

I am, Mr Price – and you are not.

Well that's a little on the nose. You gonna take the hood off now?

No, Mr Price I don't think so. You are unable to move, of course, because of the drugs my colleague gave you earlier, but I rather like you with that extra element of the pathetic. Sitting in your chair with that bag over your face, you will be able to hear what is happening and you will know in your heart what is happening but you will see it only in your mind's eye – at least until the last minute. I believe that the situation will become resonantly familiar. I think if I approach this matter correctly you will scream for me. You will lose yourself in echoes of the past and I will finally hear you in real pain.

I bought you a melon man this is totally uncalled for. An actual melon with my own money.

I do hope you will retain your good cheer. Let me explain what is happening around you. I wish the meaning of everything to be very clear to you. Sarah Kessler is on your left and on your right is your punky friend with the graphic design diploma and the regrettable sense of humour that so incensed Karenina.

Punky? Fred how the fuck old are you anyway?

I myself am not on your roof I am on another with an excellent view. I speak to you by the magic of radio. Oh, and Tuukka has a roof, too. It's a little bit lower than mine because I'm the boss and I like expensive seats. But all the same you are in a crossfire, if you understand me. Even if you should free yourself you would certainly die before you could take any kind of action. You are helpless, Mr Price. I must say I find that pleasing. Say hello, Tuukka.

Price? You are dead now.

Yeah wow that's okay that's also really pretty much direct there's just no poetry in you guys at all.

Go to hell.

Yeah again. Look Tuukka you know what your brother was into? He was really into the idea that one day he'd just completely outclass you man just like you'd finally have to acknowledge you were the family idiot and he was the smart one. He was sad. Sad his whole life and you know what? That was all because you teased him about his name when he was a little tiny Aryan farmboy. That's pretty much what made it possible for Volodya to kill him. He wanted someone to believe in his importance as an individual and not your bagman, because I mean let's be motherfucking honest Tuukka you just didn't. So yeah I had it done but it was down to you. That's got to make you feel a little bit bad.

… Fuck you Price! FFFF-FUCK YOU!

Jesus Fred is he crying? When you were recruiting your Demons did you like put an ad in *Pussy Weekly* or something?

I LOVE MY BROTHER PRICE!

Yeah man whatever. I'm just saying if you'd been a little bit nicer to him while he was alive, he'd most likely not be dead. And we all wouldn't be in this unfortunate situation right now.

GNNNNNNAAARRRRHHHHH!

Very good, Mr Price. I do commend you. Now, Miss Sarah and Miss Charlie can you hear me?

Sarah says: Yes.

Charlie says: It's Mx you fuck not Miss not Ms you fucking dinosaur Mx Charlie like a non-gendered post-hierarchical form of polite address for if you're not a total human abcess.

I shall take that as a yes from both of you. Very good. Now you will see that my colleague the doctor is placing two pistols there on the ground in front of you: if one of you has not killed the other in the next minute after I tell you to begin I will shoot you both through the head. Mr Price: if you speak at all I will likewise kill both of them. Starting three. Two. One. Now.

I'm pretty sure this is what happens. Pretty sure. I'm pretty sure Sarah looks at Charlie and Charlie looks at Sarah and right at that moment they know one another. Charlie looks at Sarah and she sees what I've always seen. She sees a good woman who deserves to live. She sees a good lawyer working the bad part of town because she's too good for the places where your clients have money and expect results. Charlie looks at Sarah she sees the whole fucking sorry story of her doing the right thing and getting fucked over. She sees her perfectly, in this weird translucent moment between life and death right this spiritual moment almost between—

When Sarah looks at Charlie she cannot quite meet her eyes. All the same she sees this emo goth design chick with all manner of weird habits and this dorm room vibe who likes books with elves and monsters in them and original Mike Hammer comic books in black and white and she sees a kid sister kinda person with this vibrant wellspring of life thing going on under the white foundation. But even so she knows what's going to happen here. Sarah knows in this bad moment that she has been wrong. She is not ultimately different from me. She's desperate to survive and she knows the cost of that choice. She can see it and as she reaches for the gun she finally meets Charlie's eyes to say god I'm sorry god I'm sorry Charlie I don't I can't I don't—

What she sees is Charlie looking back at her and there is nothing in that look at all that gives one tiny atom of a fuck.

My cocaine branding manager shoots Sarah in the head.

I'm sorry boss. I really am because I know she was your favourite lawyer and everything but you know this is an exigent situation.

That's okay Charlie I quite understand.

You do?

Yes Charlie I do. It's what I would have done.

Yeah boss that's what I was thinking back there I was like what would Mr Price do? And that was pretty much my answer.

Mr Price…

Yes Fred.

Fred on his fucking highrise. Fred with his big ol' gun. Fred Fred Fred I really want to kill that motherfucker. Fred looks down his sights and he sees that hood the doc had in her pocket and I can fucking hear his breathing as he touches the trigger.

From half a mile away Fred puts a bullet right through the damn hood.

Right.

Through.

The middle.

I tell you that was unbefuckinglievable. That guy – that was some shot man.

If I'd been wearing that hood that would really have fucked up my day.

But instead there is just melon everywhere.

Fred you ungrateful prick you fucking ruined my melon.

Price?

It's just fucking truculent is what it is. I mean a man brings you fruit as a peace offering and you shoot it in the face with a fucking M82. You should be fucking ashamed.

Tuukka, kill the doctor. Immediately.

Yeah Fred that's not gonna happen.

It's not going to happen. The doc's here with me looking doc-ish as hell and she was kind enough to take my hood off a while back so now I'm just checking out the awesome view. I tell you this place is great and oooh look over there on that second-highest tower is Tuukka but he's not alone. He's got some kind of leg brace so he can stand up and move around and his hand is all bandaged up. These things are maybe a little obscured because he's horizontal. He's bucking and twisting but it's not doing him a lot of good. Volodya has wrapped him in duct tape and he looks like an exhibit from the Smithsonian and every time he lunges too hard he cuts himself on Lucille and shrieks. After a moment or so they just roll him sideways and he goes off the top of the tower. Three or four floors down there's a kind of slanted section where the real expensive rooms in the hotel used to be and he bounces and rolls down that bit and then it's on down forty floors.

Volodya waves to Fred.

Lucille says: LUCILLE!

See the thing is Fred that you've misunderstood your situation.

Silence.

Fred if you so much as touch that rifle this conversation is gonna come to an abrupt conclusion and I do mean that. I'm gonna say a few things Fred but if you move at all you're gonna die and I'll just let the epilogue speak for itself. You've got exactly that long to think of something to say or do that's gonna save you but frankly it's gonna have to be very good. You've misunderstood Fred and it's time you get a grip on what's taking place here. I mean above and beyond being screwed obviously and yeah the doc definitely took a hand in that. Although, I have to say, I didn't know until I woke up lying here by the parapet whether you were fucked or I was but I guess that's how it is with that young lady and she and I will definitely be discussing that later I assure you. Anyway Fred here's what it is. When you came to town you were this high-and-mighty warrior with all your influence and your money and your toys and you were the fucking divine wind that slays the world. Any man has to respect that got to make way for it. But then you did something that was beneath you when you took Sean's money and still to this day I have no idea why you would do such a dumbass thing. I mean you got the Seven Demons, and they are not an organisation for this kind of thing Fred. They are for destabilising nations and killing presidents and you're gonna take on a walking business plan and a basically ordinary guy. Why would you ever do that man? That is bush league. But then something happened and this is where it all went wrong for you Fred. I moved faster than you and I killed Johnny Cubano and from that moment on you looked weak. If I didn't take you down someone else would maybe try, and your people knew that. It made them desperate or dumb or in one case horny, which is a questionable response as these things go, but no more so than the others. But then I took another and another and that was it. I can't tell you exactly when it happened but along the line you stopped being the Seven Demons. You were just Fred and his bad people and there ain't no one scared of that. It ain't an honoured order of international power it's just a PR guy with a pool-cue case and some others just hanging around.

But that's the thing Fred the Seven Demons never lose. That's what that name means. So the people you see here – Volodya and Lucille over there who just dropped a screaming Finnish burrito five-hundred-and-forty-seven feet into rebar, and Rex whose brother you killed, which was a total waste of infrastructure man, and Charlie who just shot a woman she barely knows without a second thought and who got inside Karenina's head so bad she went and arranged her own murder, and the doc and me – we're building the new Seven Demons right here. It's not you any more, Fred. It's us.

Now out of respect I'm gonna ask you one time whether you want to join these new Demons as like an elder statesman figure and do exactly what you're told and introduce us to all your expensive government contracts and so on, or whether you prefer just to go away somewhat and that's that.

Yes.

What?

Yes I will join you. Of course.

Uh well Fred that's really unexpected I kinda figured you would yell at me and scream and stuff and we'd have kind of a showdown here.

No. I am a rational man.

Well uh this is embarrassing. There's so much bad blood between us Fred.

Look into your soul, Price, and tell me that you cared for Sarah. Tell me honestly that you give a shit about anyone who has died. Anyone in the world, in fact.

Aw Fred I see what you did there. You just tried to make me say I didn't care about the doc here and get her to change sides. Or maybe you wanted me to say that I did care about her and that would get her to change sides. I'm really not sure.

Nor am I.

Well Fred that was a noble attempt but the thing is there is blood on the ground. There is darkness and suffering. I guess we could work that out but you know Fred the problem between us that is like completely fucking insoluble?

I don't believe there is one.

There is man.

And that is?

You shot the melon.

What?

That was a present man.

Price—

No man that was a present and you shot it.

Price!

You shot the melon Fred. There's no coming back from that.
Price—
Click.
And then the noise.

Say one thing about Rex and his boys when they make some place
ready to come down that fucker is coming down. And they are
professionals man so all the paper is filed and that building is off
limits to the populace. They say accidents will happen but they
don't – not with shit like this. Not unless someone like Mr Friday
and his Poltergeist friends just up and deletes the work order just
when someone like Fred is looking for a perfect place to be. But I
mean man how unlikely is that. I guess real unlikely so long as you
have a computer person on your strength but you know by that time
Karenina was mostly just a femur. Well it's tough at the top.

Especially if you are Fred.

Starting at the bottom of the Triangle building there was a ripple
in the air like the world was breaking like an old video game and then
this noise you couldn't hear because it happened inside you in your
bones and I could feel it go through me and away into the sky and
then one floor at a time there was that same pulse. WOM. WOM.
WOM. One after another until it was just a single sound and a single
standing wave in the air and as it reached the top where Fred was
standing there was a brief puff of flame and smoke. WOM WOMPF!

The whole building just stopped being a single thing and became
an inventory of falling parts.

And there at the very top I saw something just for a second: a
man running, lunging in a weird staggering pattern as if he could
evade what was happening, as if somehow he could survive, because
even Fred in the end really wanted to live. And then the thing that
was happening reached out and took him and it was as if it had
actually grabbed him and pulled him into the heart of the collapse,
and the whole giant pillar of dust and fire began to contract as if he
was sucking it down.

And then it was over.

A pile of rubble where once there was a tower.

Yeah.

My name is Jack.

And that is the Price you pay.

I'm just saying doc just saying is all that you could maybe have said to me like: Hey Jack your plan is terrible I have this much better plan and it involves my drugging you and replacing you with a watermelon and then—

Price for fuck's sake—

I mean I'm glad you liked my exploding building doc but—

Price—

No doc come on I was in fear of my life there. Also and this is a serious question, where the fuck did you get a beheaded corpse in that kind of timeframe? I mean is that like someone you just had lying around or what even is that?

Honey our relationship is real new and I just don't think you need to know every jot and tittle.

Okay that's fair actually, but let me ask you this then, are you gonna follow my instructions now that I'm like First Demon I mean is this going to be a workplace hierarchical issue?

No Price because obviously I'm gonna be the boss I mean that's just obvious.

Why would you be the boss I'm like the man who took down the whole—

Price seriously what do you care so long as you get to do appalling things and sass people and get laid?

Well that is entirely true but what do you care about job titles so long as you're basically running the whole thing anyway?

… That is true.

Of course it is.

Fine you're the boss, Price.

And so are you.

If you cross me I will kill you.

So long as you use me for sex first.

Clearly.

You know I still don't know your name.

No you don't.

So I've got this plan I'm going to shout out a random name each time we go to bed until I get the right one.

That's fine but you should be aware that I will go out and kill someone by that name each time you do.

You are officially to be known as doc forever and just you remember it.

I live to serve your every need.

Okay see that's me taking charge there.

Yes.

I mean that like electrical as well as—

Yes Price.

Did you bring your—

Yes but oh that reminds me I got you something call it a present.

Aw for me you shouldn't have—

I did here.

Is this what I think it is?

Well unless there was someone else in the building.

You found me Fred's head!

Actually someone else found it but you know they weren't all that happy about it so—

Wait one minute this reminds you of sex?

Too soon?

I can't even – nevermind – actually you know what that gives me an idea.

So Charlie you looking for permanent employment?

Hell yeah.

Well yeah okay I'm – yeah. Doc I know. Volodya you coming back to work?

Of course Price.

Rex I got to tell you there's maybe less about straightforward patriotism at work here and more about making a shit ton of money. It's illegal and really entirely wrong. You in?

Yes Colonel I understand deep cover. I'm with you sir.

Okay uh—

Tree of Liberty!

Okay and—

LUCILLE!

Okay that's about that.

We're not called the Seven Demons just because it sounds killer. We are what we are. We don't take stupid jobs and we don't take quiet ones or soft ones. The people we work for are also the kind of people who become our targets. It's a question of who pays more and when.

Me.

Doc.

Rex.

Charlie.

Volodya.

Lucille.

And Fred's severed head on a gaffing stick.

You know what they say about golfing in Florida? You don't have to be a fast runner to escape the gators. You just got to be faster than the slowest guy on the links.

If you want to join it's like that. You don't have to be crazier than me or weirder than doc.

You just have to be scarier than Fred.